THE BOONE SYSTEM

1

Every morning Harry Boone stole a couple of hours from his employers. It was his favourite time of the day. It was the time he devoted to doing what he liked best: nothing at all; the time when, finally getting out of his foetal position, he would stretch, his legs dangling over the end of the bed and his toes peeping out from the shelter of the duvet. Opening one eye and then the other, he always looked around him with the same astonishment, and always saw Maria as though he were seeing her for the first time. This was the time when, lying on his back with the sheet pulled up over his chin, he watched the sun peeping through the blinds, wondering, after what seemed to him to have been a lifetime spent in a damp grey country given over to grass and sheep, how anyone should have thought of inventing something to keep the sun at bay. This was the time when, getting out of bed quietly for fear of waking Maria, he slipped on his dressing gown and walked barefoot to the kitchen to make himself a Turkish coffee, which he brought to the boil three times. He then sipped it on the terrace as he watched the morning star gain the upper hand over the mountain, while biting into a pastry cooked in thyme and olive oil that young Jad, who was the Levantine answer to an English milkman, left on the landing every morning. And this was the time when he sometimes opened the shutters and sometimes, as he did this morning, slipped back between the sheets, warm as toast. Cuddling up to Maria, he would delicately breathe in the scent of her neck, taking care not to make a sound. Her spicy smell quickly gave him a new appetite, and before long he was licking the beads of sweat on her skin, that smelled of cumin and rose petals. His penis throbbed as it pressed against her. Stretching without moving away from him, she parted her legs slightly. Slowly, and without even touching her with his hands, he entered her with his lips pressed to the nape of her neck. Still she didn't move, just continued to lie there even as he placed a hand on her hip and gently made the bedsprings creak. Of course she was awake; but she was pretending to be still asleep, and that excited him all the more. Truth is, he'd never been an enthusiastic supporter of trading on equal terms; it would have been hard to convince him that the pleasure he derived from the buntings they served at Halim's, where they were grilled and then coated in pomegranate syrup, would have been even more intense if the poor things had got as much pleasure from being eaten by him as he got from eating them. And this, finally, was the time when he would thrust deep inside her, then go straight back to sleep with his face buried in her long damp hair.

That morning, however, an insistent ringing interrupted the ritual and broke the spell long before the last act.

'Hello,' he answered with bad grace as he pulled away from her to pick up his mobile phone.

'It's me!'

Me? Who's me? wondered Boone, looking at his manhood, which looked rather forlorn.

'It's me, Kamel!'

'It's not even eight o'clock in London, Colonel!'

'Maybe not, Boone. But it's past ten here in Beirut!'

Boone grumbled. He liked being on Beirut time in the evening, and on London time in the morning.

'Let me buy you lunch. My way of saying sorry for dragging you out of bed.'

Oh no, said Boone to himself. Not lunch with Kamel again!

'Can you meet me at the Vieux Paris?'

Oh no, Boone groaned. Please, God! Not the Vieux Paris!

Noting his reluctance, his caller was now saying: 'It's urgent. *Very* urgent, you might say.'

Urgent? Whenever Kamel expressed a desire to see him *very* urgently, it was either because he needed a visa for one of his countless acquaintances or wanted Boone to make him a present of the very latest eavesdropping gadget. Angry with him for having ruined his morning, Boone was determined to say no.

'I really can't,' he said, trying to sound sorry.

'I insist, Boone, I insist. You won't regret it.'

What did that mean? Was Kamel talking to the spy or to the gourmet?

'Can't we put it off till another day, Colonel?'

'Impossible! I need to see you today!'

'Fine.' Boone finally gave in, telling himself that public relations was part of the job after all. He sometimes thought that his work in Beirut consisted mainly of public relations. Not that he was complaining.

2

The winding road leading from the heights of Rabieh to the coast snaked through the wooded hills where Beirut's political and fashionable elite lorded it over the city in their luxury homes. Harry Boone didn't even see the gaudy frontages or the hanging gardens of the flashy villas that had been built with freshly printed money. He was far too busy trying to avoid the ruts and potholes: further proof, as if proof were needed, of the incompetence of the authorities. The government did have a Minister of Public Works, but he did his best to divert the funds he was allocated – and the bribes that came with them as a matter of course – to his own fiefdom, which was further to the south. That's the way it was in Lebanon. Infrastructures and facilities existed in parallel worlds and never overlapped; here the phones, there the roads, depending on how the ministries were reshuffled. Listening to the agonised groans from his shock absorbers, to say nothing of the protests from his thighs as they banged against the steering wheel, Boone said to himself that it was high time the Public Works portfolio went to someone else.

Once he reached the coast, the traffic became heavier. Cars that had hitherto been moving at a snail's pace now came to a complete standstill, and Boone's ancient Rover quietly joined the endless queue of metal, exhaust fumes and din. He was furious, and the idea of the lunch that lay in store for him made him even more so. He did not approve of the Colonel's choices. Cocooned inside his car, he began to imagine he was somewhere else: no longer with Colonel Kamel at the Vieux Paris or stuck in this deafening traffic jam, Boone was at the Dîwân, with a good *hummus-shawarma* in front of him. He could just see the crispy chunks in their bed of puréed chickpeas. He could smell it, and hear the delicious sizzling of hot meat in boiling oil. He could almost touch the soft bread with its light dusting of flour, taste the creamy *hummus* and feel the crunch of the *shawarma* as he bit into it. He was having vine leaves too: vine leaves so soft they melted in his mouth. His taste buds were going wild; he was on the point of standing up the Colonel and his posh restaurant.

The blast of a siren, as official as it was strident, brought him back to earth. Suddenly and as if by magic, the horns fell silent and the cars coming in the opposite direction pulled sharply over to the side to give way. It was like the parting of the Red Sea. Boone, who half expected to see Moses looming up in his rear-view mirror, saw a limousine bearing down on him at full speed. The big black Mercedes with smoked windows flashed past him seconds later, followed by a Range Rover escort, all its windows wound down to give the submachine guns some air. Boone couldn't stop from making a gesture of annoyance. He still couldn't get used to these

10

armed queue-jumpers who, more than anything else in this country, symbolised the gulf between the ruling caste and the masses. He wondered what happened when one queue-jumper met another one coming in the opposite direction. Armageddon, no doubt.

Yet Boone felt quite at home in Beirut, ruts or no ruts, queue-jumpers or no queue-jumpers. He wouldn't have swapped the Lebanese lack of public-spiritedness and potholed roads for the smooth tarmac and bland social life of a European capital for anything in the world. He had been here four years, and he was beginning to put down roots – for good, he hoped. At first, he had operated from the British embassy, under the cover of a commercial attaché (although 'operated' was hardly the right word to describe the way he went about his work). As he clearly preferred the company of the Lebanese to that of his fellow Europeans, and Levantine delicacies to English food (and who could blame him?), he had suggested to the Clubhouse espiocrats who employed him that they would be better off setting up a discreet outpost that would be beyond the reach of the Foreign Office stuffed shirts. When he was informed of the plan, Her Majesty's Ambassador was delighted. He was genuinely thrilled to be able to get rid of Boone, having quickly labelled him GPO (Garden Party Only), meaning someone one ought not to be seen with. As the Clubhouse took the cautious view that a British trade mission might attract too many bona fide enquiries, it opted for a regional variation, praying devoutly that the local bazaar merchants would not develop a sudden interest in Northern Ireland's many different species of sheep and terrorists. The Ulster Trade Mission, the cornerstone of the Boone system, was born.

As soon as he had acquired some premises, Boone – who had an innate understanding of how civil servants operated – immediately installed a monumental safe to keep his secrets in, a coded communications system to transmit them to his bosses when he couldn't do otherwise, and armour-plated doors and windows to keep the whole lot secure. Then he rented the flat on the same floor and moved in with Maria, his Lebanese mistress. Within a few months of his arrival, he had succeeded in creating a *fait accompli* that had remained in existence ever since.

When the time came for the unending yearly discussions about budget allocation, mean spirits at the Clubhouse never failed to point out that the Ulster Trade Mission and its director – to say nothing of his mistress – were a burden on the Service's finances. Stubborn accountants then regularly drew up clever plans designed to close down the Mission and bring Harry Boone back in line.

It was then that the problems arose, and that the watertight defences Boone had established really came into their own. He had taken the precaution of having the safe set in the wall of his office, and the bureaucrats determined to do battle with him suddenly became aware that their codes and secrets were in the safe, and that said safe was in the office. Hence the armour-plated door and windows. Any savings the Clubhouse might be hoping to make by closing down the Mission wouldn't be worth all the administrative bother involved in moving the safe and the communications system, to say nothing of the definitive loss of the armour plating. Boone's system worked. It was a coherent whole. Interfering with one cog meant interfering with the whole thing, and interfering with the whole thing would create more problems than it solved. When some new recruit suggested, with the zeal of a neophyte, that moving Boone and his mistress into the office would help cut costs, there was always someone wiser or more blasé to point out that Boone's flat was next door to the office, and they couldn't run the risk of having just anyone move into it. Security had to be the first priority. And so, once a year, the Clubhouse devoted long hours of its accountants' time trying to bring down the Boone system before throwing in the towel and swearing to give it another go next year.

Year in, year out, Boone succeeded in beating his critics at their own game. Confident in his system and taking full advantage of the force of inertia he had succeeded in generating since coming to Beirut, he was slowly but surely going native. At the Clubhouse, some even thought his case was hopeless, and found themselves wishing he would soon assert his right to a very early retirement or at least have the decency to accidentally drown himself in the Mediterranean he seemed to like so much.

The Clubhouse. The secret service where Harry Boone had finally ended up deserved its nickname for the very good reason that it had been born on a golf course while Cecil Devereux and Robert Walker were playing a particularly impassioned round. Walker had just joined the government as Minister in charge of the war the Prime Minister had solemnly declared on all sorts of foreign thugs, and Devereux, just back from an ambassadorial posting to Athens, was looking for a new niche. In the course of that memorable round, Walker came up with an idea: why not set up an intelligence service devoted exclusively to money laundering, drug trading, illegal transfers of technology and, of course, terrorism? The idea was picked up at 10 Downing Street, and when the Bunkers protested from their cosy new citadel on the Albert Embankment, Whitehall put their minds at rest by telling them that the new service would not duplicate theirs, as its mission would be to deal with *flows* and not *structures*: flows of people, money, drugs, arms and technologies. Truth to tell, no one was able to provide a convincing explanation of what possible difference there might be between 'flows' and 'structures'. But as the Bunkers were out of favour at the time – the

13

Prime Minister had described them as 'pathetic' – Walker was given the henchmen he wanted, and Devereux got the prestigious title of 'Director' that he coveted so much, plus nice premises on Russell Square.

The Bunkers did not give up, though. Having lost the Whitehall round, they moved the battlefield to Fleet Street and launched a full press campaign in an attempt to discredit their rivals. The Clubhouse nickname dated from those days. Being good sportsmen, Walker and Devereux played the game. They even took a liking to it, and golf and its jargon entered the language of Russell Square: the Service's steering committee became known as the Royal & Ancient; Research and Archives became the Green; Logistics became Caddy; the training centre was nicknamed Practice; the field became the Rough; the Albert Embankment troublemakers became known as the Bunkers; and the largely female population at the Millbank Security Service became known as the Proettes. All of which left Harry Boone pretty cold. Contrary to Walker and Devereux, he was no golfer. And when he did venture onto a golf course, he made straight for the nineteenth hole.

He was right there on that ill-fated day in the previous year, contentedly sipping his whisky, when a young diplomat had opened a breach in his first line of defence, and he had thought his whole world had collapsed. This diplomat, Richard Cholmondeley, had not meant to cause trouble. But he did come up with the unfortunate idea of getting himself shot in broad daylight shortly after he arrived in the Lebanese capital, where he had been looking forward to testing the historical and linguistic knowledge his Cantabrian teachers had knocked into him against harsh Middle Eastern realities.

At first, Cholmondeley astounded the city's Westernised middle-class ladies with the purity of his classical Arabic. (In the hope of seducing him, one of them even went so far as to enrol in a course on pre-Islamic poetry taught by an elderly Dominican friar.) He then ended up annoying his opposite numbers at the Lebanese Ministry of Foreign Affairs, who couldn't keep up with him. As he couldn't find anyone in the capital with whom to practise his Arabic, Cholmondeley decided to look elsewhere. He therefore travelled to the north of the country in search of a worthy adversary in more traditional circles. Everything suggested that he had succeeded better than he could have hoped. Alas, when he was not involved in literary jousts, Cholmondeley had the unfortunate idea of taking an interest – a little too close an interest, maybe – in learning the Arabic for 'anthrax bacillus' and 'smallpox virus'. He also, it seems, became interested in a Red Crescent clinic that was thought to specialise in their manufacture. Some of the people he talked to were undoubtedly impressed by his remarkable Arabic, but they were also so impressed by his precision and grasp of detail that they simply decided to eliminate him, even if it meant depriving the language of the Qur'an of an ardent defender.

Cholmondeley was still lying in a pool of his own blood on the pavement when a communiqué claiming responsibility for his murder reached one of the capital's main dailies. Signed by the Sons of Jihad, it stated that a commando had just executed an English spy (sic) and threatened even greater atrocities against the British government. All this in an Arabic whose purity would no doubt have appealed to the late diplomat.

The news of young Cholmondeley's violent and untimely death sent a shockwave through the whole of Whitehall. It even reached Buckingham Palace: Richard Cholmondeley was not just anyone.

Generation after generation of his distinguished family had provided the Crown with innumerable colonial administrators and officers, and one of his aunts had even married a distant cousin of the Queen. At the Clubhouse the consternation was just as great, as the purists really could not understand why anyone should silence a diplomat in this way when he might have become an invaluable source of intelligence if kept alive. Once again, there was talk of Muslim barbarity and irrationality. They really didn't play by the rules, did they? Green Keeper Nico Mowbray-Smyth, who had a smattering of Marxist culture, coined the term 'lumpenislam'. The expression caught on.

As a result of all this, HMG ordered the immediate and temporary evacuation of all embassy staff, and Harry Boone really thought he had had it. Richard Cholmondeley looked likely to win a posthumous victory for the Clubhouse, where all its pen-pushers had failed so miserably.

So Boone stepped into the breach and volunteered to replace the departing Consul General. He would stay in Beirut and take care of all the administrative formalities concerning the repatriation of poor Cholmondeley's mortal remains. Whitehall and the victim's parents had indeed decided that, whatever Rupert Brooke might have to say about it, there would not be some corner of a Lebanese field that would be forever England. Acting hand in glove with the unavoidable Colonel Kamel, Boone promptly launched an investigation into Cholmondeley's murder, knowing full well that it would not get anywhere. The Clubhouse, which had come to regard Boone as an indigenous agent rather than one of Her Majesty's subjects, fell for it. Boone was able to breathe again. His system had survived the ordeal intact.

Since then, he had done everything that needed to be done to strengthen it. In other words, he had done as little as possible. The Boone system was allergic to zeal, initiative and upheavals of any kind. Like the sea that washed the shores of Lebanon, it was both placid and temperate, and Harry Boone was keen to see that it stayed that way.

3

'Strange things are going on inside the Apparatus,' the Colonel was saying. 'As you know, they were all in Quetta. Quetta, in Pakistan.'

'I *do* know where Quetta is!' said Boone with irritation. He was still angry with Kamel and bitterly missing his *hummus-shawarma*, his vine leaves, and Maria.

'Of course ... I was forgetting the Empire... I was forgetting you are English.'

'Irish, Colonel!'

'So they were all in Quetta a month ago,' the Colonel went on, as though he hadn't grasped the distinction, 'for a meeting with their Arab, Pakistani and Afghan friends.'

The oysters were rather fatty and the Chablis was over-chilled, but Boone didn't take offence. What Kamel was saying was beginning to interest him.

'For a pow-wow,' he said, for the sake of saying something.

'That's it! A pow-wow, as you put it.' Boone almost expected to see him take out his notebook and write the word down. Kamel was working hard on his English, or, should one say his American.

'They were all there,' said the language student.

'I heard rumours.' Boone hoped that the Colonel would see his evasive answer as one of those understatements the English were supposed to like so much. The Clubhouse had sent him a detailed list of intelligence requirements, but apart from what he had read in the press and the scraps of information he had picked up at dinner with a rich carpet merchant just back from Pakistan, he hadn't succeeded in learning much about that business.

'And as you also know,' Kamel went on – after a brief pause to let the flock of waiters hovering around them change their plates – 'the Arab sheikhs who financed the Apparatus and similar outfits are pulling out.'

'They've taken fright. They're adapting to the new order.'

'That's right. As you say, they're adapting to the new order.'

'Chequebook diplomacy is over.'

'For years, the Gulf sheikhs have been buying peace and quiet and begging forgiveness for their well-known liking for whisky and women by financing religious fanatics,' said the Colonel, with the usual petty-bourgeois scorn for other people's money.

'And now Washington is asking for proof of where their loyalties lie.'

'The Arab princes have suddenly realised that they have more to fear from the Americans than from the Islamists.'

'So they're dropping their old friends like hot potatoes.'

'Yes, Boone, hot potatoes, as you say. And as you can imagine, it's a real windfall for people like us.'

The Tournedos Rossini were overcooked and the 1963 Nakad far too young for the year given on the label, but Harry Boone paid no attention. The Colonel was beginning to worry him. Ever since Cholmondeley's death he had been terrified that his profession might catch up with him. And all at once, his fears were being realised thanks to the unexpected intervention of a happy-hour Lebanese *Sûreté* Colonel he had never taken seriously. He began to wish that Kamel had just wanted to ask him a favour.

'I took advantage of the windfall,' the Colonel went on with a triumphant look, 'and I thought of you.'

At a signal from Kamel, a *Sûreté* agent sitting at a nearby table got up and put a sealed envelope in front of Boone.

'Open it! Open it!' the Colonel encouraged him.

Boone felt ill at ease. This was really not the place for this kind of business. He looked around the room. The Vieux Paris was a smart restaurant that had cannibalised a grand old house. It was a favourite meeting place for the big shots in the Lebanese *Sûreté*, who used it to entertain their opposite numbers from the various services that had some kind of accreditation in Lebanon. Despite its name, the Vieux Paris looked like a small Venetian palazzo. It had it all: chandeliers, mouldings, crystal, iridescent glass and marble colonnades and tiles. All around the main dining room, doors draped in purple opened onto small private function rooms that remained depressingly empty. Shutting themselves away in there would never have crossed the minds of the Vieux Paris's regulars. They were indeed rooms without a view, and those who graced the Vieux Paris with their custom wanted to see, and to be seen.

To their left, smoked salmon and Lebanese *mezze* lay promiscuously side-by-side on a kitschy table where the Iranian consul was sitting next to a Brylcreemed Lebanese Army colonel who, as everyone knew, was bankrolled by the Americans. Strange mixture, Boone said to himself, thinking of the food as much as the people eating it. Further away, the Libyan *chargé d'affaires* was methodically chewing a steak while listening with half an ear to a local journalist who was boasting about his latest article. Boone knew the journalist well. He'd taken money from all sides at one time or other, and this was the second time he had got into bed with the Libyans. Once back at his embassy, the Libyan would lose no time in sending a coded message to his superiors to tell them about suspicious clandestine contacts between the Iranians and a Lebanese official who was working for the Americans, knowing full well that the Iranian would be warning Tehran that the Libyans had just recruited a local journalist who had been working for the Islamic Republic until now. That was the way of cocktail spies. They all went to the same restaurants and bars, wore the same safari suits and sported the same Ray-Bans. They all sent their greedy masters exaggerated reports that confirmed their paranoia and justified the fabulous budgets that allowed them to live in style. Mixing with all these stoolies had dispelled any illusions Boone might once have had about his cover. He crossed his fingers and hoped that the Iranian and Libyan would be too absorbed with one another to take any notice of Kamel's little game.

'Dessert?' asked the Colonel as their table was being cleared. 'No? You're sure? I recommend the tiramisu. Homemade, Boone ... Absolutely sure? Coffee, then. No sugar, right?' Kamel liked to surprise his guests by remembering their culinary likes and dislikes.

CORK COUNTY LIBRARY 169 0618

Opening the envelope, Boone pulled out a dozen or so official documents bearing the Apparatus's logo, and a four-page report in poor English that revealed the identity of the members of an Islamist network based in the UK. It also listed their safe houses and arms caches. Why was the report written in English, he wondered. Why had Kamel taken the trouble to have it translated? Not for his benefit, that was for sure. For the Americans, perhaps? He realised that some of the names were those of men who had recently been arrested in Cardiff, and quickly forgot about the Americans and the unexpected translation. Contrary to all expectations, he had to admit that this was four-star intelligence. It would have been hard to find better. Nothing like the rumours and gossip Kamel usually brought him. Boone should have been delighted, but the fact was that he was becoming frightened. These documents could easily make waves that could rock his system.

'I understand your police have just arrested some Islamists in Wales. Pure chance, I'm told,' said the Colonel, waving a black crocodile-leather cigar case.

Refusing the Cuban monster he was being offered, Boone searched through his pockets and finally produced a crumpled Dutch cigarillo.

'Wales is in England, isn't it?' asked the Colonel.

Not really feeling up to explaining the difference between England, Great Britain and the United Kingdom, Boone nodded.

Kamel used the gold cigar cutter he kept on a chain together with his keys, and the same *Sûreté* agent jumped up from his chair and produced a foul-smelling flame from a Zippo. Dismissing him with a scornful gesture, Kamel beckoned the Vieux Paris's *sommelier*, who rushed over with the usual cedarwood matches. It was not for nothing that the Colonel mixed with the Lebanese upper classes.

22

Quite apart from providing him with a lucrative business – and the Jaeger Le Coultre Reverso on his wrist was there to prove it – moving in these circles had taught him that good cigars do not get on with petrol lighters, just as it had taught him which wine, or at least which colour wine, went with what. As he watched him, Boone thought of all the Western intelligence officers who spent their undercover lives posing as businessmen and ended up retiring on pitiful pensions. Fools, all of them. And there was Kamel, a sensible man who never bothered with anything except his well-being, and who saw intelligence as nothing more than a pretext for lucrative business. Boone couldn't help but envy him.

'Interesting, isn't it?' asked Kamel, proudly blowing out smoke.

'Tell me, Colonel ... Have you shared this intelligence with anyone else?'

'Product from this source is for you, on an exclusive basis,' replied Kamel, avoiding a direct answer to the question. 'No other service will have access to it. I promise. This will stay between you and me.' He gave Boone a conspiratorial wink. 'And in exchange for this little favour, the *Sûreté* would like to have those new mobile phones ... the digitally coded ones.'

'Will there be any more? Or is this a one-off?'

'There'll be more, Boone. I guarantee it. You can even get it yourself.'

'If I understand you correctly, you're offering me a source.' Boone was getting seriously worried. He suddenly had a vision of all this getting out of hand and interfering with his quiet life.

'And it's not just any source! Not just any source!' said the Colonel, leaning towards him with a knowing look on his face. 'The Sharif,' he whispered. 'The Sharif, Boone ...'

'The Sharif?'

'The Sha-rif,' Kamel stressed both syllables and settled back in his chair. 'The Sha-rif,' he repeated, puffing on his cigar.

'How the hell did you get to him?'

'Does the name Hammud mean anything to you? Sheikh Ahmad Hammud?' Kamel tugged at his moustache, looking impishly at Boone.

'Hammud, as in the Union of Islamic Students? The Apparatus's recruiting agent?'

'Yes, that Hammud,' replied Kamel. He stopped tugging his moustache and was concentrating on his cigar. 'Hammud is very close to one of my sources. A professor. He's a Christian but his speciality is Islam. He and Hammud see each other from time to time. Cultural and intellectual intercourse … You know the kind of thing I mean.'

Boone knew what he meant.

'And how was the Sharif recruited, Colonel?'

'Well, to be perfectly honest, he wasn't actually recruited … Not in the true sense of the word.'

'What does that mean?'

'Last Saturday, this professor went to visit Hammud. So he turned up at the Sheikh's at the appointed time, and found him in the company of another man with a beard and half his face missing. Without even introducing himself, the stranger immediately took things in hand. The Sheikh slipped away. The stranger picked up a briefcase, opened it, put two or three books inside it – they were of no importance – tapped the bottom to suggest that someone should take a closer interest in it, and handed it to the professor, telling him to come back and see Hammud the following Saturday. The stranger doesn't ask; he gives orders. But my source will tell you all about that in detail. There's no doubt about it, Boone. It really is the Sharif. My source tells me that the whole right side of his face has been ravaged. Looks as though it's been ploughed. As you may remember, he was seriously injured and burned in a car-bomb explosion ten years ago.'

'So the Sharif is under threat.'

'The times are changing, and he is presumably taking out a little insurance policy. He's offering to sell his intelligence before his old protectors give it away for nothing. And him with it.'

'Did you share your source with anyone else?' Boone knew only too well how Kamel worked.

'Share it, Boone?'

'With the Syrians, perhaps?'

'No, no.'

'The Americans, then?' Boone looked doubtful.

'The Americans? Certainly not! Why should I share my source with the Americans? I'm a patriot, Boone!'

Boone knew that the Colonel was a good patriot when it came to dealing with the Americans, but not quite so good a patriot when he was dealing with the Syrians.

'And now, Boone, I suggest that we go and meet him. His name is Shartuni. Dr Sami Shartuni. He's waiting for us in a chalet at the Marbella Beach seaside resort. A *Sûreté* safe house.'

'Fine,' said Boone reluctantly. 'Let's go see your Mr Shartuni.'

'*Doctor* Shartuni, Boone! *Doctor*! He has a doctorate. A PhD from the United States of America. You'll see, he's a very distinguished man. English education.'

Boone allowed himself a little smile. He knew from experience that in this part of the world, the people who claimed to have had an 'English education' were not so much the ones who could speak English properly as those who didn't understand a damned word of French.

25

Clamping his Cuban cigar between his teeth, Kamel made a big noise of pushing his chair back. The bodyguards at the next table all did the same and stood up as one man. Boone observed that they paid far too much attention to their boss and not enough to what was going on in the room. Good courtiers but not very effective bodyguards, he concluded, abandoning the stub of his cigarillo and standing up in his turn.

4

A tiny one-bedroom flat on the second floor of the Marbella Beach; so much for Kamel's 'chalet'. Leatherette chairs, a low formica table, and a bed trying very hard to look like a sofa. It was more of a bachelor pad than a safe house.

'As I was telling you, mister...'

Sitting with his back to the window and resting his elbows on his knees, Shartuni was busily plaiting a paper handkerchief. Boone was sitting opposite him in the other armchair. Colonel Kamel had opted for the sofa-bed and put some distance between himself and the other two, as though to suggest to Shartuni that he would be dealing with Boone from now on.

As soon as they had come in, the Colonel had pulled the curtains and plunged the room into semi-darkness. So as to impress Shartuni, presumably. As though he wasn't nervous enough already. The hand he had offered Boone was damp, and he was constantly mopping his brow.

'I went to see the Sheikh at his home. I've been going there regularly for the last few months. At the request of the President himself ... The President of the Republic,' he hastened to add, in case Boone hadn't got the point. 'I'm an academic! Your espionage is nothing to do with me! It was the President who introduced me to Mr Kamel, and it was at his request that I agreed to Mr Kamel's suggestion that I should re-establish contact with the Sheikh.' He mopped his brow again. 'And I did it because I think we shouldn't break off communications. I think that a better understanding between the various religious communities in our country is essential. But there was never any question of spying, secret documents or secret compartments in briefcases ...' More brow mopping. 'I intended to speak to the President about it, as it happens,' he said, as though he was hoping that a mere promise would revive his failing courage. His conversation was full of 'the President this and the President that', but he wasn't too convinced that he had impressed his listener. He was getting more and more nervous, and the paper handkerchief he was playing with was beginning to look like a piece of lace that had been made by someone having a fit. He glanced at Kamel, but got no help from that direction. The Colonel was keeping to his role, and Boone was determined to keep the pressure on.

'Your friend Hammud left you alone with the stranger?' he asked, tucking his legs under the low table.

'Yes,' sighed Shartuni. That act of treason was obviously a painful memory for him. 'He left me alone with him. The man picked up a

28

case, tapped the bottom saying that there were some documents in it, and told me to give it to Mr Kamel.'

'Mister' Kamel. Shartuni seemed to like 'Mister' better than 'Colonel'. As though the word 'Mister' were enough to put some distance between him and the secret world that was catching up with him.

'Then the man with the limp turned up with some books,' he continued.

'What man with a limp?'

'Just a servant. With a limp. He's often at the Sheikh's when I go there. That day, he came to bring the books on jurisprudence I'd been asking the Sheikh for. I'm doing some work on Hanbilite jurisprudence. The stranger picked up the books, put them in the case, closed it and handed it to me ... I took it, naturally. It all happened so fast. He told me that Mr Kamel would know who to give it to, and that the next time I paid the Sheikh a visit, I had to bring him a reply ...' The image of that terrible interview with the stranger must have become unbearable, as Shartuni stood up and then sat down again almost as suddenly. 'He also told me,' he went on resignedly, 'that if I didn't have a reply, there was no point in my coming again. That the Sheikh would not see me.' He wiped away a ribbon of sweat running down his right cheek with what was left of the handkerchief. 'I was caught off balance,' he said in an attempt at self-justification. 'I didn't know what to say. So I picked up the case and went to see Mr Kamel.'

Shartuni had gone straight to Kamel. He didn't go to see his friend the President. Boone had met a lot of Shartunis in his time. They went abroad to get their degrees and came home laden with important-sounding academic titles and sophisticated Western concepts. Already picturing themselves as the powers behind the

29

throne, these would-be *éminences grises* then drew up feasibility studies and cleverly worked out forecasts (complete with graphs, diagrams and footnotes) for their masters. The plans ended up gathering dust in forgotten filing cabinets in the alcoves of power. The big chiefs flattered them, calling them 'Doctor' and 'Professor', showing them off as though they were performing dogs and phoning them whenever they didn't have a dictionary to hand. *Hello, Dr Shartuni? Dr Sami Shartuni? Just a moment, please, the President would like to speak to you.* And there's Shartuni standing to attention. Oh, for a video phone to immortalise the moment! *Hello, Shartuni? Tell me, my friend ... The capital of Mauritania is ... Nouakchott, you said. That's what I thought. You see, my dear! Dr Shartuni really is a mine of information! Thank you, Shartuni!* Then the big chiefs tire of them, just as they tire of everything else, and pass them on to their more pragmatic henchmen in the security services, who make more extensive use of them. Thus the Shartunis of this world become the Kamels' messenger boys. Boone did not like this Shartuni one bit. But he would have to do business with him.

Standing up, he went to the window and pulled back the curtains. A tired autumn light made an unconvincing attempt to invade the room, its task made all the more difficult by the sorry state of the French window, which generation after generation of cleaners had neglected. Boone slid the filthy glass open. The cool wind of a seaside evening swept into the room, bringing with it the familiar sounds and smells of the outside world Shartuni was still trying to cling to. Down below, a Sri Lankan housemaid was going mad trying to calm down three screaming kids fighting by the side of a swimming pool. Taking no notice, their mothers were patting a ball backwards and forwards across a sun-faded net, watched by a dejected tennis coach they had unilaterally appointed ball boy. Further away, a keep-fit enthusiast was working out while eyeing a woman who was trying to catch the last rays of a yawning sun.

'Dr Shartuni,' Boone finally said. 'It seems to me that, in the course of your legitimate quest for a constructive relationship between Lebanon's religious communities, you have accidentally stumbled across someone who has, shall we say, an advanced vision of dialogue. You have to admit that such opportunities are too rare for us not to take advantage of them.'

'An advanced vision of dialogue!' Shartuni leaped to his feet. 'You mean "spying", don't you?' The title of 'Doctor' Boone had just bestowed on to him had obviously boosted his morale. 'My relationship with the Sheikh is political,' he went on. 'We are both working towards a meeting that would bring together the spiritual leaders of the various communities, and I was planning to speak to the President about it. Now it's all ruined.' Discouraged at the thought of this failed summit, the would-be Sherpa sat down heavily.

'I do understand your disappointment. But you have to agree that the Sheikh's views about the prevailing situation are personal, and therefore subjective. Whereas the documents that were handed over to you give a more objective insight into the situation. They shed a new light on this whole business.'

'I don't even know what these wretched documents are about! I haven't even seen them! As far as I'm concerned, it could just as easily be a list of garrisons, arsenals and military positions! I really don't see how that will help us reach a better understanding of Islam!'

'Do you want me to show them to you?' Boone bluffed.

'Certainly not! I don't want to see them. What's all this got to do with me? The Sheikh could have found someone else.'

'Dr Shartuni, you tell me you are on friendly terms with the Sheikh. Presumably it was in the name of that friendship that he introduced you to his friend and asked you to do him this favour. He put his trust in you.'

Shartuni stopped protesting. Seen in this light, his role seemed more acceptable. Boone thought to himself that the job was half done. Shartuni had been won over to the idea that he had done nothing so far that might tarnish his self-image. It was now up to him to persuade the good doctor to go the whole way.

'Dr Shartuni, what is going on in the Muslim world is of the greatest interest to all of us. The Sheikh and his friend are now waiting for our answer, and you are going to take it to them.'

'But it's nothing to do with me! It's none of my business!'

'Dr Shartuni,' Boone continued, speaking as softly as he could, 'If you let me down, I can replace you easily enough.' Boone was lying. Given the state of his network (if it could be called a network), it would take him weeks to find a suitable courier. What was more, he would have to expose himself. No, he thought, he would be much better off using Shartuni as a cover. Boone was a great believer in letting other people front for him, and his system made extensive use of cut-outs of all sorts.

'Having said that,' he added for the benefit of this particular cut-out, 'I make no secret of the fact that I'd rather do business with you. The Sheikh and his friend trust you, and –'

'But I am an academic, not a spy!'

'We're talking politics, not espionage! Islam is going through a crucial stage in its history. Alliances are being made and unmade. Yesterday's friends are today's foes, and *vice versa*. Totally new regional and international alliances are taking shape. Everything is up in the air. Do you want to play your part? Or would you rather miss out on all this and stay on the sidelines of History?'

'But I'm not a professional,' Shartuni pleaded.

Got him! Boone said to himself. He didn't say 'spy', he said 'professional'. It was not a matter of principle any more, just a matter of competence.

5

'So just who is he, this Sharif?'

Cecil Devereux was finishing reading Boone's report, and peered over the top of his genuine horn-rimmed glasses as he asked Archie Briggs the question. A full meeting of the Royal & Ancient was in session at Russell Square. Also present were Nico Mowbray-Smyth, Alec Rose and, of course, Guy Fennell. As was only fitting, Fennell was sitting to Devereux's right – on the right hand of God the Father. This was so because Fennell was in charge of the prestigious East-West department. In the days when the Russian mafia's money, duly laundered, used to flow into the Western banking system with no questions asked, Fennell's Inlands had been the darlings of the transatlantic Cousins. Then a new president had more or less got things under control in Moscow and inaugurated an era of co-operation with the United States. This threatened to put Fennell out of a job at the very time when Washington was beginning to lose interest in the Russian mafia, concentrating instead on the Islamist threat. Politicians now only had to read the papers to find the intelligence that Fennell had been secretly passing on to a carefully chosen audience. Or they could get it directly from yesterday's enemies. (*Delighted to be able to do this little favour, my friend, but please don't forget the loan we discussed.*) Since then, Fennell had been looking for a new niche. Good espiocrat that he was, he quite naturally came up with the idea of an internal shake-up. With Devereux's agreement, he set up a think-tank (all very informal, of course, and with himself and Devereux as its only members) to decide how the Service should adapt to the new world order. Archie Briggs was only too well aware of what was really going on behind all this planning and thinking. Now that the wind from the east had dropped, Guy was looking for a southerly wind to keep him going. He was eyeing Briggs's North-South department, otherwise known as Links.

'His name is Ali Al-Husayni,' Briggs finally replied in response to Devereux's puzzled look.

'Ali what? All these names are terribly confusing. We were just getting used to the Russians, to say nothing of the Czechs – all those consonants – and now they come up with these Arab names. Quite unpronounceable.'

Briggs refrained from pointing out to his director that, when it came to impossible names, the English gave as good as they got: 'Deverooks' for Devereux, 'Chumley' for Cholomondeley, and 'Broom' for Brougham. To say nothing of Pontefract, which was pronounced 'Pomfret.'

'He also goes by the name of "Abu Hasan",' was all he said, hoping to make things easier for his boss.

'So he has several names? Abu Hasan ... Sharif ... Ali whatever-it-is ...' Devereux seemed annoyed.

'He's descended from the Prophet. That's why he's called the Sharif.'

'Descended from the Prophet, you say ...'

Devereux seemed to have recovered something of his good humour. Briggs noted to himself that the Sharif's noble ancestry must have appealed to his snobbery.

'He's a bigshot in the Apparatus, which is the Islamist movement's intelligence service,' Nico Mowbray-Smyth said. 'He's spent his whole career in it, and he's still under thirty. They rise through the ranks quickly, though they often fall even faster. He's married and has at least one child, a boy, Hasan. He's originally from Mastaba, a small village to the west of the Beqaa Valley, not far from the border with Israel. Ten years ago, the population of the village was decimated in a car-bomb attack. The whole of the Sharif's family died. He was badly wounded, and still bears scars on the right side of his face. He was later recruited into the Apparatus, and is now a member of its international committee, as well as heading its organisation in Lebanon. What we don't know is how long that will last.'

'And we want to employ this *terrorist*?' Guy Fennell butted in. 'I'm not sure that our American friends will like that. This Sharif must be on their Most Wanted list.'

'He isn't a terrorist,' said Mowbray-Smyth. 'The Apparatus is an intelligence service, not a terrorist group. The Sharif is a spy, pure and simple. He has no executive power. We've never found any evidence that he's been involved in any terrorist activity.'

'Even so! He's no angel! He can't be white as snow!'

36

'I should hope not, Guy,' replied Briggs. 'I sincerely hope he knows who's doing what, when, where and why, and that he will tell us.'

'I hope so, too. But there might be a high price to pay. If this source is as good as you claim, he could become a financial burden.'

'True,' intervened Alec Rose, who, as Caddy Master, was in charge of the Clubhouse's budget. We'll have to think about the financial side of things. He might swallow up the whole of Archie's budget.'

'I wonder if the Minister would agree to extending our credit.' Devereux seemed worried.

'No point in asking him for more funds,' said Fennell, who had just found the opening he had been looking for. 'As everything is fairly quiet on the eastern front, I can easily find the funds required for this operation out of my own budget.'

'Good idea,' said a relieved Deveureux. 'We'll draw on Guy's budget, that way we can keep it in the family.'

'Spiffing idea,' exclaimed Alec Rose, who was rather fond of dated expressions.

'We'll have to find him a code name,' said Devereux. 'What about "Tiger Woods"? We don't have a Tiger Woods on the books, do we?'

'We don't,' said Mowbray-Smyth. 'And it's high time we did. All the sources we employ have dreadful handicaps.'

The Director decided to ignore his Green Keeper's sarcastic remark. 'Gentlemen,' he announced solemnly, 'this operation is now a matter for the Royal & Ancient, and it becomes the Service's number one priority. So send me the file on the Sharif, Nico. Only what you have to hand. No inter-service requests, right? No point in bringing him to the attention of the Bunkers and the Proettes ... Archie, warn your man in Beirut that we're going ahead ... Alec, you

37

will be in charge of the budget ... Guy, you will be responsible for distributing the product outside the Service. No names, of course. For the moment, we will keep the source's identity to ourselves. Then we'll see. We might let the Americans in on it, but not immediately. Only when we're sure about our source.'

He's done it, Briggs said to himself. Guy's done it. That's the niche he wanted. Guy's back in the saddle. Well aware of the market value of the Sharif and of the profits he could make from it in Whitehall and in Washington, Guy had jumped at the opportunity. He had played his cards well. Guy knew that the best intelligence – the intelligence his masters were really interested in – was not be found in the field but in the corridors of power. And Guy knew all about those corridors. At one point he'd had hopes of becoming deputy director. Which, Devereux being what he was, would have made him the real boss. But his dreams were shattered the day when, at eleven in the morning, he went to see the Minister wearing patent leather shoes. All of Whitehall got to hear the story of that gaffe. Guy had staggered under the blow, but it did nothing to diminish his burning desire to rise through the ranks. He simply put his ambitions on the back burner, until the story of his over-polished shoes had been forgotten about and until he himself had acquired the polish the system demanded. And he'd gone to a lot of trouble. He went to Leslie King's golf academy to improve his swing, and to a posh Savile Row tailor to brush up his dress etiquette. He even went so far as to take an intensive French course because he once heard someone say that all toffs had French *au pairs*. Yes, Guy had played his cards right. But Briggs was not displeased; he had played his cards right too. Better to hand over the Sharif with good grace than to have them poking their noses into his business. Briggs was a realist. He knew that the Sharif was too much for him to handle. Too political. If he had insisted on keeping complete control over his source, they would have quickly begun to go through his accounts with a fine-tooth comb: Alec Rose would call him to ask for Boone's expense account, Cecil Devereux would tell him that the Prime Minister himself was asking about the Sharif, and at the Royal & Ancient's weekly meetings Guy would slyly ask if he had learned anything new about Cholmondeley's murder or about the latest terrorist attack on the Americans. Briggs told himself that, all in all, he had come fairly well out of this. The Sharif might eventually escape him, but Guy was now too busy with his new hobby horse to go on 'thinking' about restructuring the Service.

6

In the weeks that followed, Boone and Shartuni met regularly at the chalet that Colonel Kamel had so graciously put at their disposal. Boone had got Kamel to promise that he would stop using it for secret meetings, professional or romantic. He went to the Marbella Beach every Saturday morning and debriefed Shartuni when he joined him there. Then he gave him the double-bottomed Delsey containing the money for the Sharif and the latest requirement list. Shartuni went to the Sheikh's, then came back in the afternoon with the case. Boone spent long hours debriefing him and even longer hours reassuring him about his role in all this business, which was quite beyond him.

Money was not the way to Shartuni's heart, or at least not the thousand dollars Boone gave him for his troubles every month. The key to Shartuni was his ego. Boone had to flatter him constantly, giving him to believe that the political and philosophical discussions he had with the Sheikh were at least as important as the secret documents he ferried back and forth. Boone could be a very good listener when he had a bottle to hand. At such times, his patience and receptivity knew no bounds. Shartuni, who ran on logomania rather than liquor, took full advantage, launching into interminable lectures on Christianity and Islam that inevitably ended with solemn recommendations that Boone, equally solemn, promised to pass on to those in high places. Boone found that side of the job especially painful, but he still attached great importance to it, knowing full well that he had to play at being Shartuni's mentor and confessor, and at being the outlet for a stream of verbal diarrhoea which would otherwise have landed on Kamel or, worse still, his friend the President. So he bought Shartuni's silence by listening to him talk nonsense within four walls.

Once the switch had been made and Shartuni recovered his nerve, he would go home with a black Delsey. It was identical to the one he shuttled between the Marbella Beach and the Sheikh's house, and had been specially bought by Boone so that Shartuni's friends would get used to seeing him carrying a briefcase. To make way for the Delsey, Shartuni had had to get rid of the old leather satchel he had brought back with him from the obscure American university he'd attended. That had caused some gnashing of teeth. But in the end, reason prevailed, and Shartuni nobly agreed to sacrifice his fetish for the sake of his own safety.

So, week after week, the double-bottomed case delivered its precious intelligence, which was duly appreciated by the Royal & Ancient and by all the friends and allies who were knocking in ever greater numbers at the Service's main door, not to mention the back

41

door. For years, they'd all been trying to get to grips with this ill-defined nebula which, for want of a better name, they called 'Islamintern'. They had sought to understand this fluid structure, whose rhizome-like tentacles seemed to defy all attempts at rationalisation. They had finally given up on the grounds that the Islamist scene defied all analysis, while the minds of its leaders defied all logic. Then the Sharif turned up, promising to answer all – or nearly all – the questions that obsessed them, and here he was outlining the Apparatus's organisational structure, dissecting its internal and external links, and finally providing a rational political explanation for all its seeming irrationality. Though this be madness, he seemed to imply, Bard-like, yet there's method in it. And all this he did without any embellishments: his style was as clinical as it was spare, and he reported with a very un-Oriental economy of words. A courier, a double-bottomed briefcase and an exchange that was as regular as it was fair: banknotes and lists of requirements on the one hand, answers on the other. Week after week, and as regular as clockwork, the Sharif supplied new intelligence. At last the intelligence community was able to bring itself up to speed after long years spent looking for a mare's-nest, picking information off the grapevine, recruiting sources who proved not to be sources after all, and cultivating contacts who always called collect.

Barely three weeks after the start of the operation, a yellow van delivered two boxes to Russell Square. Syd, the Clubhouse's old porter – no doubt warned of this imminent delivery – was waiting on the steps when it arrived, and immediately informed Alec Rose, who rushed down to sign the delivery slip in person. Further enquiries revealed that the boxes contained the scrambler phones that Colonel Kamel was waiting for with such impatience. A few days later, the

42

Clubhouse's car pool was further enriched by a black Jaguar and a blue Ford which cheekily squatted in parking places that were in theory reserved for the staff of the nearby university, with which the Clubhouse always did its best to blend in. In the meantime, armed with his new title of Liaison Officer, Guy Fennell hadn't wasted any time getting hold of the files on the Islamist militants who had been arrested in Cardiff, and on the other activists who had subsequently been picked up on the basis of intelligence supplied by the Sharif. He had then invited Nico Mowbray-Smyth to lunch at a bistro in Chenies Street (knowing that the Green Keeper would never have agreed to lunch with him at his club), and over a glass of Sancerre and another of Badoit, he had succeeded in borrowing Blaker. *I need a good Arabic speaker, Nico, and I was thinking of young Simon Blaker. He's not been with you for very long, so it would be quite easy for you to manage without him, wouldn't it?* In Fennell's view, Blaker had the great virtue of being a Rookie, a newcomer to the Service. His loyalties were still uncertain and he owed nothing – or very little – to either Nico Mowbray-Smyth or the other members of the Royal & Ancient. He was malleable, could easily be won over and could just as easily be turned if the need arose.

That same afternoon, Simon Blaker reported to Fennell, his only luggage a *Hans Wehr* Arabic-English dictionary. Fennell himself put him in a little office not far from his own. He then solemnly handed him the file on the Islamists and asked him to trace every reference to contacts the network might have established in Europe and America. Having stressed that the task was urgent and that it was strictly confidential (*You will report your findings to me, and only me!*), he wished him good luck. Suiting his action to his words, he then tiptoed out and quietly closed the door. Two minutes later he was back. Gesturing at Blaker to sit down and pretending to let him into the conspiracy, he asked him to make a note of anything to do with Islamists in Russia and the Caucasus (*We do have to adapt to the new climate of international co-operation, don't we?*).

Blaker proved to be an excellent recruit. He had been working for Fennell for only a few days when he gave him a telephone number in Paris. It was in Arabic and had been scribbled down by some Islamist with a poor memory. Fennell immediately passed on the tip to the French head of station in London. After a week of telephone-tapping and shadowing suspects, five Algerians were finally arrested. The evidence against them was not very substantial, but on the eve of a trial involving members of a North African network accused of being involved in a series of murderous attacks perpetrated in Paris a few years earlier, the French authorities had no scruples about casting a wide net. The French services, who had been harshly criticised by the media and accused of doing too little too late at the time, took advantage of the opportunity to boost their fortunes with a series of deliberate leaks. Their many contacts were only too happy to publish them, and the leaked intelligence was quite naturally picked up by the Arab press.

7

Two weeks afterwards, Tiger Woods managed his first Birdie. That Saturday, Fennell had shown up at the Clubhouse just after three in the afternoon to wait for Boone's weekly transmission, and had immediately checked to see that Simon Blaker was at his desk. Then he called in his secretary Joan and asked her nicely to go over to the Caddies and get them to inform her as soon as any message came in from Beirut.

On the stroke of six, and after three false alerts, Joan knocked on his door and told him that a message from Boone had just come in.

'Thank you, Joan,' he said, admiring her leather-clad legs. 'Go and bring it please, and ask Blaker to come and see me. Also, find out if Archie and Nico are in today. Discreetly,' he added, still looking at her legs. 'Discreetly, please.' Fennell was always saying 'please' to Joan's legs.

Ten minutes later, Joan and Simon Blaker came into his office. Nico Mowbray-Smyth apparently hadn't been seen all day, but Archie Briggs was in his office. So, said Fennell to himself as he broke the seal on the brown envelope Joan had just given him, Archie already knew roughly what was in Tiger Woods's latest dispatch, or would do very soon.

Joan left and closed the door behind her as Fennell took four sheets out of the envelope. The first was a brief message from Boone explaining that Tiger Woods's latest information suggested that a terrorist attack on Paris was in the making. The second sheet contained a text in Arabic that meant nothing at all to Fennell. The last two sheets were sketched maps.

'Park yourself there, you and your dictionary,' he ordered Blaker, who was still standing with his arms folded across his *Hans Wehr* as though he were afraid someone might steal it from him. 'Tell me what all this is about,' he added, giving him the Arabic text and the maps but keeping Boone's message to himself.

Taking the sheets, the Rookie sat down, put his dictionary on his knees and had a quick glance at all four documents as though to get an initial idea of the scale of the task that lay before him. Then he concentrated on reading them, slowly, his lips moving as he read. He looked like a diligent schoolboy. From time to time he frowned and touched his *Hans Wehr* as though in search of inspiration. He had already been reading for a good five minutes, frequently going back and forth from one sheet to another and turning the drawings as he tried to get his bearings. Fennell was beginning to lose patience. He was mentally comparing Blaker's reading speed with that of Briggs and his people.

46

'I don't need a literal translation! Just give me the gist of it. We'll worry about the details later!'

Blaker almost fell off his chair. He obviously didn't like working under pressure; he was an academic.

'Well, sir,' he said at last, when he had cleared his throat. 'These are the names and addresses of six Arabs ... The addresses are all in France, and they belong to garage owners or car dealers.'

'What does this list correspond to? Isn't there an explanatory note?'

'Just a list.'

'What about the drawings?'

'One of them is of a car park in Paris. Seems to be an underground car park, the one in ... I don't know Paris well, sir, but judging by the Arabic text, it would seem to be the car park in the Blâs Dûfîn.'

'Blâsdûfîn? What's that mean, Blâsdûfîn?'

'Blâs Dûfîn, in two words, sir. Blâs and then Dûfîn.'

'Dûfîn, Dûfîn, Dûfîn ... Got it! It must be *Dauphine*. The Place Dauphine, at the bottom of the Avenue Foch,' said Fennell, whose knowledge of the French capital was restricted to the seventh, eighth and sixteenth *arrondissements*.

'Quite possibly, sir. You see, Arabic renders the sound 'o' as 'oo', and there's no 'p' in the alphabet. The Arabs replace 'p' with 'b'. It's true that some reformers place two points under the letter 'b' to turn it into the Roman alphabet's 'p', but –'

'What about the other drawing?' interrupted Fennell, who was not at all interested in hearing a lecture on Arabic phonetics. 'What does it show, exactly?'

'A ... a square,' stammered Blaker. He'd been wrong-footed. 'The same Place Dauphine, according to what it says here, with the Palace of Justice to the east.'

'You mean the Palais de Justice ?

'So it would seem, sir.'

'The Palais de Justice in the Place Dauphine? Are you sure?'

'That's what the Arabic text says,' replied Blaker, who was no longer sure about anything.

'Go and get me a map, then.'

'A map?'

'Yes, a map! A map of Paris! A street map! There must be one somewhere around here!'

'Yes, sir,' said Blaker, dropping both the papers and his *Hans Wehr*.

As soon as he was alone, Fennell picked up the phone and dialled an internal number.

'Archie? Guy here. Have you seen our friend's latest dispatch? So what do you think? Boone seems to believe they're planning an attack … But the documents don't say anything of the sort. Elliptical, isn't it?'

Elliptical! Fennell would never have admitted to Briggs that he was completely at sea.

'Ah, you've got a vague idea? Perhaps we should talk about it. OK, I'm on my way.'

In the corridor, he bumped into Blaker on his way back. He was brandishing a little leather-bound red book that made him look like some young Chinese communist with his *Quotations from Chairman Mao*.

'Later, later,' he told him without pausing to slow down. Fennell was edgy. The idea of going to see Briggs cost him dear. His acute sense of his own importance made it feel almost humiliating. But he needed Briggs.

'It's the Place Dauphine in the first *arrondissement*, Guy! It's the *Porte* Dauphine that's at the bottom of the Avenue Foch in the sixteenth, not the *Place* Dauphine.' Poring over a map of the French capital, Briggs pointed to the Île de la Cité. 'Here, look for yourself. The west side of the Palais de Justice is on the Place Dauphine ... And there, look, "P" for "Parking". With an entrance on the Quai des Orfèvres.'

Looking at the map like some doubting Thomas, Fennell imitated Briggs and pointed to the Place Dauphine. His finger then traced a route that went downriver along the *quais*, round the Place de la Concorde, up the wrong side of the Champs-Elysées (Fennell's index finger was English and drove on the left hand side of the road), round the Place de l'Etoile, down the left side of the Avenue Foch, until it finally reached the Porte Dauphine. Apparently convinced, the index finger then went off to scratch Fennell's head as he sat down.

'What makes Boone think that they're planning something?'

'Must be the trial.'

'What trial?'

'The North Africans' trial, at the Palais de Justice.'

'Of course! When does it start?'

'On Monday.'

'This Monday? The day after tomorrow?'

'The trial begins at noon the day after tomorrow. If Tiger Woods is to be believed, the Islamists are planning a bloody spectacle to mark the event.'

'The documents say nothing of the sort. Boone's talk of an attack is pure speculation.'

Sitting back in his chair with his arms crossed over his stomach, Briggs looked at Fennell with the half-weary, half-amused expression of a patient teacher dealing with a rather dim student.

'What do you think is going on, Guy, when a source as important as Tiger Woods sends us a sketch of the Place Dauphine, another of a nearby car park, and a list of people who appear to be garage owners in the Paris area who have links with the Islamists?'

Fennell said nothing. Briggs could guess what was going through his mind. Guy understands all right, he said to himself, but he wants me to draw the conclusion for him.

'I don't know what you think, but it looks to me like a car-bomb attack, almost definitely inside the car park in the Place Dauphine, probably during the trial and perhaps on the day it opens.'

'Tiger Woods's documents are far from explicit, Archie. Why doesn't he spell things out clearly?'

'My dear Guy. How could a written message give us anything more than these documents? Someone with the right authority obviously asked him to reconnoitre the area immediately around the Palais de Justice and to supply a list of Apparatus agents and correspondents in the Paris area – second-hand car dealers and garage owners. Tiger appears to have supplied the intelligence he was asked to supply. That more or less keeps his cover intact, because the documents are far from him now, and because there is more than one copy in existence. But if he had sent us an explicit note, which is what you seem to want, he would have blown his cover. He would have been taking a huge risk if by any chance the message was intercepted. The game wouldn't have been worth the candle. Tiger doesn't know who will carry out the attack, or when or how. He doesn't even know if any attack will actually take place. After all, we plan enough operations and then abandon them ... So

50

any explanatory message he sends us would be vague in the extreme. No *who*, no *what*, no *when*, just a *where*. If the message did get into the wrong hands, this very haziness would point the finger at him. He's being careful. You can't hold that against him; he's watching his back.'

Pulling a face, Fennell stood up and began to walk in circles. Briggs quite understood his dilemma. By covering himself so well, the Sharif was leaving Guy dangerously exposed, and Guy did not like sticking his neck out.

'So you think someone is planning an attack ...'

So it is *I* who think so, Briggs said to himself. Guy was protecting himself as best he could.

'What I think, Guy, is that these documents suggest that an Islamist group we know nothing about at the moment is planning – or has at some point planned – a car-bomb attack on the Palais de Justice in Paris.'

'What should we do?'

'Given that you're the liaison officer, I think you should pass this intelligence on to the French without any further delay. Get hold of Dupond-Aignan right now. After all, we don't have a lot of time.' He glanced at his watch, as though to suggest that time was already running out. 'The trial opens in less than forty-eight hours.'

'Listen,' said Fennell, who was still pacing like a lion in a cage. 'I've got the frogs eating out of my hand ... Our hand, I mean,' he immediately corrected himself. 'The intelligence we have supplied them with so far has been much appreciated. Really appreciated. We can't spoil everything by giving them false intelligence, can we? Our credibility is at stake, Archie!'

'The fact remains that we do have this intelligence, true or false. We can't act as though we didn't have it. Imagine what would happen if an attack really did take place.'

A long silence followed while Guy Fennell weighed the pros and cons.

'Perhaps we should tell Cecil first,' he said at last. 'And perhaps the Minister. After all, this isn't just an intelligence matter. If Tiger turns out to be right, this is political. Very political!'

'As you like, Guy.'

'Right, right ... That is what we'll do, then. We'll ring Cecil and then ask Dupond-Aignan to drop by and see us.'

He's done it, Briggs thought. Guy has finally covered himself. The idea that an attack was being prepared was mine, not his. And Guy, who is usually so jealous of his prerogatives, makes sure that he does not see the Frenchman alone. That way, if the red alert triggered by the Sharif's intelligence proves to be groundless, he can always accuse me of being an alarmist. If the reverse is true, he can claim the credit for it on the grounds that he's the liaison officer.

As he was going home from their meeting with Cecil Devereux and Henri Dupond-Aignan, Briggs figured Guy would sleep badly that night. He could just see him tossing and turning, and hear the plaintive squeaks from the bedsprings and Mrs Fennell's sighs of exasperation. He could just see him getting up in the morning, feeling more exhausted than when he went to bed. He would go to the Clubhouse early in case Dupond-Aignan phoned. Once there, he would have some breakfast brought to his office, hover around the phone, pick up the handset at regular intervals to make sure his line was connected and resist going for a pee in case the noise of the flush stopped him from hearing the phone ring. During all that time, he would dream up scenarios. He would draw up a plan of attack should the Sharif's intelligence prove to be accurate, and at the same time prepare a fallback position in case things went wrong. Whatever happened, he had to be the first to get the information. So he would be in his office tomorrow morning in any case; and he would have a bad night, in any case.

Not so Briggs. Briggs had a peaceful sleep that night, hardly upset by the odd bad dream – he dreamt that a touch of frost had got his daffodils, which had flowered too early.

8

When Briggs got to the Clubhouse on the following Monday, he could tell from the frantic activity that the Sharif had been right and that Guy's vigil at-arms had paid off. His secretary Gladys confirmed his suspicions by informing him that he was expected at a meeting in the Director's office in five minutes.

'Do you know what's going on?' Mowbray-Smyth asked him as they met in the corridor. 'I really don't like these impromptu meetings. I've not even finished reading the papers yet.'

So Guy hadn't even bothered to take the Green Keeper into his confidence. That was a mistake, Briggs said to himself. Guy should be more careful.

'I have a vague idea,' he said. 'I think it's about Tiger Woods.'

Alec Rose was already outside of the Director's office, and the secretaries had joined forces to make the coffee: an obvious sign of a crisis meeting. A little red panel light finally turned green and one of the secretaries pressed a button. An electronic bleep sounded, and the heavily padded door opened outwards, forcing visitors to retreat before they could go in: a visible sign of power. Briggs, Rose, Mowbray-Smyth and the coffee team joined Devereux and Fennell in the office. Fennell, who was all smiles, remained seated as they entered: another visible sign of power.

'Bullseye!' he said as soon as the last secretary had left the room.

'It's a Birdie, you mean,' said Devereux, who was enthroned on a caster-wheeled Chesterfield behind a mass of mahogany that stood between him and common mortals.

'I did think of ringing you, Archie,' Fennell was saying, 'but it was after one when Dupond-Aignan rang me, and I didn't want to wake you.'

'I do wish someone would tell me what's going on,' protested Mowbray-Smyth.

'All right, all right,' Devereux condescended. 'Sit down, boys. Let me hand you over to our liaison officer, who will bring you up to date with the latest developments in Paris.'

'Right, then,' said Fennell, addressing his words to Nico Mowbray-Smyth, whom he felt he should appease. 'Early on Saturday evening, a message was transmitted from Tiger Woods warning us that a car-bomb attack on the Palais de Justice in Paris was being planned, probably in the underground car park that runs along the west side of the Palais ... So I discussed this with Archie – you weren't here, Nico – and after consulting Cecil' – a deferential nod towards the man on the Chesterfield throne – 'we finally decided to ask our friend Dupond-Aignan to be so good as to join us, and

55

alerted our friends in Paris without further ado ... It was delicate, of course. Our credibility was at stake. But with less than two days to go before the trial of an Islamist network opened, we did have to act quickly, didn't we?'

Indeed, thought Briggs as he looked at Fennell, who wore the expression of false modesty much as a leader who'd just taken a personal risk for the good of all.

'And it appears that we were right,' the risk-taker continued. 'Yesterday, at nineteen-hundred hours local time – eighteen-hundred hours our time – a grey BMW was driven into the Place Dauphine car park. A young woman was at the wheel. Our French friends, who were keeping a discreet watch (discreet because they still didn't quite believe us) asked the police officer stationed at the entrance a few questions. The officer knew both car and driver well. A local resident, a Uruguayan national by the name of –'

'Carmen Ferreira Rios,' Devereux finished Fennell's sentence for him after consulting a file.

'That's her ... Carmen Ferreira Rios, resident in France for two years. Lives on the top floor of Number 14b, a small flat sublet to her by an Argentine diplomat she's friendly with.'

'Number 14b is opposite Yves Montand's former flat,' said Devereux. 'Montand, the French crooner ... the actor... now deceased ... A bit too far to the left. Montand, not the flat. Sorry, do go on, Guy.'

'Six weeks ago, Miss Rios acquired a car – the BMW – and habitually left it in the car park. So Miss Rios parks her car on level one and quietly goes home. Nothing unusual so far.'

'Until ...' Devereux intervened. Success had made him somewhat jovial.

'Until ...' Fennell went on, delighted at being prompted by his boss, 'until one of our French friends, a certain Edouard ...'

'Labat,' Devereux again took the words out of his mouth. 'Captain Edouard Labat ... Oh yes, there are still a few military men in the French secret service.'

'Until our friend Captain Labat went to take a look at the BMW. Just to set his mind at rest.'

'And what does our conscientious and observant friend notice?' asked Devereux, in an attempt to keep up the suspense.

'He notices that the back of the car is sagging badly and that its shock absorbers look as though they're doing the splits. Which suggests that the car must be heavily loaded. Having used his torch to look inside and having checked that there was no bulky parcel that might explain why it looked overloaded, he then does something that no British law enforcement officer would dream of doing. Ignoring the danger, to say nothing of the law, he delicately picks the lock on the boot, hoping that he'll find something to explain why the tyres were in such agony and why the shocks were groaning.'

'But the boot is empty,' announced Devereux, sounding more like a ham actor than ever.

'The boot was indeed empty. Our French friend scratches his head, trying to think of another explanation. It is true that the car belonged to a lady, which might explain why it had been badly maintained and why the shock absorbers were in such a poor state. On the other hand, the tyres were new, and the car was a recent model. Faced with this enigma, and having exhausted the resources of both his intellect and his imagination, Captain Labat was overcome by a mixture of fear and exhilaration. And this time, he did what any model civil servant would have done: he alerted his superiors.'

57

'Then he conscientiously stood guard outside Number 14b, in case Miss Rios took it into her head to go out,' said Devereux, who had apparently decided Captain Labat deserved the Croix de Guerre.

'Two hours later, the bomb squad discreetly turned up and found an explosive charge of three hundred kilos under the back seat and into the side panels of the BMW.'

'Three hundred kilos, gentlemen!' Devereux interrupted. 'Over six hundred pounds!'

'A charge of three hundred kilos of dynamite primed to go off at nine-thirty the next morning.'

'Just a few hours before the start of the trial,' explained Devereux.

'The impact of the weight alone on the shock absorbers was obvious ... I leave you to imagine the impact the explosion would have had on the Palais de Justice. It would have shaken it to its foundations!'

A moment's pause, and a sip of coffee. Fennell was enjoying the effect his story was having on his audience.

'Incredible,' Mowbray-Smyth finally exclaimed.

'Flabbergasting!' added Alec Rose.

Briggs treated himself to a small biscuit.

'Indeed,' said Fennell. 'True professionals ... They came so close ...' Having risked his credibility in his heroic attempt to foil them, he was all the more inclined to praise the courage of the terrorists. 'Needless to say,' continued the hero of the day, 'there was no further call for discretion, and the Latin character of our French friends quickly came to the fore. The whole area was cordoned off by armed men from every force and ministry, roadblocks were thrown up across all the bridges to the island, and the French burst into the Uruguayan's flat. They found her sitting in front of her Mac, wearing only a bra and panties. They unceremoniously bundled her into a car and then subjected her to the kind of strong-arm treatment she had left Latin America to get away from. Obviously shocked and in a state of panic, she denied everything and just kept saying, "It's impossible, it's impossible,"' in a dazed tone.

Another pause. Another round of coffee.

'Just after midnight,' Fennell continued, 'our Captain Labat –'

'Who wasn't born yesterday,' Devereux butted in, just to prove how much he admired him.

'... It occurred to Captain Labat that perhaps he wasn't dealing with a terrorist of the Tupamaros vintage or with a zealot who had recently converted to Islam, but with a poor sucker. So, he gave her a hot drink ...'

'... And his coat to cover her nakedness,' said Devereux, who wanted Labat to be a gentleman as well as an officer.

'Miss Rios gradually calmed down, and Labat was able to put the whole story together. Three months earlier she had attended a reception at the Argentine embassy, where she met a charming young Lebanese businessman.'

'One Akram Harbi,' said Devereux, after a quick glance at his file. 'Nothing on record.'

'Good-looking, well-dressed, speaks perfect English and French, obviously quite well-off. And young Carmen Ferreira Rios, who was on the rebound –'

'The artist she had come to Paris for had just dumped her,' explained Devereux.

'... Allowed herself to be seduced by this handsome stranger. A real man about town, very different from her former lover, who was something of a tormented soul. She fell in love with him. And, if she is to be believed, he fell in love with her. Our lovebirds were having an idyllic affair and met whenever Akram's work brought him to

Paris, never in her flat but always in his suite at the Royal Monceau. Six weeks ago, Akram gave his lady-love a BMW. Second-hand, but nearly new. A dealer friend who owed him a favour; and the friend in question ...' At this point, Fennell paused and waited for someone to finish his sentence for him.

'The friend in question,' continued Briggs, who wanted to give him a little treat, 'is on the list of car dealers and garage owners supplied by Tiger Woods.'

'Ex-act-ly!' said Fennell. 'His name is Rami Makhzumi. He is Lebanese and he calls himself Rémi because it sounds more French. He has a garage dealing in second-hand German cars in Evry, just outside Paris. Carmen is delighted ... Akram phones her on Friday evening. He's in town for the weekend. The next morning they both go off in the BMW to have lunch in the country, then go back to the hotel and stay in their room until the evening. When they go down to get the car, they find that vandals have scratched the paintwork and slashed the tyres. Carmen is devastated, but Akram takes things in hand. No problem. He will ring his friend Rémi, who will send a tow truck, change all four tyres, touch up the paintwork and check that everything is in good working order while he's at it. It is well-known that the Lebanese are always willing to lend a helping hand, and that they don't balk at working over the weekend. Young Carmen is delighted that everything is being taken care of. She finds Akram such a comfort. The next day, in other words yesterday, she finds that her car has been repaired, washed and polished and given a re-spray. Handing her the keys, Akram says goodbye. He has a plane to catch. No need for Carmen to drive him to the airport: with everyone coming back to Paris after the weekend break, she would be caught up in the jams. It's really not worth it, they'll see each other next week, he'll call tonight or tomorrow ... "*Bonté divine*," says Captain

60

Labat to himself, "*Bonté divine*," or whatever it is that the French say in such circumstances: he might phone. While Carmen is telling him how Akram had walked her to her BMW, our French colleague takes her by the hand and drags her into the street. As she is describing their goodbyes, he bundles her into a car and takes off for the Place Dauphine. He thinks he still might have a chance to catch this Akram. But Akram didn't phone that night. Nor the next day. He's still running.'

Another pause for a mouthful of cold coffee. Briggs thought to himself that Guy owed much of his success to his talent for telling stories.

'After that,' continued the storyteller, 'the French, who'd been keeping our friend Rémi under close surveillance, arrest him and search his house and garage. I'll spare you the details of everything they found. Dupond-Aignan phoned me during the night to inform me that the operation had been a success, and he sent us his report first thing this morning.

'The classic honey trap,' said Briggs.

'A honey trap that marks the start of a new honeymoon for us and the French,' Devereux declared. 'They are delighted and they insist on thanking us in person. So Guy is going to Paris. Guy, I'm counting on you to re-launch the Entente Cordiale, and so on and so forth ... That's what I call a job well done, boys. But I do have to admit that these frantic weekends wear me out ... Archie, are you sure that Boone can't find a way of communicating with Tiger Woods earlier in the week, rather than on Saturdays?'

9

London was gearing up for the Christmas break. The TV and radio hammered home the message that there were only six more shopping days. Only six short days to take part in the serial cloning of Santa Claus and make a child, a lover or a maiden aunt happy. Screamed at by adverts and directed by neon signs, Orwellian figures – shoppers who couldn't make up their minds or who had left it a bit late – pushed and shoved and carelessly trod on each others' toes on the crowded pavements and in the stuffed department stores, where the alluring Christmas carols competed with the ringing of insatiable cash desks.

Only a hundred yards away from all this, and cut off from all the commercial pruritus by the sober bulk of the British Museum, Russell Square was an oasis of calm. The absence of activity was so conspicuous that the place seemed to be sulking. There were no fashion boutiques here, and no toy shops. No decorations lit up the square's leafless trees and the blank facades of the sleepy buildings. Deserted by its American clientele, which was suffering from a new bout of isolationism, the Russell Hotel was dozing. Forsaken by their students, the various faculties had gone to sleep. The bank and university clerks who made up the rest of the local population were champing at the bit and counting the hours to the long weekend. Overlooked by the advertising world and forgotten by everyone, Russell Square appeared like a black hole in the festive galaxy.

Only one thing jarred in this picture of catatonia: the Clubhouse. This year, the Clubhouse was the scene of activity as frantic as it was unusual. Nestling quietly between the Commonwealth Institute and the Centre for Slavic Studies, the Clubhouse usually went into hibernation during holiday periods. For it normally marched in step with its masters, and when they finally withdrew to their damp country houses and Caribbean retreats, leaving the Queen to pass on their best wishes to those they governed, the Clubhouse followed them like Mother Courage. Ever since it had come into existence, the Clubhouse had been at Whitehall's beck and call. And when Westminster and Fleet Street took a break, and Whitehall could at last breathe again, the Clubhouse dropped its guard and put everything on hold.

Not this year, though. This year, the Clubhouse had broken the habit of a lifetime, and was listening hard. But it was listening to the Sharif, and not to Whitehall. Devereux, who had been planning to take a holiday in Bermuda, had stood up his family and an under-secretary of his acquaintance and was putting in unprecedented weekend appearances in Russell Square; Fennell had been so zealous as to move a cot into his office; and Old Syd, whose main job until now had been to politely redirect the odd waylaid student, had turned overnight into a fearsome watchdog, taking an obvious pleasure in being high-handed with the Clubhouse's many official visitors and suitors.

The Clubhouse's staff knew that something important was going on and that the Service was the object of everyone's attention. The lights, especially on the fourth floor, burned until late at night, and on the lower floors the tea breaks were alive with rumours. Even those who normally cleared their desks at five-thirty were there until after seven, hanging about in case the top floor needed them.

As it happened, the top floor didn't need anyone from downstairs. The top floor needed the Sharif. For some time now he had been playing hard to get. A real prima donna. Ever since the Place Dauphine triumph, nothing. Having been impressed by the brio of his debut performance, the audience was getting impatient: Devereux, the master of ceremonies, was beginning to regret his ruined weekends and his holiday with the under-secretary, while Fennell, the impresario, was on the verge of depression. Feverish activity may have been the order of the day on the lower floors, but upstairs on the fourth the atmosphere was somewhat morose.

'What's going on, Archie? Since the Place Dauphine business, your source has given us nothing but scraps.'

Fennell had just come out of a meeting with Tom Van Dusen. Having failed to give the American anything he could get his teeth into, he was in a filthy mood.

'*My* source, as you put it, is a man, not a machine!'

'Archie, Archie ... Don't lecture me about the difference between human and technical sources of intelligence. My people do deal with sources, you know. We don't just plant microphones, interpret satellite photos and read the phone tap reports that the Big Ears are kind enough to send us! I know perfectly well that a source can be blown, cut off from his handler or denied all means of communication. I know all that! And I also know that your source has none of those problems. We know that Tiger Woods is still in place, we know that Boone is still in contact with him, and we know that the courier is working normally. So allow me to ask you again.' He had jumped from his chair and was staring at Briggs, one hand on Devereux's desk as though that would lend him some authority. 'What's going on? Perhaps Boone's not handling him properly.'

'You're laying it on a bit thick. Harry doesn't handle Tiger, nor does he handle the Sheikh, who's the cut-out between Tiger and us. Harry just handles the courier, and the courier is doing his job perfectly well.'

'But his production is tailing off. Not only does he send us warmed-over and rehashed stuff, he also refuses to answer our questions. Nothing about Cholmondeley's murder, and nothing – absolutely nothing – about the attacks on the Americans. Not a dicky bird!'

'He's frightened.'

'Frightened? You ... you mean he doesn't want to go on working for us?' The prospect must have made Fennell go weak at the knees. He slumped into his seat.

'I don't think so. He's still producing, isn't he? He's still in touch. The only thing is, he wants to work at his own pace, not ours. And if we want to keep him, we'll have to adjust to his rhythm.'

Fennell's working rhythm – and even his biorhythm – matched that of the different organising committees, restructuring committees, liaison committees and co-ordinating committees whose meetings filled his diary. The prospect of working to the Sharif's rhythm didn't seem to have much appeal for him.

65

'And I suppose you've made a study of his *rhythm*?'

'Harry has. He thinks he has worked out how Tiger Woods's mind works.'

'And what does your man think?' interjected Devereux, who seemed to have taken no interest in the discussion until now. Ensconced in his armchair, with his back to his subordinates, he had passed the time clicking the top of a biro and admiring the mahogany William IV console he had recently acquired. Pushing against the silky carpet with his foot, he swivelled himself around and joined in the discussion.

'Well, Archie?'

Briggs did not reply immediately. He had taken off his glasses and was wiping them with his handkerchief. The handkerchief was finding it difficult to cope with the smooth surface, and Briggs was silently cursing his optician, or rather his optician's son, who had persuaded him to buy non-reflective lenses. He held his glasses up to the light, pulled a doubtful face, and put them back on his nose. He then carefully folded his handkerchief before putting it back in his pocket.

'Harry looked into when Tiger sent his dispatches, and he noticed something. He noticed that Tiger first contacted us after the chance discovery of an Islamist network in Cardiff. He could have done so immediately after he came back from Quetta. It was already obvious to him then, that he would take the plunge sooner or later. But he didn't, did he? He waited until the arrests in Cardiff had been made before supplying us with any intelligence about Islamist networks in this country. And all that time, he went on ignoring our urgent requests for information about Cholmondeley's death and about terrorist attacks on US targets ... The second time he came up with anything was after the arrest of the Algerians in France. It was immediately after that that he gave us the Place Dauphine operation.'

'What are you driving at?' Fennell was losing his patience.

'Harry made the connection, and he reached the conclusion that Tiger always waits until arrests have been made, and been made public, before sending us four-star intelligence. Why? To cover his back, obviously. To make sure that his masters don't suspect a leak. To lead them to the conclusion that we are getting our information from someone we've arrested or from some notebook we've found in a safe house or other. It's a red herring. He probably does know who killed Cholmondeley, he probably does know who is carrying out attacks on the Americans, but he's careful not to breathe a word to us before making sure that we have a lead, no matter how tenuous it is. A lead that can explain the leaks and help him cover his back. He won't be hurried. He insists on working at his own pace and deciding what he sends us and when he sends it.'

There was a long silence as the espiocrats who had never done any fieldwork nor gone anywhere near the Rough slowly digested this lecture on espionage. Briggs, who had been eyeing the plate of biscuits for some time, took advantage of the silence to delicately lift up a wafer with one finger, hoping to find a chocolate biscuit underneath it.

'Well, it sounds plausible to me,' Devereux finally sighed. 'But having said that, this leaves the problem intact so far as we are concerned. We've pulled in the punters and raised the bidding, but we won't get very far without the goods. For the moment, we've still got the wind in our sails. But if we have to rely on Tiger Woods for a good wind, I fear, gentlemen, that we will end up by missing the tide. So the question is this: what can we do to bring our source back to life? Perhaps you have a suggestion, Guy?' He turned to Fennell who, coming out of his lethargy, had got to his feet and was now pacing the room with his hands in his trouser pockets.

'I do,' he replied, coming to a halt and speaking to his shoes. 'A Drop.'

'A Drop!' exclaimed Briggs.

'A Drop, Archie! We're going to exfiltrate him from Beirut! He's going to defect and come here. We'll offer him an easy way out, all the money he wants, a new identity, and a new face if he wants one. The whole works.'

'Impossible!'

'Impossible? Why is it impossible? If he's frightened, if he feels he's in danger, a Drop will solve both his and all our problems. He'll be safe, and we'll have our source close to hand. We'll provide our own good wind,' he continued, looking at Devereux, 'and we won't miss the tide.' Fennell was a good armchair tactician.

'It won't work,' moaned Briggs. Matching actions to words, he pulled a doleful face as though to show that he was genuinely sorry.

'I agree with Archie,' said Mowbray-Smyth. 'I really don't see the Sharif defecting, changing his identity, opening a numbered bank account in Curaçao and settling down in a cottage to grow roses. Still less do I see him publishing a book called *I Spied for Islamintern* and going on the American lecture circuit. Might have been good enough for the Russians, Guy, but it's not an Arab's cup of tea.'

'That's true.' Devereux sounded annoyed. 'These people are … how shall I put it … different.'

'I don't want to encroach upon Nico and Archie's territory,' replied Fennell. 'I have every confidence in their understanding of the Arab and Muslim mentality. But they tell us that Tiger is frightened, that he is sitting in an ejector seat and that his protectors are abandoning him. So I say to myself: what do we have to lose by trying?'

'Things are already weighted in his favour as it is,' said Briggs, and then realised that he'd have done better to shut up.

'Who's responsible, if not Boone?' Fennell was again on the attack.

'It would look as though we were begging. We wouldn't be able to control him.'

'Control him, Archie? Did you say control? We have to get hold of him before we can control him. You yourself admit that we have no means of bringing pressure to bear.'

'Psychologically, such a suggestion would put us in a very uncomfortable position.'

'Psychologically! I'm interested in intelligence, not psychology! Art for art's sake? Not for me, Archie!' Fennell was pushing his advantage home now. 'To tell you the truth, I don't give a damn if Boone feels his source has the upper hand. My problem is finding satisfactory answers to the questions we have been asked. And if Tiger's defection helps us do that, I don't see why we should hesitate. Tell Boone to contact him. Tell him to go and see him in person and make him an offer. That's what I suggest.'

Briggs turned to Mowbray-Smyth, but the Green Keeper was miles away. He had decided to devote all his attention to his gaudy socks. No hope of any support from that quarter. Briggs knew that he was fighting a rear-guard battle from now on.

'Assuming that he does take our offer seriously, his defection would deprive us of a prime source. An irreplaceable source of intelligence about the Apparatus's plans ...'

'The Apparatus's plans?' Fennell butted in. 'Let's talk about these plans! The plans your source tells about in drips and drabs, when he feels like it and always in a roundabout way. You see, Archie, given the setbacks it's been suffering, I'm wondering if what the Apparatus plans to do, or what it can do, matters as much as what it has done already ... If Tiger Woods came here, that would at least help us to clear up all these obscure questions.'

Fennell was staring at Devereux, who was scratching his nose and sniffing his fingers, perhaps to make sure they hadn't already been burned. Everyone waited patiently for the boss to complete his nasal analysis.

'Guy's right,' said 'the nose' after making a one-hundred-and-eighty-degree turn. 'Cholmondeley, the attacks against the Americans, anthrax spores, smallpox virus and flying schools – that's what the Minister is interested in. Whitehall knows that we are dealing with a senior Islamist source, and Whitehall still doesn't understand why all these questions remain unanswered. They are beginning to think that things are moving a bit slowly. For the moment we still have a short reprieve, but as soon as the holidays are over the pressure will be on and things will heat up.'

'The Drop will give us the respite we need,' Fennell reassured him. 'As soon as the Minister has been informed that we plan to bring our source here, he will be able to calm Whitehall down.

'That's true.' Devereux's face lit up. 'Guy's right. That'll calm Whitehall down!'

Deciding that Whitehall was too much for him, Briggs threw in the towel. Taking off his glasses, he placed them in his breast pocket and retreated into a reassuringly out-of-focus world.

10

The chairs had been set out Eastern-style around the walls, and the centre of the room was taken up with an immense carpet. A tawdry chandelier hang from the ceiling. Shartuni had gone straight to a velvet armchair beneath a calligraphic Qur'anic verse in a gilded frame. Boone assumed that this was his usual place, and that the Sheikh sat opposite him by the telephone. Their discussions then took place across the big Persian carpet. Between them, he thought, the Sheikh and the professor must have an answer for everything. They must even have answers to questions that did not yet exist.

Ever since they had got here, Shartuni had been looking quite serene. Nothing like the man Boone had met at the Marbella Beach two hours earlier. That Shartuni had been sweating heavily, and had difficulty in controlling the fear that was gnawing away at him. To cheer him up, Boone had given him a little reward – a crested invitation requesting the honour of his presence at a conference Chatham House was organising on the role of Islam in the new world order. Shartuni immediately forgot his fears. The Shartunis of this world set great store by conferences and other international talking shops. They gave them the opportunity to travel, fill their address books and add to CVs that were already lengthy. So, thanks to the Clubhouse and thanks to the Sharif in particular, Dr Shartuni, author of a number of obscure articles published in even more obscure journals, could go off to England in the spring, his briefcase duly filled with the off-prints he would hand out as though they were business cards.

Boone couldn't identify the noise coming from the terrace outside. It sounded like a piece of machinery that needed oiling. Puzzled, he was getting up to go and investigate when the drapes dividing the public space of the house from its private space parted to reveal a boy of about ten and a bearded man floating in a black robe. Looking like a bat, Sheikh Ahmad Hammud made straight for Boone and embraced him. The boy gave Shartuni a kiss on the cheek and called him 'uncle'. The Sheikh held Boone in a wordless embrace, and the piercing noise of the badly oiled machine could still be heard. Finally letting go of his prey, the Sheikh gestured towards the French windows, and Boone thought he was about to reveal the source of the mysterious noise. He was in fact inviting Boone to follow him onto the terrace. All four of them went out, the boy holding Shartuni's hand and the Sheikh's batwings brushing against Boone's arm.

The terrace overlooked an orchard, and the noise that was puzzling Boone came from a couch hammock with an awning. A man was sitting in it and swinging back and forth, causing the ball-bearings to squeak. Boone could see him in profile. He was smoking and staring straight ahead. Leaving Boone standing, the Sheikh did his bat act again and joined Shartuni and the boy amongst the orange trees and the medlars.

Boone approached the man with the cigarette and sat down beside him. This was the last thing he had been expecting. He had been expecting untimely halts, sudden changes of direction and vehicle, underground car parks with multiple entries and a brief meeting in some badly lit cellar or in the back seat of a moving car. But here they were in broad daylight, sitting in the sun on a flower-patterned hammock! He began to hope that this business would be less traumatic than he had feared, and that all would go smoothly as it should between civilised Levantines.

They remained silent for a few moments, and then the smoker flicked his cigarette away, used his foot to stop the hammock and turned to him.

'Harry Boone,' he announced to no one in particular.

The right side of his face was disfigured by ugly scars running down from his temple, across his eyebrow, cheek and ear, and then disappearing down his neck.

'Are you well, my friend?' he asked in good English.

He had the harsh voice of a man capable of impressing an audience despite his young age. This was a voice that was accustomed to giving orders, a voice that spoke plainly, without any of the false humility of the average cleric.

'I'm very well,' replied Boone in his halting Arabic.

'I imagine there must be a problem somewhere. Otherwise you wouldn't have insisted on meeting me.'

'It's London.' Boone lit a Dutch cigar to disguise his lack of composure. 'London is worried.'

'We are all in His hands,' said the believer.

'It's the quality of the intelligence that worries them,' Boone continued in more prosaic terms. 'The dispatches are becoming irregular.'

'We are not the masters of Time,' explained the Prophet's descendant, lighting another cigarette. 'But we can sort this out. We'll find a way, you and me.' He had adopted an informal tone that suggested some closeness, some shared history.

'London has an offer to put to you.' Boone felt embarrassed.

'I'm listening.'

'London thinks you are in danger.' Boone was beating about the bush. 'They'd like to reassure you. Get you to safety.'

'They want me to go to England?'

'They've got a bee in their bonnet about it,' replied Boone in a tone that implied that this crazy idea was nothing to do with him.

'They want me to *defect*?' He smiled. 'Like in the good old days of the Cold War? Like in the movies?'

'Something of the sort.'

Boone felt awkward. He hated Briggs for having put him in this position.

The Sharif said nothing and started swinging again. Faster and faster. Boone was beginning to feel sick.

'I accept,' the Sharif finally said, and suddenly stopped the swinging.

'You ... you accept?' Boone was flabbergasted. He had been caught off-balance.

'On one condition. We do it my way.'

'You accept?'

'In a fortnight's time, you will send Shartuni to see the Sheikh as usual.' He gestured towards the bat and his acolyte. 'You will stick to the same routine. While they are together, my car will take a very specific route and you will arrange for it to be totally destroyed.'

'What?'

'I won't be in it of course,' said the Sharif, pretending not to see why Boone was so surprised. 'But it will be my car, and my bodyguards.'

'You mean a bomb?'

Boone suddenly saw his cushy life being turned completely upside down. If he got mixed up in a car-bomb attack, nothing would ever be the same again.

'A bomb attack, yes. A car-bomb, with my car as the target.'

'A car-bomb,' Boone repeated in a monotone as he tried to relight his cigar.

'If I have to disappear, we might as well do things properly.'

'You want us to plant a bomb to cover your defection?'

'To cover my tracks,' said the Sharif, throwing his cigarette away. 'They mustn't know anything. They have to be convinced that I'm dead.'

'A car-bomb! I don't know if they'll agree to that,' said Boone, praying with all his might that London would say no to this diabolical plan.

'I didn't ask for anything,' said the Sharif, setting the hammock in motion once again. 'You came looking for me. It's either that or nothing.'

He's got a nerve, Boone said to himself. He really has.

'And I want a real bomb. Not some little firecracker. The Mercedes has to be blown to pieces, and it has to be impossible to identify the remains of the passengers.'

He wants to implicate London, thought Boone.

75

'If you can't get your hands on some C4, make sure you use at least three hundred kilos of semtex and cakes of plastic explosive.'

He wants London to be in it up to the hilt, thought Boone.

'To make sure that the explosives take care of the car's armour plating, use hollow charges, mortar shells, and anti-tank mines.'

What am I doing here, Harry Boone asked himself. What am I doing here, sitting under a flowery awning in an orchard, listening to a complete lunatic issue deadly instructions as though he were giving me a recipe? And why am I saying nothing?

'You will wait for me at the Museum,' the Sharif was saying. 'Near the French ambassador's residence. I'll meet you immediately after the explosion. Those are my conditions.'

'Some conditions!'

'If London wants me, then London will have to pay the price.'

And what a price! The Sharif was going to cost London dear. And the more he costs them, the more precious he would be and the more they'd want to hold on to him. Once they had paid the price, they would pamper him and defend him tooth and nail.

Boone was in a state of near panic. He hadn't been thinking of days like this or of getting mixed up with the dirty tricks brigade when he joined the secret service once his wife had made him a free man again. At the time, he had been teaching in a minor Catholic boarding school deep in the country, and neither the atmosphere nor the climate had been to his liking. He wanted to see the world, he had said to himself, and he also wanted to be looked after without having to do anything in exchange. No point in forcing yourself, he had said to himself. Taking holy orders had seemed like a good idea at one point, but the fact of the matter was that he was not very keen on the vows of chastity that went with the job. He had also thought of marrying a rich heiress but, quite apart from the fact that it would have been difficult for him to find one (Boone did not exactly move in the right circles), some lingering sense of Christian morality had got in the way. Which left the public service. That would give him both the chance to travel and ensure that a cheque would arrive at the end of the month without him having to worry about it. Boone had ruled out the Army from the start: too violent for his liking. Its forays abroad were usually synonymous with wartime expeditions. As for the Foreign Office, he was well aware that he would never get the kind of posting he wanted and would probably spend the rest of his life in some obscure office in London. He hadn't been to the right kind of school for that, and the closest he'd ever been to the elite of this country was when he'd watched them over the red brick walls of the plebeian college he'd attended at Oxford. That only left the secret service, which he had finally joined in the hope that *secret*, and not *service*, would be the magic word, and that he would be able to exploit this secrecy to hide the inaction he intended to cultivate. It had worked, too. At first with the Bunkers, and later at the Clubhouse. But now his hand was being forced. He was being driven to forsake his natural idleness and get mixed up with actions (and violent actions, at that) that would probably not remain secret for very long. Actions that threatened to upset the system he had so patiently put in place.

11

It was after two in the morning and London still hadn't reacted to his message. They must be doing some hard thinking in Russell Square, Boone thought. The Royal & Ancient must have called up all the troops. A decision of this importance required nothing less than total unanimity, consensus being the essential precondition for a successful career for everyone. Harry Boone had his system in Beirut, and the Royal & Ancient had its own system in London.

He could just imagine the scene. Guy would begin by crying wolf so that, if need be, he could say later that he had tried to warn them all. Nico would disagree, and say that he didn't think it was a trap. Archie would say that the Sharif's suggestion was consistent with his approach. But Guy wouldn't give in. Caution was his middle name. Having come up with this idea in the first place, he would play devil's advocate, and Devereux and Rose would naturally agree with him. Then, slowly but surely, and because their desire to get their claws into the Sharif outweighed their bureaucratic anxieties, they would let themselves be convinced. In the meantime they'd have worked out a fallback position. They'd build up a file containing all the evidence, tenuous as it might be, that suggested that the Sharif was playing a double-cross game. Every scrap of intelligence, every rumour that linked him directly or indirectly to Cholmondeley's murder, planes that had been crashed into office blocks, water towers that had been poisoned and a dozen or so similar atrocities. If things went wrong, and if the Sharif's proposal did prove to be a trap, they could always say that they had been making a serious attempt to eliminate the murderous bastard and that, sorry and all that, you can't make an omelette without breaking eggs. After all, they would say, our American cousins and Israeli allies don't discriminate.

Finally, the Royal & Ancient would come to a unanimous agreement. Not about the operation itself but about the safety net. Once that had been worked out, Devereux would go to see Walker at his house in the Cotswolds. Walker would receive him in his wood-panelled smoking room, Devereux would state the facts; Walker would dwell at length on the fallback strategy and quickly give it a spin for the politicians and the media; if the spin was to his liking, he would give the operation the green light. That was decision-making at its best.

The telephone finally interrupted Boone's train of thought, and he picked it up at once before it could wake Maria, who was sleeping in the next room.

'I hope I'm not dragging you out of bed,' said Briggs's voice on the other end of the line.

'Not at all. I was waiting for your call.'

'Let's go onto the scrambler.'

Shit, thought Boone, pressing a button on his mobile. His boss's voice came back immediately, sounding metallic and out of synch.

'Agreed, Harry.'

Shit, shit, shit. Boone could see what was coming next.

'Our friend's suggestion has been accepted.'

Hence the phone call, of course. No written traces, not even any electronic traces.

'But we would like the job to be done by a Pro.'

A Pro! London was being careful. In the snobbish terminology the Service had picked up on the golf course, a Pro was a mercenary. Nothing to do with the so-called Gentlemen who were the Service's backbone and who also supplied it with its honourable correspondents. Pros were not in-house, and they were never invited to the Clubhouse.

'Acting directly is out of the question. Subcontracting this business to our friend the Colonel is also out of the question. You understand?'

'Perfectly.'

'The Pro you choose has to be convinced that this is a real job, not a mere diversion. Understood?'

'Understood.'

'Do you think it can be done?'

'I'll be able to tell you that next week. Perhaps as early as Monday.'

'Very good, Harry. Phone me when you know more.'

Phone me! Meaning don't commit anything to writing!

'We'll pay whatever we have to pay. No limits. Understood?'

'Understood.' Boone quite understood that, for the Royal & Ancient, a comfortable margin of deniability was essential. Pros were paid very well to compensate them for their bastard status. The Service would never admit to having anything to do with whatever it was they did. It wouldn't raise a finger to get them out of any trouble they might get themselves into.

'Have a good weekend, Harry.'

'You too,' said Boone as he hung up, thinking of the pious Sunday that lay in store for him.

'Well?' asked Maria through the closed door. So she wasn't asleep.

'They've agreed,' he sighed.

'They're mad!' she shouted as she came out of the room, legs bare and wearing his pyjama top. 'They're completely mad!'

'Mad or not mad, I have to do what they say.'

'A car-bomb attack in the middle of Beirut is complete madness. That war on terrorism's given them a taste for blood!'

'This is just the beginning ...'

Boone told himself that he should never have left his minor school in the country.

'Surely you're not going to do it yourself, Harry!'

'I was thinking of passing it on to Kamel and using him as cover, but they won't wear it.'

'They might be mad, but they're not stupid.'

'Pity. Having the Lebanese *Sûreté* on board would have made life easier.'

'Anyone else in mind?'

'Theo, maybe'. Boone always told his mistress everything, and he also made sure that the Clubhouse knew it. Maria was just as much part of his system as his flat, his office, his safe and his armour-plated door. She was in on all his secrets. Some people in London might have wanted to recall him, but others realised it was safer to keep him in Beirut, if only to make sure that his mistress didn't go telling everybody all she knew.

'Isn't Theo getting a bit old for this kind of thing?'

'He's old, and he's been sidelined. So he'll be all the more willing to do it.'

'And then? After the car-bomb?'

'The Sharif will meet me by the French embassy, at the Passage du Musée, and I'll drive him to Halate. I was talking to Roger Trad this afternoon.'

'King Roger himself? Nice to know you have friends in high places!'

'He's agreed to lend me his yacht for a trip to Limassol.'

'The *Jolly Roger II*? Or is it already the *Jolly Roger III*? Maybe even *IV*? You know he ordered a hundred Jolly Roger ties, with skull and crossbones, from Benson & Clegg? He blithely hands them out to all his friends. Or should I say his victims ... They wear them with pride, as though they were his trademark. Putting the rope around their own necks, so to speak.'

Boone ignored her teasing. He knew that Maria had once been Trad's mistress, and that it had ended badly.

'He won't be needing his yacht that day,' he said.

'A weekend of *après-ski* at Faqra, I suppose? I hope you won't be away for long. You know I don't like you going away.'

Boone knew she could not put up with long periods of widowhood, and that she usually found some charitable soul to console her. He was furious, and cursed the Sharif and the Royal & Ancient for having got him into this mess.

12

The priest had just finished reading the Gospel in Armenian. Then he bravely began to read it again in Arabic. The eleven o'clock mass at Saint Michael's Armenian-Catholic Church catered for a congregation of assimilated bourgeois who had all lost touch with their mother tongue to some degree. That was why the priest celebrated mass in two languages. It was now time for his second sermon of the day. He stammered his way through it in a halting Arabic that offended even Boone's profane sensibilities. He listened with half an ear, looking around the church in the hope of catching sight of a frail figure with a shock of white hair. There was no shortage of little old men that morning, all of them bowing and kneeling, some waiting for others to do so first as if to highlight their self-importance. But none of them had the *gravitas* or the ostentatiously contemplative air

Boone was looking for. He made a special effort to recall the liturgy and its high points, when crowd movements might allow him to catch out a certain someone who would be watching even more carefully than he. His prayers were answered when the moment came for communion. The man he was looking for was there, all right.

At the end of the service, the man left the priest and his flock to gossip on the church porch and made his way down the steps without looking back, crossing the little bridge over the dried-up Beirut River and entering the Armenian Quarter. Boone followed him on the opposite pavement. The man walked a further hundred metres without looking back, and then disappeared into Number 83 Rue Arax. In the Armenian Quarter, each street had its name on a clearly marked street sign; each block of houses had its letter and each building had its number. The Armenians were good Cartesians. Things were different elsewhere in the city, where space was organised around a local landmark such as a nearby mosque or church, or even some 'mini-supermarket' or other. Addressing a letter to someone living there was like playing charades ('Mister so-and-so, Building this-or-that, behind the old school, opposite the grocer's'). It was a real stylistic exercise for the sender and a tough job of interpretation for the postman. Failing which, the post stood no chance of reaching its destination. Not so in the Armenian Quarter: there, the rational division of space was the rule.

Crossing the street, Boone entered the building. In the dingy stairwell, a sheet of paper taped to a door told the visitor he had found his way to the ERA: Ecumenical Relief Agency. Very funny, Boone thought to himself. The door was ajar, but he still pressed the doorbell, which played religious music. The Padre seemed to have kept his sense of humour.

'Come in, Harry, come in.'

So he had seen him in the church. That's why he had missed out on all the gossip, even though he usually enjoyed it. Boone pushed the door. It creaked open to reveal a little man with a short white beard. His face broke into a wide carnivorous smile. He was holding a bottle and two glasses.

'Come on in, Harry!'

'Hello, Theo.'

'Come on, we can't drink on the doorstep!'

Closing the door behind him, Boone found himself in a room that needed a good sweep and a lick of paint. There were maps everywhere – tourist maps of the region, military maps of Lebanon, even aerial photographs of Beirut. A large crucifix hung above the unmade bed. Other features included a cupboard, a table, three chairs, and piles of books and folders on the bare floor. The windows had no curtains and the shutters were closed. Theo Damiano had obviously fallen on hard times.

'Welcome to ERA,' he said, putting the bottle on the table.

They sat and drank in silence. Boone thought Theo had aged. But his eyes were still the same. They had lost none of their liveliness and mocking sparkle. And he still had the same white teeth – the teeth of an American film star, of a predator.

'It's been a long time, Harry. How's my niece?'

'Maria isn't your niece, Theo!'

'Her father was my best friend. So I have every right to call her my niece, don't I? Oh, never mind ... Is this a private visit, Harry, or are you here on official business?'

'Let's just say I've not been here.'

'Spoken like a true Englishman!'

'I'm Irish, Theo.'

'You really wouldn't think it. You've become more English than the English. I think I liked you better the way you were.'

A hint of criticism now, that signalled a full-scale attack was about to come.

'How are you?' Boone was trying to duck. 'Everything all right?'

'We get by, Harry, we get by. We have our refugees, lots of them; and we have our benefactors, not so many of them; and we still hand out such gifts as our slender resources allow us to hand out. No religious discrimination.' Now the hint of ecumenism.

'And what about your other business?'

'My other business? You'd know more about that than I do, Harry. What you call my *other* business has been hit by the competition from the major department stores ... Ever since your outfit and other outfits like it withdrew their custom ... And for what, I ask you? To give it to those idiots in the *Sûreté*.'

He was on his feet now. Time for the full guilt trip, Boone said to himself. Theo Damiano was a past master at making people feel guilty. Not for nothing did they call him Padre.

'Times have changed, Theo. Liaison ... That's the name of the game these days. Our masters swear by it. Liaison with the more or less friendly services ... That's the new philosophy of intelligence.'

'Bah,' sneered Damiano, sitting down again. 'That's how you end up living on the frozen food that our friend Kamel is kind enough to dish out to you ... Bah.' Another sneer. 'Listen to this, Harry. Last year, Kamel went to France at the invitation of the French secret service. He had the brilliant idea of including in his delegation Captain Jaafar Nasrallah from the Passport Department. The guy's never been near a source in his life, Harry. A real pen-pusher, his fingers stained with ink from his rubber stamps. The sort of guy who takes his thumb-piece to bed with him. But never mind all that,

Kamel takes him to Paris. He's clever, is Kamel. At the time, all eyes were on Hezbollah's Sheikh Hasan Nasrallah. So Kamel turns up in Paris with a Nasrallah, and passes him of as the other man's cousin. At dinner, Captain Nasrallah finds himself sitting next to the French Director General, no less. The Frenchman couldn't keep his eyes off him. Kamel had, of course, omitted to tell his hosts that Nasrallahs are ten a penny here... What do you think of that? What do you think of the way the Western services are so taken with the *Sûreté*?'

'They're not taking any risk, Theo. They don't want any nasty surprises. Beirut is the new Vienna: Vienna in '46. Without the tragedy, but with added greed. Everyone in Beirut has intelligence to sell. One in two Lebanese has a brother, a friend, a cousin or a friend of a cousin's who is in the Apparatus, in Hezbollah or with the drug lords. If not all three. If junk bonds existed in the intelligence world, Theo, Beirut would be the perfect place to trade them.'

'Beirut is far worse than Vienna ever was, Harry,' said Damiano, shaking his head sadly. 'These days, they don't just sell the same intelligence over and over again. In triplicate, at that. They even sell the questions one puts to them. These days, it's the questions that are valuable, not the answers. It's very lucrative, the questions business. Very lucrative, and very dangerous.'

'You thinking of Cholmondeley?'

'God rest his soul, poor lad. But you didn't come here to talk about the past, did you, or to wish me a Happy New Year.'

'I want your opinion about something.'

'Oh! You've come to consult me!' Damiano sat back in his chair and glanced discreetly at his watch like a lawyer working out how much he could charge for his time. 'I'm all ears.'

'Actually, it is about Richard Cholmondeley.'

'Is it, now?'

'We know who was behind his murder,' Boone lied.

'And who might that be?'

'The Apparatus. The Sharif's people.' Another lie.

'The Sharif, you say? You surprise me, Harry. It's not his style.'

'Our intelligence is good.'

'Did you get it from Kamel?'

'No, no, Theo. This is from the horse's mouth.'

'The horse's mouth? A source inside the Apparatus?'

'A reliable source.'

'A mole, Harry? You have a mole inside the Apparatus?'

'London doesn't want to see this murder go unpunished.' Boone ignored the question.

'I see ... Judgement Day. London is settling the score by taking advantage of the fact that the whole region is in chaos.'

'Something like that.'

'What sort of retribution do you have in mind?'

'A car-bomb.'

'A car-bomb? So that's why you've come to see me. I don't deal in car-bombs. Blind violence isn't part of ERA's ecumenical vocation. I'm surprised at you, Harry.'

'Theo –'

'Don't interrupt, please. Intelligence is fine by me. And targeted assassinations, in extreme cases. But not blind violence! What about the teachings of Our Lord, Harry?'

Boone thought to himself that the Padre was taking his version of Christian charity a bit too far. But he'd been out in the cold for so long that it was only to be expected.

'Listen to me carefully, Theo. I can find killers. Most of them would probably miss their target while killing innocent civilians. What I am asking you for is to find me someone who can do a clean

88

job, target the Sharif's car and restrict the loss of human life, insofar as that is possible.'

'Mmm ... A clean job, you say.' Damiano seemed to be getting younger by the minute. 'If you really – and I mean really – want to go ahead, Harry, I can probably help you find a professional who's skilled enough to limit the – what do you call it – the "collateral damage". Collateral damage! What a euphemism. A clean language for a clean war. Well, if it really is a case of sparing innocent lives, I am willing to help you.'

Amen, said Boone to himself. The Padre was at last at peace with his rather strange conscience.

'When?' asked the apostle.

'A week Saturday.'

'That's less than two weeks. It's a bit short notice, Harry ... Very short notice.'

'But it can be done?'

'Why a week Saturday, Harry? Is it an anniversary date? Or is it the day before the budget is decided?'

'Can it be done, Theo?'

'Hmm ... Yes, it can be done. Where?'

'The Sharif will leave his office in Mazraa at three o'clock to go to the Beau Rivage hotel. He will be in a white Mercedes – armour-plated, of course.'

'Your mole has given you all the details?'

'At half past three, the car will drive past the Cité Sportive and slow down at the entrance to the sports ground –'

'The entrance to the ground? On a Saturday afternoon when there's a match on? This is going to be messy.'

'Not as messy as it would be if an amateur was involved, Theo. The man you choose might make the difference between five dead

89

and fifty dead. I'd rather there were only five, but I'd also like to be sure that there will be nothing left of the Sharif's car.'

'Don't worry, Harry. There'll be nothing left. But it's going to cost you ...'

'How much?'

'Oh, somewhere around sixty thousand.'

'How much?'

'Dollars, Harry! Sixty thousand dollars, not pounds!'

'It's too much in either dollars or pounds!'

'Too much? It's the Sharif we're talking about. Not just anyone. It's very risky. Plus, there's the time factor: two weeks is not a lot of time.'

'Two weeks might be a bit short notice, but sixty thousand dollars is far too much!'

'Just you listen to me, Harry. Ten thousand for the hardware, and ten thousand for the software –'

'Software? Hardware? So we're doing it by computer these days, are we?'

'Shut up, will you. The hardware is the equipment – car, explosives, munitions and cables. The software, well, that's the men. Just bear with me. Two thousand for the car –'

'Two thousand for a stolen car? Your guy could get one for five hundred!'

'You think so? We can't use any old banger. You don't want it to break down, do you? Agreed? Good. So we were saying two thousand for the car, and eight thousand for ... let's say, the spare parts. See, Harry, I'm getting used to euphemisms ... And ten thousand for labour costs, including the guy who's going to set up the operation, a bomb-maker for a thousand, a lookout for another thousand, and the driver ... That's a fair price, isn't it? The driver alone will get two thousand. Half in advance, half later.'

Half later! Boone had no illusions. The driver would never see the colour of his money. Wouldn't see anything, come to that. No professional would leave an empty car parked outside the grounds. The driver would still be at the wheel when the car exploded. The thousand-dollar lookout would see to that.

'Even if I accept your inflated figures, Theo, that's still well under sixty thousand.'

'Listen, Harry. If you'd come to see me two or three years ago, this would have cost you thirty thousand. Not a cent more.'

'Galloping inflation, is it?'

'It's not inflation, Harry. It's just that you and I were still in business together in those days. And then you disappear. No sign of life from your people. They've been very off-handed, Harry. "Don't call us, we'll call you", that type of thing. Then you turn up as though nothing had happened, as though we'd seen each other yesterday, and you expect me to give you a cut-price deal. You call that fair? Because I don't. So three times my cost price seems to me to be a fair price for a job well done. Discreetly done.'

This isn't an estimate, thought Boone. This is a claim for damages. The Padre wants London to pay for its infidelities, for the way he's been sidelined in favour of Colonel Kamel, for his loss of influence, for this dump of a flat, even.

'It's too much, Theo,' he said, emptying his glass and getting to his feet. 'I can't fork out sixty thousand dollars.'

'Right, well ...' Damiano gestured to him to sit down again. 'I'm not going to haggle with you, Harry. I'll settle for forty thousand. Double my expenses. But only because it's you. Because you're Irish, and a Catholic. Your Chancellor owes you a lot, Harry. If it was just up to me, I'd take their last penny. Fucking pen-pushers!'

13

Boone looked at his watch: one minute to half past three. If all went according to plan, he thought (he couldn't bring himself to say 'if all went well'), a dozen or so poor sods, some innocent and some not so innocent, were living their last moments on earth, and before long a further twenty or so would never be the same again.

Three-thirty. Now, he said to himself. But nothing happened. He wound down his window. Still nothing. Just the polite silence of what used to be a upper-class neighbourhood still finding it difficult to get over the war. Boone relit his cigar stub. His watch showed three-thirty-eight. Still nothing. Opening the door, he got out of the car he had borrowed from Roger Trad that very morning. Suddenly a huge explosion ripped through the air. Boone glanced surreptitiously at his watch: three-thirty-nine. The Padre's disciple appeared to have carried out his bloody contract. All around him, worried passers-by were rushing towards the soldiers on guard outside the French ambassador's residence, as though being close to men in uniform would give them God alone knows what protection, and God alone knows what answer to their anxious questions. Boone followed them.

'It's a bomb!' someone shouted. 'Look!'

The sun in his eyes, Boone looked to where the man was pointing and saw a thick column of smoke to the southeast.

'Does it never end?' wailed someone else.

'It's over by the Cité Sportive,' added someone who knew the city well.

Not bad, said Boone to himself as a second explosion, less violent than the first, ripped through the air, which had scarcely recovered from the first blast.

'Another bomb!'

Boone looked mechanically at his watch: three-forty-five.

'Look!' shouted the man with the local knowledge, pointing towards the smoke rising in the west. 'Over by Sabra!'

Three-thirty-nine at the Cité Sportive, and three-forty-five in Sabra. Boone didn't understand. Was the Padre's disciple still handing out such gifts as ERA's slender resources allowed him to hand out, and still without any religious discrimination?

Losing all hope in the soldiers, who seemed to be just as confused as they were, the bystanders scattered and went off home to discuss the news with their neighbours. As the cars began to disappear from the Passage du Musée, a ramshackle old banger pulled up ten yards away from Boone and dropped off a traffic cop in a khaki uniform. As the nervous driver made a U-turn and drove off west with a reflex reminiscent of the civil war, the cop walked past the soldiers and overtook Boone as he made his way towards the eastern part of the city. Boone had already seen that ravaged profile. This clean-shaven off-duty cop carrying a pathetic grocery bag was the Sharif. Getting back into his car, Boone drove off slowly and caught up with him two hundred yards down the road.

For a long time, they drove without saying a word and it was only when they had crossed the city limits that Boone at last broke the silence.

'Everything go as planned?'

'Everything went perfectly well.'

'The traffic cop was a nice touch,' said Boone in an attempt to lighten the mood.

'No one's frightened of traffic cops. They're despised by everybody. No one ever pays any attention to them.'

'True enough,' nodded Boone, thinking of the twenty-four-hour-a-day rodeo that took place on the roads. 'But the second explosion ...' He fell silent and waited for an answer that did not come.

'What's next on the agenda?' asked the Sharif.

'We're going to Halate. There's a boat waiting for us.'

'A boat? So we're going to Cyprus, are we?'

'We'll get there tonight and then take a plane to England.'

They had just reached Juniyeh, fifteen or so miles north of Beirut, and were driving along an elevated motorway. It was a relic from pre-war Lebanon, in the days when a president, who was better at management than warfare, had cherished the mad dream of building a state in a country ruled by tribes and clans. All that remained of his dream was this fine piece of engineering, and the casino where it ended as though at a toll booth. It looked for all the world as if the stretch of motorway had never been anything more than an immense red carpet that had been rolled out for the exclusive use of the roulette and baccarat players. Anything to improve the cash flow.

As they drove into the coastal village of Halate, Boone cut his speed. 'Halate-sur-Mer': the sign must have come straight from the French Bureau of Road Signs. Boone turned left into the beach complex, went over some bumps and stopped at a metal barrier. He then hooted impatiently, stepping on the accelerator at the same time. The racing engine and the horn were signals designed to inform the man on duty at the entrance that he was not dealing with just anybody. The man the signals were addressed to finally emerged from his hut and sauntered casually towards them. Being familiar with the semiology of power, he had decoded the signals all right, but he had seen it all before and was not easily impressed. But as soon as he realised that the car belonged to Roger Trad, he rushed to raise the barrier.

Turning left, Boone drove around the central building and onto the quay that separated the luxury chalets and manicured lawns from the sea. This was a world away from the Marbella Beach, with its cramped spaces, lower middle-class women in war paint, swarms of screaming kids and hordes of underpaid Sri Lankan maids. Halate-sur-Mer looked not so much like a holiday complex as a futuristic submarine base. The architecture was pure and cold: all marble, glass and concrete. Asceticism and sobriety were the order of the day, and even the waves were muted. When the killing went on here (as it inevitably did from time to time), silencers were part of the dress code.

The *Jolly Roger II* was moored by the jetty, with its black skull and crossbones fluttering in the wind. Boone drove past it to the car park.

'Right,' he said when he had cut the motor. 'I'll just ring Shartuni to tell him that I have to go away for a while. I wouldn't like him to worry.'

'I wouldn't bother, if I were you.'

'What?'

'I was just saying that it's not worth calling Shartuni.'

'Not worth it?'

'You won't find him.' He had turned to face Boone, and the look in his eyes said it all. 'You understand?'

No, Boone didn't understand. Boone didn't want to understand. Boone wanted everything to be spelled out for him.

'The explosion ... the second one ... Hammud was the target. Your Shartuni was still there, patiently waiting for someone to give him his precious briefcase. But the briefcase was primed to explode as soon as it was opened.'

Boone immediately turned on the car radio. The announcer had just finished reading the headlines and was moving on to the main news of the day. *A black day in the capital,* he said in the sombre tone his elders had adopted when they were covering the civil war. *At three-forty this afternoon, a car-bomb exploded outside the main gate to the Cité Sportive. The police and rescue workers who rushed to the scene have already found forty-seven bodies, and the death toll could still rise as no fewer than one hundred and fifty wounded have been found, some of them in serious condition* ... Forty-seven dead! One hundred and fifty wounded! Theo hadn't kept his word. *A few minutes later,* the radio went on, *an explosive device went off in a house in Sabra. The explosion is reported to have killed three people. This wave of attacks occurs at a moment when –*

Boone turned the radio off. He wasn't interested in their dubious analyses, and he was in a hurry to get in touch with Shartuni. He dialled the number half a dozen times as the Sharif sat peacefully beside him and smoked a cigarette. The pre-recorded woman's voice told him again and again that the number he was calling could not be reached. Giving up, Boone put his phone in his pocket. It immediately began to ring. He hastened to answer it, hoping that Shartuni would be on the other end of the line. It was Colonel Kamel.

'Hello, Boone? Heard the news?'

'I've just heard it on the radio.'

'What a blow! Must have been a professional job.'

'Do you know who the target was?'

'Seems it was, you know... the guys we were discussing at the Vieux Paris ...'

'No!' Boone did his best to sound astonished.

'Yes, yes!' said the Colonel, proud to be the first to give him the news. 'We have to talk it over.'

'That might be difficult.'

'Oh! Pity. I wonder whether our mutual friend ... the other one... The professor ... You know ... I was wondering if he might have something to say about this business.'

'Our mutual friend went to his weekly rendezvous this afternoon and I haven't seen him since ... I waited for him in vain.'

'He didn't come back to see you?'

'No. I thought he might have gone to see you.'

'Me? No.'

'I can't reach him.'

'You mean ...'

'I have no idea where he might be.'

'You mean ...'

'I fear so. He should have been at his friend's house when it happened. He didn't call me, and as I just said he can't be reached on his mobile.'

'But we have to talk! We *have* to!'

'Unfortunately I'm leaving right away. I had planned to go away as soon as I'd seen our mutual friend and, after what's happened, my bosses will certainly want to see me. I've got some explaining to do.'

'I understand, I quite understand. It's a real shame it had to end like this. Well ... That's life, what do you expect? It's all part of the job. I sometimes say to myself that I'd have been better off if I'd gone into business, like my brothers ...'

As though you weren't in business as it is, thought Boone.

'What do you expect, my friend,' the frustrated businessman was saying, in the weary tones of someone who sees his life flash before his eyes. 'There are no second chances. That's the way of the world. Have a good trip, my friend. See you soon, *inshallah.*'

That's that, Boone said to himself as he rang off. All the suspicion was gone, washed down with a glass of melodrama and a dash of self-pity. Kamel wouldn't say a word to a soul about either the Sharif or Shartuni. He must have been relieved that Boone had broken the eggs, and not him. No, Kamel would keep quiet.

'You're a very good liar,' the Sharif complimented him once he had finished his call.

'And you're very heavy-handed. You've eliminated both Hammud and Shartuni!'

'I'm playing for high stakes. May as well clean up after myself.'

Clean up! Boone thought to himself. The few brains Shartuni had had in his empty head now decorated what was left of the walls of Sheikh Hammud's lounge. Dr Sami Shartuni, man of culture and symbol of 'Lebanon the cradle of religions and crossroads of civilisations', wouldn't be going to London in the spring after all to enlighten his peers. No more conferences or brainstorming sessions for him. The would-be *éminence grise*, who was in fact just a little short on grey matter, had ended his career prematurely thanks to a few pounds of chemicals and a cheap detonator. A sad end. He'd never go into orbit now. At least he had died in good company. If God does exist, thought Boone, the professor and the Sheikh must be somewhere in the constellation of Gemini. Tomorrow's papers would write that a cowardly hand had dealt a severe blow to inter-religious dialogue. As for Shartuni's widow, she would fondly keep his old leather satchel, his unpublished thesis and his off-prints as though they were relics.

They got out of the car. The Sharif was in shirtsleeves, holding his cap and his uniform, which he'd rolled into a ball. Once they were out of the harbour, he would weight the bundle and consign it to the waters, even though the sea wouldn't keep it for long. It would surface in a week or two, depending on the currents. But it would be in shreds, and as unrecognisable as the fish the Lebanese still insisted on catching with dynamite. Boone prayed that it would be the last explosion marking this lethal affair.

14

Boone was asleep and dreaming a very tactile dream. A hand was touching his bare shoulder and rocking him.

'Sir!'

There was sound in his dream now. The hand that was rocking him was linked to a voice, and the voice was in control. The urgency apparent in the voice had been communicated to the hand, which wasn't rocking him any more. It was shaking him.

'Wake up, sir!'

So that was it. Opening one eye, he saw someone leaning over him: Travers. Opening the other eye, he looked at his watch. Two-twenty. In the afternoon, to judge by the rays of sunlight that had managed to find their way through the barrier of the curtains. Boone hadn't heard Travers open the door. He hadn't heard him cross the room. In fact, he hadn't heard anything at all, and for a few brief moments he hadn't known where he was. Another man might have felt embarrassed at being caught out like this. Another man might well have tried to play the pro to the bitter end with a 'Yes, yes, I heard you, I wasn't really asleep,' so as to let Travers know that his tiptoeing hadn't caught him off-guard. Not Boone. He simply stretched lazily, without even trying to brush the young man's hand away.

'Mr Fennell is here.'

'And our friend?'

'In his room. Still asleep.' He spoke with a Northern burr that belied his feline demeanour.

'Tell Fennell I'll be down in a moment.'

'Very good, sir.'

When Travers had left the room, Boone slowly dragged himself out of bed, shivered, put a towel around his shoulders and went to the window. The curtains were warm to the touch, and he waited a few moments before tentatively trying to open them. He wasn't sure the cord would work. But it did, and the curtains slid back along the rail with no difficulty. Boone blinked. The hot Cornish sun that had been beating down on the glass for some time didn't wait to be invited in and invaded the room, flooding the flowers on the carpet and the wallpaper. Boone had forgotten how much the English liked flowery patterns.

The bathroom was suffused with the same sunlight, which fell on the same carpet as the bedroom. Boone wanted to shave, but the washbasin had no mixer tap. He began by scalding himself, tried in vain to find a plug, and then alternated between the hot tap and the cold while philosophically pondering that, in this as in so many other circumstances, temperance was a matter of simultaneity rather than of succession of opposites. He then tried to take a shower, but the unit was just a larger version of the washbasin – Fahrenheit apartheid was the rule there too. In desperation he ran a bath, even though he detested them. At least he had the satisfaction of knowing that he was keeping Fennell waiting.

'Fennell will chair the debriefing committee,' Briggs had told him the night before as he trotted down the tarmac at his side. A few minutes earlier, the *Jolly Roger II* had berthed at the British base of Akrotiri in the southern part of Cyprus. Briggs had waited for them quayside. Wrapped up in an Ulster that was too long for him, wearing his Anthony Eden and with his bag in his hand, he looked like some obscure French prefect who had joined the Resistance and was waiting for a British submarine to take him to General de Gaulle. After the usual 'Pleased to see you' and 'No names mentioned', an RAF Land Rover had dropped them off a couple of miles further on, at the end of a beacon-lit runway where an old Hawker Siddeley 125 was waiting for them.

'As soon as we land in Plymouth, I'll leave you and go back to London,' Briggs said, clutching his hat to his head. 'You're going to Cornwall. We've rented a house down there, at Mullion Cove near Land's End. Alec Rose's Rutters are in Plymouth, and they'll drive you down. I shouldn't think Guy and his team will get there before tomorrow.'

Once they were on board the plane, Boone informed his boss that the Sharif had, so to speak, completed the job Theo Damiano had started by cleaning up after himself. No more Hammud and no more Shartuni. Briggs's only reaction was to take off his glasses and stare myopically at the ceiling. Then, after a few moments' silence – in memory of Dr Shartuni, Boone thought to himself, unless it was in memory of the operation that was slipping through his fingers – he

102

put his glasses back on and changed the subject without warning, explaining to Boone that Fennell had brought in Sam Catlow, the king of debriefings. This was the man who had brought down Nemeth, the fake defector from Hungary. If Guy was to be believed, or so Briggs had said, every man in his department was a king. Kings without a kingdom, now that the Russians were in bed with the Americans. Catlow would be bringing Le Pelley with him, of course, and Nico's Simon Blaker to handle the Arabic. Doggett and Latimer, just back from Langley, would also be joining the team. They were already polishing their new toy. They couldn't wait to show off everything they had learned on the other side of the pond.

They reached Plymouth early in the morning. Steel and Travers, the two Rutters Alec Rose had sent to babysit them, were waiting at the end of the runway in a Range Rover that looked more country squire than military. There was even a tartan rug carelessly thrown over the back seat. More handshakes with Briggs, more 'Pleased to have you with us and no names mentioned', and then they set off for Land's End.

The Range Rover made good speed, its turbo engine greedily gobbling up the asphalt of the A38, which was empty on this early Sunday morning. Once they had gone past Dobwalls, the noose began to tighten. They were now quite a long way down the peninsula, and there wasn't much land left. The country grew narrower and narrower, until they finally reached Land's End. Boone observed to himself that it was typical of the Royal & Ancient to want to shut the Sharif up in the Cornish *cul-de-sac*, with his back to the sea. Point of No Return. Leaving Truro and its Protestant cathedral behind, they took the A39 to Helston and then headed due south along yet more constricted roads to Mullion Cove.

The place the Clubhouse had rented for the occasion overlooked the sea. From his window Boone, who was enjoying a leisurely smoke after his bath, could see, over the boundary wall, the steep path that led to the point where the dark green cliffs plunged into the Atlantic.

'Sir ...'

Travers was knocking at the door. Fennell must have been finding it a long wait.

15

Catlow, Le Pelley and Blaker stood up when he entered the room. Fennell remained seated, legs crossed, swinging his left leg as though to emphasize how long he'd been kept waiting. He had dug out his country outfit for the occasion: heavy brown Derbys, whipcords, tweeds, checked shirt and woolly tie. Perfect in every detail. Boone nodded to all of them and settled on the couch, opposite the gentleman-farmer.

Gentleman or not, Fennell swiftly went on the attack: 'Fifty dead, Boone? One hundred and fifty wounded? Your famous Pro wasn't such a pro after all, so far as I can see!'

Boone said nothing.

'An extremely heavy toll ... At the very time when Lebanon is licking its wounds. This is going to create waves. Big waves.'

Boone still said nothing. He wasn't sure what Fennell was getting at.

'Are you sure it can't be traced back to you?' Fennell asked. He looked as though he hoped the answer would be 'no'.

'Yes, I'm sure.'

'Absolutely sure?'

'Absolutely, Guy!'

Fennell raised an eyebrow. He didn't like Boone calling him by his first name. Familiarity on the part of his superiors was a source of great satisfaction to him. Familiarity on the part of his peers was acceptable. Coming from a subaltern, it was quite unacceptable, especially when the subaltern was Boone.

'In any case,' he went on, 'you're going to take a little rest until the dust settles, and until we've had time to decide whether or not we should be thinking of replacing you. We wouldn't like you to suffer the same fate as poor Cholmondeley, would we? To say nothing of the embarrassment it would cause the government.'

So that's it, Boone said to himself. Now that he had the Sharif under lock and key, Guy had to make sure he would not be disturbed. He would have to replace Boone with a man he could trust. The Boone system was in danger. Mortal danger. If Boone wanted to save it – and he most certainly did – he had to get back to Beirut without further delay. He cursed the day he had agreed to have lunch with Kamel at the Vieux Paris.

'Our guest is still asleep,' Fennell was saying. 'Dead to the world. Doesn't snore, doesn't talk in his sleep. But he does grind his teeth.'

The wonders of technical intelligence-gathering, Boone thought. Catching the subject unawares, watching him without him knowing, waiting for his exhausted unconscious to come up for air, using up miles of tape and megabytes of hard disk, comparing today's belches with yesterday's and the evening's yawns with the afternoon's. The laboratory approach: the truth was supposed to emerge from recurrent slips that could be plotted on a graph, not from any rapport between source and controller. The experimental approach, with the source as guinea pig and the controller as lab worker.

'Both his bedroom and this room are bugged,' Fennell went on. 'The debriefing will take place in here, and Catlow will take charge.' He gestured towards Sam Catlow and Julian Le Pelley with his right hand. Catlow was sitting with his hands folded across his paunch like a buddha. Le Pelley was concentrating on filling his pipe. 'Our young friend Blaker will take notes and will help Catlow and Le Pelley when the Sharif's English lets him down.' Fennell waved his left hand in Simon Blaker's direction. Blaker was so intimidated that he scarcely dared to perch his bum on the edge of his straw-bottomed chair. 'That's the reception committee taken care of,' Fennell concluded, arms stretched out. Unlike Blaker, he occupied every inch of the wing chair he had chosen to honour with his behind. He was silhouetted against the French window giving on to the garden as though he were standing in front of a picture. From where Boone was sitting, the bare branches of a cherry tree made him look as though he'd grown antlers. A real Stag King, Boone thought to himself. King Arthur and his Knights of the Round Table.

'We'll need to hear your opinion about a lot of minor details, of course,' Catlow-Lancelot addressed Boone.

'That's right,' agreed King Arthur. 'So you'll be staying in Cornwall for a few days. Then you can go back to Beirut to pack your bags,' he added, still thinking of his strategy.

'We'll start with a recap of the last few months,' Catlow continued in a stage whisper. He sounded like a psychiatrist slyly taking control of a group session and letting his patients believe they were in charge.

'That's right,' agreed Fennell. 'A recap to begin with, and then a session with the flutterer. Doggett and Latimer are ready to start, and I would like that to go ahead as soon as possible. The debriefing can't begin until our guest has passed a lie detector test.'

Obviously not, thought Boone.

'As for the debriefing, I think that the traditional approach – let's begin at the beginning, where were you born and so on – is a bit dated, don't you?'

Boone didn't see why Fennell had to express his views on that subject. But Fennell seemed to want to impress him.

'So we will adopt a simultaneous approach,' the expert went on, 'alternating attacks on three fronts: biographical details ("What's your name?"), operational details ("Who killed Cholmondeley?") and psychological details ("We heard you screaming in the night"). Catlow will ask him random questions about his childhood, his work, his fears and his plans for the future. The total approach.'

Total approach indeed. Boone wondered whether Fennell had followed Dutch football in the seventies, or whether he had picked up his 'total approach' from the flutterer.

'A lot will depend on the subject's psychological state, of course,' stated Catlow.

'Yes, of course.' Fennell nodded in agreement. 'But if we ask random questions, we stand a better chance of trapping him, don't we? Gentlemen, I do realise that a man is innocent until proven guilty in this fine country of ours. But that very English custom doesn't really apply to our friend the Sharif, does it? He's guilty until proven innocent. It's not up to us to prove him guilty. It's up to him to prove himself innocent. A bit like the French system. Once we are convinced he's the genuine defector he claims to be, we can start to distribute the product in all the right places.'

Fennell had a faraway look in his eyes. More Stag King than ever, Boone said to himself. He must have been thinking of the heads of all the friendly services lining up to ask him for right of access to his rare pearl. *Could you ask him one little question that means a lot to us? And would it be too much to ask you to let us see him for a few moments? Not alone of course, but with your People who know him so well and who are doing such good work. And why not pass him on to us when you've finished with him? We could give you Mendoza in exchange ... the man from the cartel. Yes, it's true, Mendoza is a bit past his sell-by date. But he's not bad at all. You'd be surprised.'* A sort of sabbatical exchange.

'And once the debriefing is over,' said Catlow, interrupting his boss's daydream, 'Julian will discuss the practical and financial details of his reinsertion with him.'

Le Pelley puffed out a cloud of smoke.

'Well gentlemen,' declared Fennell, getting to his feet and shedding his antlers, 'as we are all agreed, we might as well ask our guest to join us.'

16

Harry Boone didn't hear the door open. But he could guess from the way all heads turned as one that the Sharif was there. Fennell had the proprietary look of an owner whose horse has just won the Grand National, and Catlow was sizing up the new arrival in the way that a Sumo wrestler sizes up an opponent. Le Pelley was frantically puffing away at his pipe, and Blaker had the blank look of a man who has just seen the flesh and blood translation of a description spat out by a dating agency's computer.

'Mr Al-Husayni,' announced Fennell as he got to his feet. The others followed suit. 'Come in, come in … Let me introduce you.'

Walking towards his hosts, the Sharif held out his hand to Fennell, who took it in both his hands, shook it vigorously, his face creased into a complicit smile.

'I believe you already know Harry Boone ... This is Sam Catlow ... Julian Le Pelley ... That's Simon Blaker. My name's Fennell.' He spoke slowly and clearly. 'Guy Fennell,' he immediately added in the solemn tone of a man who was doing a favour by giving his first name.

A smiling and docile Sharif greeted everyone in the order Fennell had introduced them. Handshakes and muttered greetings were exchanged. It was like being in a brothel in Istanbul. Once the punters had sat down with the mother-pimp, the girls made their entrance one by one. Eye contact was made, and handshakes established physical contact. The girls smiled and the men stared. The ritual was both mercantile and courteous. It allowed the customer to weigh up the goods. An Ottoman version of Hamburg's plate-glass window brothels. Having done the rounds, the Sharif sat down on the couch next to Harry Boone. Next to his pimp.

'Blaker speaks Arabic.' Fennell was trying hard for common denominators.

An embarrassed Blaker felt obliged to confirm what his superior had just said and came out with an *Ahlan was Sahlan* that was worthy of the owner of a Lebanese restaurant in London.

Smiling back at him, the Sharif produced a packet of American cigarettes and, with typically Oriental good manners, offered it to all present. They all refused politely.

'Blaker speaks perfect Arabic but, if you don't mind, our discussions will take place in English. You do speak our language, I believe.'

'I get by.' The Sharif lit his cigarette. 'It's not Shakespeare.' He inhaled. 'But it's not ... What do you call it? ... It's not pidgin English either.' He breathed out the smoke.

111

Fennell obviously hadn't been expecting that. Slightly taken aback, he must have been thinking that it takes all sorts to make a world, and that even a Muslim Arab could find someone with a skin darker than his own.

'I see that we were not misinformed about your linguistic gifts,' he said eventually. 'So, welcome to England. We've done a good job together and I am sure that our co-operation will prove even more fruitful in the months to come. You do realise that you are someone of great importance here?'

The Sharif smiled politely with an air of false modesty and waved his cigarette in protest.

'Seriously. Your reports are read at a very high level. The highest level. And they are greatly appreciated, I must say. Yes, yes ...'

The Sharif smiled doubtfully and just puffed on his cigarette. How many times had he not played the same little game, diligently massaging his sources' ego?

'Let me explain how we are going to proceed. We'll begin with a quick update on the events of the last few months. Then a short polygraph session.' Fennell had decided to use the scientific term to soften the blow.

'Polygraph? You mean a lie detector? Don't you trust me? After everything I've given you?'

'Let's just say that the polygraph is there to satisfy our bosses. We all have our bureaucrats to deal with. What do you expect?' Fennell was playing the field operative, trying to show the Sharif that the two of them had a lot in common.

'Do those things really work? I read somewhere that all you have to do to cheat them is clench your toes.'

'Really?' Fennell couldn't tell if the Sharif was being serious or not. 'Very funny. Very funny. Clenching your toes ... No, it works, I can assure you. But it's just a formality. So, no objections?'

'No objections. But I do hope you won't insist that I take my shoes off.'

'Take your shoes off?'

'My toes. To convince you I'm not trying to cheat the machine. In my country we take our shoes off to pray, not to take lie detector tests.'

Fennell's attempt to smile made him look as though he was pulling a face, but Julian Le Pelley couldn't stop himself from guffawing. He had the choking laugh of a smoker. Young Blaker took advantage of the general relaxation to settle back into his chair. For the first time that day, he felt he was a full member of the team. And that was thanks to the Sharif.

'Where were we?' Fennell was trying to get a new grip on things. 'Oh yes, the polygraph. We'll get down to serious business after the polygraph. My estimate is that it will take between six and eight months to cover everything properly. Our government attaches very great importance to your intelligence. Both the Minister and my immediate superior – the head of the Service – have asked me to take care of you personally. I will therefore be visiting you on a very regular basis.'

In just a few words, Fennell had succeeded in telling the Sharif that he was not dealing with just anyone, but with the Service's second in command, no less, and with someone who also had direct access to the government.

'Over the weeks to come,' the Clubhouse's Number Two continued, 'you will have time to gradually familiarise yourself with our way of life. After the debriefing, Julian will bring you up to date with all the details regarding your reinsertion: a new identity, financial compensation, a new face if you want it. We might be able to do something about those ... those scars.'

'We'll see.' The Sharif stubbed out his cigarette.

'It's not just a matter of cosmetics, you know. It's a security issue too. And in the meantime, things will certainly have calmed down and we can think about bringing your family over.'

'We'll see. We'll see.'

Taking out another cigarette, the Sharif tapped it on the back of his hand in annoyance, as though it had no filter and had to be tamped down, and then put it in his mouth without lighting it.

'You know, we'd be very happy to have you stay in this country if that appeals to you. But if you'd rather settle down somewhere else...' Fennell seemed to have been put out by the obvious display of bad temper.

The Sharif lit his cigarette and kept silent.

'Fine, fine, fine,' Fennell said, after waiting for an answer that did not come. 'And now, I'm afraid I must leave you.' He got to his feet. 'But I'll be back to see you very soon,' he promised.

Not before he's got the results from the flutterer session, Boone said to himself. Fennell would keep his distance until Doggett and Latimer had given their verdict. There was no question of him getting involved without getting the go-ahead from the machine.

'I just hope,' said Fennell as he took leave of his guest, 'that you don't do what the Egyptian pilot who flew his MIG to Israel did ...' He paused to make sure that he had everyone's attention. 'The Israelis gave him a new identity, and then sent him to live in Latin America with a very healthy bank balance. But as soon as he got there, he had the bright idea of sending a postcard to his family in Cairo to say that he was fine. You can imagine what happened next.'

When they're embarrassed, some say nothing and some yawn, thought Boone. Fennell made jokes that were in bad taste.

17

'Why us?' asked Catlow. 'Why choose the Brits? Why not the French? Or the Germans?'

'Because you're barbarians.'

'What does that mean?'

'It means that you don't negotiate. You refuse to give in to ... what's the word?'

'Blackmail?'

'That's it. Blackmail ... Take the hostages ... You remember the hostage crisis. The French and the Germans did negotiate. They handled the crisis. They are civilised people. And they play along with our own civilised people. The ones you call "moderates". The radicals aren't civilised. Either they kill, or they let things drop. They don't bargain. They don't handle crises. They don't ... comprom-ise ... Is that the word?'

'It is indeed.' Catlow seemed as impressed by the Sharif's words as he was by his English.

'You're a bit like that. Barbarians. And for someone in my position, that's reassuring. Because your civilised people and ours reach agreements. And I don't want them doing so at my expense. Just imagine what would have happened if I'd contacted the Germans. I can assure you that their Minister for Foreign Affairs, who's a real moderate, would have gone behind my back and come to an agreement with my old friends.'

'You mean the Germans are involved in secret negotiations with your former friends?'

'The Germans, and the Belgians! There's a secret agreement. They don't interfere with us, and we promise not to carry out operations in their countries, and not to target their nationals.'

'Incredible!' exclaimed Le Pelley who, despite his Huguenot background, was a fanatical Eurosceptic.

'Incredible or not, I'm giving you notice now that I categorically refuse to meet either the Germans or the Belgians. I don't trust them. And I also refuse to allow my intelligence to be passed on to them.'

'We'll bear that in mind,' Catlow promised.

'And while I'm at it, I ought to add that I also refuse, for different reasons, to meet any Jews ... Israelis ... They killed all my family.'

The limitations of Fennell's much-vaunted 'total approach' were quickly becoming obvious. No matter how cleverly Catlow and Le Pelley tried to plan their attacks, the Sharif's answers always defeated them. When asked questions, he wouldn't budge. His inquisitors, on the other hand, were beginning to get lost. Blaker had spent weeks studying the monumental *Encyclopedia of Islam* and the more than dubious *Encyclopedia of Jihad* in preparation for this clash of cultures, but he certainly had not expected this. He was fascinated. If Boone hadn't intervened, the interrogation would have rapidly degenerated into something out of the *Arabian Nights*.

'What about the man with the limp?' he asked.

'Sorry?' The Sharif stubbed out yet another cigarette.

'The man with a limp ... The man who was at Sheikh Hammud's when you met Shartuni there.'

'Oh, him ... Another cut-out I used.'

'What else?'

'He was Hammud's assistant.'

'Was?'

'Hammud is dead, isn't he?'

'What's his name?

'His name? Tareq.'

'Tareq what?'

'Tareq Bizri.'

'And before he worked for Hammud?'

'He used to work for me.'

'Did he die in the explosion? The one that killed Hammud and Shartuni? I didn't see his name on the list of victims.'

'I don't know. He was at Hammud's that day. I don't know any more than you do.'

'Did you warn him?'

'Warn him about what?'

'About the car-bomb, the car-bomb we staged.'

'Of course not.'

'Who else, apart from us, knows about your defection?'

'No one. It's my secret. And yours.'

'Not even your wife?' asked Catlow.

117

'I told you. No one.'

'How did you avoid being in the car when it went up?'

Sitting back in his armchair, the Sharif crossed his legs, lit a cigarette and took a deep drag on it before replying as he blew smoke through his nose.

'When I left the office, I stopped off at one of our safe houses. In Sabra. The building has underground parking. My car dropped me there and left without me.'

'A decoy,' said Catlow.

'A trick,' replied the Sharif, who preferred words he understood. 'To deceive the enemy. Then I went up to the fifth-floor flat we use as a safe house. I had a transceiver tuned to the wavelength used by my car. I waited. When I heard the explosion, the transmitter went dead and I went out on to the balcony. I could see a column of smoke rising from the scene of the explosion. And I could see Hammud's house, no more than a hundred metres as the crow flies. I waited until they opened the booby-trapped case I'd sent them. Once it had exploded, I had a shave, put on the cop's uniform I'd hidden in the flat a few days earlier, wrapped my own clothes up into a parcel, went down to the basement and threw the lot into the furnace. Then I went to a grocer's to buy a few things – I don't like walking around empty-handed. Looks aggressive. And then I jumped into a taxi to go and meet my friend Harry at the Passage du Musée.'

'Why didn't you make contact with us earlier?' asked Catlow once he had taken in all the details of this meticulous plan. 'Why did you wait so long when you got back from Quetta?'

'I was waiting for the right moment.'

'Cardiff?' interrupted Boone.

'What?'

'The Cardiff network. The Islamist network. The one that was rolled up here.'

'Yes, the network ... You see, I knew that one of the people you arrested had access to the kind of intelligence I planned to pass on to you. That gave me enough cover.'

'And after that, the rhythm of your dispatches ...'

'Was always dictated by the arrests you made. I couldn't take the initiative without putting myself at risk.'

'And the car-bomb you asked us for?' asked Catlow. The bomb that killed so many people at the Cité Sportive. Was that to cover your tracks as well?'

'Of course. But I also wanted to make sure you were serious.'

'What about the planned attack on the Palais de Justice in Paris? You waited until the very last minute before warning us.'

'I had to be sure that the French had a lead. The Algerians were arrested at just the right moment.'

'If I understand you right,' said Catlow, 'you'd have done nothing if the arrests hadn't given you a cover. You would have kept your information to yourself, and the attack would have taken place.'

'Sure.' The Sharif didn't seem to be at all worried.

'Don't you think you're taking caution a little too far?'

'Too far? No, I don't think so. You can never be too cautious. But there's no need to worry, I'd have sent you the information afterwards.'

'Afterwards? After the attack? After the deaths?' Le Pelley had taken offence.

'Yes, afterwards. So what? What are you, some kind of doctor? You want to save human lives? Well you did save them. Satisfied? What good did that do you, you and your French colleagues? A pat on the back, that's what.' He was on his feet and pacing up and

119

down now. 'But if the attack had taken place, and if, thanks to my information, you had succeeded in getting your hands on those responsible a week or two later, what do you think would have happened?' He stopped pacing and stared at each of his hosts in turn. 'I'll tell you what would have happened. You would have been promoted by now! Your masters would have given you everything you wanted. All the funds you needed! Why? Because you'd have been avenging the dead. More important still, because you would have spared the survivors. Not just any survivors! I'm talking about your superiors, my friends, and your politicians.' He sat down and stubbed out his cigarette. 'Prevention is better than cure. That's what they say, isn't it? That's what they teach you. But not in our line of work. In our line of work, curing is always better than preventing.'

'That's not the way our society works!' Le Pelley's legalistic sensibilities had been offended.

Guy wouldn't agree with Julian, Boone said to himself. Guy would have loved to hear that.

'You were saying,' interrupted Catlow in an attempt to get back to business, 'that you decided to contact us because, unlike our European colleagues, we're what you call "barbarians". But so are the Americans. Why didn't you approach them?'

'Why you and not the Americans? Well, because you've some experience of dealing with Arabs and Muslims. Over a long period of time. The colonial period, true, but nonetheless ... Because the skins of your soldiers, your administrators and your missionaries were tanned in our countries and because their bones were bleached white beneath our sun. Not the Americans. What do the Americans know about us? What do they really know, apart from what they pick up indirectly, or from satellites and spy planes?' He lit another cigarette. 'What experience of Muslims, Arabs or the East do the Americans have? And while we're on the subject, what experience do they have of any human being that doesn't live in the United States and doesn't have the right to cast a vote there? The Americans!' He breathed out more smoke. 'Let me tell you a story I heard about the American landing in Somalia. You remember when they got it into their heads that they should police the Horn of Africa.'

The Brits remembered only too well. A dozen Rangers had been killed when a surface-to-air missile hit their helicopter. One of the missiles Washington had supplied to the Afghans in the hope that they would be used against the Red Army. Or so the story went.

'So the Americans landed in Somalia, taking their mascot, a big bruiser of a cat, with them. The cat immediately left the base to throw his weight around and let everyone know that he was the king of the jungle now. As he was strutting around, he came across a Somali cat who was so thin that he could barely stand. The American cat couldn't resist the temptation and decided to teach his distant African relative a lesson. He pounced on him, but all his strength and all his fighting skills didn't stop him from getting a good mauling. Defeated, covered in scratches and above all puzzled, he goes back to base and tells his colonel everything. Obviously, the colonel is furious at seeing his mascot cutting such a sorry figure in front of the natives, and tells him so. "You are an American cat," he reminds him. "You're well trained, you have all the combat skills that are needed, and you represent the best army in the world. I won't have you being humiliated by some shit of an African cat. So get back out there and show him who's boss." After the pep talk, the American cat goes off to pick another fight with the Somali cat. And once again, the Somali cat wins, and the American is out for the count. A bit later, as he begins to come to his senses, he opens one eye with difficulty and sees the Somali cat looking disdainfully down at him.

"I don't get it," he tells the winner. "I am an American cat. I'm part of an elite force, I'm well fed, stuffed full of vitamins, highly trained, and I get beaten hollow by some starving, mangy Somali cat. I just don't get it!" And the Somali cat looks at him with big eyes and protests: "A Somali cat! I'm no Somali *cat*, I'm a Somali *lion*!"'

After that they were all on first-name terms, chatting happily as if they were in an Oriental coffee-shop. Later that afternoon, Blaker went into Helston and came back with some spicy sausages ('pure beef,' he assured the Sharif), basmati rice, a tub of *hummus* and some pita bread he'd found in a shop in Meneage Street. The Sharif cooked his new friends a meal, and then tried to teach them how to use the bread instead of knives and forks. There was a lot of laughter that evening, and a lot more stories were told. Even Catlow was won over and forgot about his strict diet. First round to the Sharif. Even though he was not exactly keen on the idea of the flutterer, Boone said to himself that it was high time Doggett and Latimer put in an appearance and spoiled the party mood.

18

The weather changed in the morning. As though to disprove the local tourist office's pet theory that Mullion Cove enjoyed a microclimate, the sun had disappeared and the serpentine rock locked onto the dark sky. At about midday, an east wind brought heavy clouds and a black estate car. The clouds deposited their load of rain and the estate car deposited Doggett, Latimer and a large attaché case. Politely but firmly declining Steel and Travers's offer to lend a hand, Doggett and Latimer quickly rearranged the furniture to build a cosy little nest where they could be alone with the Sharif while keeping the others at bay. Latimer carefully opened the case and, to the bewilderment of the laymen, began unrolling a tangle of electric leads, tubes, cables and electrodes connected to the monitors that lay dozing in the case. There was a momentary panic when the English socket refused to take the plug that betrayed the machine's transatlantic origins, but order was restored when Travers returned with a universal adapter. Shortly afterwards the Sharif, now stripped of his cigarette and his heavy jumper, found himself being wired up to the machine.

'Did the Apparatus order you here?' asked Doggett as Latimer switched on the screen and the graphs.

'No.' The Sharif stared at the lid of the case that prevented him from seeing the machine he was fighting. An invisible enemy.

'The Islamists sent you.'

'No.'

'You are here of your own free will.'

'Yes.'

'Your wife is called Fatima Dandash.'

'No.'

Your wife is called Fatima Kronfol.'

'Yes.'

'You have spied on the British and their allies.'

'Yes.'

'You have taken part in terrorist attacks against the West.'

'No.'

'You have helped to plan terrorist attacks against the West.'

'No.'

'You have intelligence on terrorist attacks on the West.'

'Yes.'

'You are a believer.'

'... Yes.'

'No smiling please ... No, no laughing ... You mustn't laugh ... We'll start again ... You are a devout Muslim.'

'Yes.'

'The Apparatus knows that you're not dead.'

'No.'

'The Apparatus knows you're in England.'

'No.'

'You were born in Beirut.'

'No.'

'The information you sent us was transmitted with the consent of your superiors.'

'No.'

'Your son is called Ali.'

'No.'

'You had an assistant with a limp.' Doggett asked the question Boone had insisted upon.

'Yes.'

'The man with a limp is called Tareq Bizri.'

'Yes.'

'You are telling me the truth.'

'Yes.'

'You were born in Mastaba.'

'Yes.'

'Your son is called Hasan.'

'No.'

'Your wife knows you're here.'

'No.'

'Your son knows you're here.'

'No.'

'Good,' Doggett said as he disconnected him. 'We'll take a short break.'

'Can I smoke?' asked the discharged prisoner.

'I'd prefer it if you waited until we're finished with this.'

'As you wish.'

'When you were asked if your son was called Hasan, you said "no",' objected Latimer after consulting his papers.

'That's right.'

Latimer handed a graph to Doggett. The Sharif's answer had left nothing but a straight, flat line. No wiggles. No disturbance.

'But your son *is* called Hasan,' said a puzzled Doggett.

'I don't have a son.'

'You don't?'

'My wife and I have no children.'

A programming error. Doggett and Latimer shot angry glances at Catlow, and Catlow shot an angry glance at Blaker.

'B... but ...' the Rookie stuttered as he fumbled through his papers, '... you're called Abu Hasan ... That means "father of Hasan". Abu Hasan isn't your *nom de guerre*, is it? Your *nom de guerre* is "the Sharif".'

'That's right. They call me Abu Hasan because my father's name was Hasan, not because I have a son who answers to the name Hasan.'

Programming error or no programming error, Doggett and Latimer should have kept quiet, said Boone to himself. They'd opened up a breach in their defences, and the Sharif had rushed into it.

'It's a local custom. We give young men nicknames like Abu Hasan or Abu Ali because they will eventually have sons to whom will give their fathers' names. But that doesn't mean that they *already* have sons ... Can I have a cigarette now?'

Boone looked at Blaker, who seemed to have lost all interest in his notes. The Rookie had just come face to face with the limitations of academic papers and bookish culture.

Doggett and Latimer then went on with their work, but they appeared to be getting more depressed as the Sharif's answers became more cheerful. The episode of the non-existent son had disturbed them deeply. They had lost heart. Their questions were no longer as confident as they had been. They were having doubts, and their machine was beginning to share them. Before long, the British team split into two groups: Catlow and his people on one side, and the trinity of Doggett, Latimer and the flutterer on the other. The Sharif had taken the initiative.

While the Sharif was playing a game of cards with his guardian angels that evening, Catlow called the others to a meeting upstairs to evaluate the afternoon's High Mass.

'The subject has a fairly high level of emotivity,' Doggett was saying. 'You can see that from his answers to harmless questions. But he is not English, after all.'

'Is he a heavy smoker?' asked Latimer.

'He chainsmokes,' said Catlow, who had given up smoking two years earlier and put on twenty pounds since.

'He scarcely smoked at all,' said Doggett. 'That ought to have made him nervous.'

'To say nothing of having to speak English.'

'All things considered,' Doggett concluded, 'we can say that the subject hasn't lied to us about anything important, and that he's being sincere when he says that he is speaking the truth.'

'Perfect, then.' Catlow got to his feet.

'Be that as it may,' Doggett stopped him and wagged a finger, 'could I remind you that these tests only work if the data we are given is accurate. It appears that, at least on one point, the intelligence you supplied us with is mistaken. We will of course have

127

to mention that in our report. If a mistake has been made, it's not down to the machine. It's human error. All agreed?'

Boone imagined the report that Doggett and Latimer would submit to the Royal & Ancient. It would say: 'Yes, but'. Doggett and Latimer would hide behind their machine, and they would hide their machine behind Catlow and his poor programming. When you played this game, the golden rule was to commit yourself without ever becoming involved. But Boone had other fish to fry. He was in a hurry to get back to Beirut to try to salvage something from the wreckage.

19

Guy Fennell sat in the leather backseat of the Jaguar taking him to Grosvenor Square. He had both his feet up, one leg crossed over the other, and a good half of his sole was visible to the passers-by as if in royal salute. From where he was sitting, the capital had never looked so beautiful – at least not since that unfortunate rapprochement between Moscow and Washington, which had rendered useless all the painstaking work he'd done on the Russian mafia. He usually found the crowds in Piccadilly offensive, but today he felt kindly towards them. Today, he could forgive their intolerable frivolity, and he felt vaguely responsible for their well-being. *Go on, go on, my good people*, he seemed to be saying, *you can go about your business in peace and sleep soundly in your beds tonight. You don't know it because my war is fought in the shadows, but I am watching over you.* He was perfectly content. If a tramp had asked him for money, he'd have given him a crisp fiver without a second thought. In Regent Street, he felt a real regent, and as the car entered Mayfair on its way to the American embassy, he told himself that, in his own discreet way, he was making a contribution to all this opulence. The fact is that Guy Fennell was over the moon. His protégé had been proved innocent by the flutterer, and armed with that acquittal from a judge who was both impartial and above suspicion, he was preparing to offer him to the Americans – as an engagement ring, or, rather, as a ring to celebrate their happy reunion.

When the car drew up outside the embassy, he was not displeased to see that Tom Van Dusen had sent someone down to meet him and get him through the checkpoint without any fuss. He made a note of this act of courtesy, and began to wonder if Van Dusen might have suspected the importance of what he wanted to discuss with him. Led by his guide, he went through the cordon of Marines without a hitch, telling himself that on a day like this, he would happily have complied with all the heightened security checks they might want to put him through (just the once wouldn't hurt). He would have done so with good grace because, today, the source of his strength was not his usual self-importance. It was the secret he was keeping and the treasure that, good privateer that he was (Fennell lacked the guts to be a pirate), he was about to hand over to the London proconsul of the New Roman Empire. With a spring in his step, he followed his guide to the soundproofed room in the basement where Tom Van Dusen had seen fit to meet him.

'I've come to talk to you about Tiger Woods,' he said once they were alone.

'Tiger Woods? Your source inside the Apparatus?' asked a casual Van Dusen. Everything about him exuded the discreet chic of New England. Fennell felt quite jealous.

'The very same. The man who gave us the Palais de Justice operation in Paris.'

'A good catch. It's a real pity he still hasn't given you anything on the Islamists' anti-American operations.'

'That is just what I've come to talk to you about.' Fennell was anxious to spill the beans, if only to make up for his late failings. 'Now that we have this business well in hand, I am in a position to admit to you that Tiger Woods is with us, Tom. I had him exfiltrated, and I've put him somewhere safe.'

'Exfiltrated? Where from?'

'Beirut.'

'So Tiger Woods is Lebanese, is he?'

'He is. Now that he's well and truly in my hands, we can put as much pressure on him as we like. You'll see, before long he'll be telling us all he knows about his friends' anti-American activities – and I'm sure he knows a lot.'

'May I ask who he is?'

'Ali Al-Husayni! The Sharif!'

'The Sharif? The guy who used to run the Apparatus's Lebanese operations?'

'The very one, Tom.'

'I thought he was killed in a car-bomb attack in Beirut a fortnight ago.'

'It was faked. I faked it to get him out discreetly.'

'So the car-bomb was you, was it? To think that we got the blame. Reputations shape reactions, I suppose.'

'It was us.'

131

'Sneaky!'

'We weren't being sneaky at all,' Fennell apologised. He had taken the comment literally and was afraid he was being criticised for his lukewarm Atlanticism. 'So long as the intelligence he was giving us was of no direct interest to you, there was no point in telling you about it, was there?'

'I understand, I understand,' Van Dusen reassured him.

'But now that he is here, and free to answer all our questions, I thought I should give you the right of first refusal, and take the opportunity to tell you that Cecil and I would like you to be fully involved in the debriefing.'

'Very generous of you.'

'Not at all. We're on the same side in democracy's fight against the forces of obscurantism and barbarism.' Just for a moment, Fennell forgot he was talking to the Company's London representative. Just for a moment, he was addressing Congress.

'Very generous indeed ... Tell me, Guy, did you kidnap this Sharif of yours?'

'Why should we kidnap him?'

'Are you holding him prisoner?'

'Of course not. He's here of his own free will. He defected.'

'I see ... So the debriefing you want me to take part in is not so much an interrogation as a casual chat about this and that.'

'No need to grill him. No need to bring any pressure to bear. He's talking to us about everything. Freely.'

'Freely, you say?'

'Absolutely,' smiled Fennell.

'So I'd be right to assume you and he have been working together for some time now. '

'If you want to put it that way.' Fennell was intrigued. He couldn't quite grasp the point Van Dusen was trying to make.

'If we join in now, the three of us would be working together.'

'The three of us ... I suppose so.'

'Hmm.' Van Dusen ran his hand across his cheek, trying to find rough patches of bristle that might reflect his state of mind. There were none; his barber in Curzon Street shaved him very closely each morning.

'If a *ménage à trois* doesn't appeal to you, Tom, we could hand him over to you lock, stock and barrel.' Fennell was already thinking about how to persuade Cecil Devereux to hand the Sharif over to the Americans, and about the price he could get from Van Dusen.

'No, no,' protested the recipient of Fennell's gift. 'You misunderstand me. We don't want to handle him by ourselves.'

'I'm not with you, Tom.'

'You see, Guy, if you had kidnapped this Sharif, he'd be a prisoner of war and I'd be free to interrogate him to my heart's content.'

'I still don't understand.' Fennell was worried, and thought that Van Dusen might be trying to get him to lower the price.

'It's a question of – how shall I put it? – it's a question of where we stand. With respect to him, I mean. If he was a prisoner of war, there would be a barrier between us, and being on the other side of that barrier I could go on interrogating him until I broke him. But if I got it right, that is not the case, is it? Your Sharif is here of his own free will. So you have been colluding with each other.'

'Colluding? Colluding in what?'

'I don't know... In a car-bomb that served as a smokescreen to cover his disappearance, for instance. And in all the innocent lives it claimed.'

Fennell was becoming more and more confused. And the more confused he became, the more anxious he became.

'There's a certain intimacy between the two of you, Guy. To be perfectly frank, I can't risk getting involved in your twosome.'

'Why ever not?'

'You may not realise it, but a good many of the bombers we are now hunting down were, at one point or another, being run by us. By us, Guy! We trained them, armed them and bankrolled them. To fight the Reds, obviously enough. But some of them have turned their arms – our arms, rather – against us. We once colluded with some of them. We used to be on intimate terms. Just as you are on intimate terms with the Sharif. The Company cannot afford to get involved in this matter. Our field operatives are busy eliminating their former agents, and some are carrying out their task with a real vengeance, if only to atone for their past errors. Do you understand?'

'The Sharif passed the flutterer test brilliantly.'

'The flutterer doesn't have to justify itself before the Senate! We do!'

'The Sharif is an invaluable source of intelligence.'

'I don't give a fuck about that.' Van Dusen's Bostonian mask had just slipped. 'The Company got its fingers burned, Guy. Half the Administration and half of Congress still hold our old links with the Islamists against us. If I talked to him, the Company would have to inform both the President and Congress. And believe you me, the Company doesn't want anyone reminding it that it used to be in bed with the Islamists.'

'So you don't even want to talk to him?'

'We're no longer intelligence officers, Guy. We've become policemen of some sort or other. We are less interested in the information people volunteer to give us, than in the confessions we can get out of them.'

'Don't you even want to meet him?'

'I want to, but I can't. I cannot allow my name, or that of the Company, to be associated with him. We cannot possibly allow ourselves to be associated – either directly or indirectly – with his past atrocities, and above all not the car-bomb that allowed him to get out of Beirut.'

Fennell was speechless. This was the last thing he'd been expecting.

'And what's more, your Sharif doesn't seem to have anything that is of direct interest to us. For the moment, the game isn't worth the candle as far we we're concerned.'

Fennell still said nothing.

'I will of course be in the market for any information you see fit to pass on to me, but meeting him or telling anyone in Washington that Tiger Woods is the Sharif is quite out of the question.'

Fennell, who had been imagining himself testifying before the Senate Intelligence Committee, was shattered. His American Dream was over. His yearling would not be running in the Kentucky Derby.

'As far as I am concerned,' Van Dusen said, driving the point home, 'this conversation never took place, and I have never been informed of the real identity of your source.'

Hence the interview in a soundproofed basement room, Fennell said to himself. Hence the privileged entry Van Dusen had so graciously permitted, so that he could slip unnoticed past the Marine checkpoint.

As he left the embassy, he felt like a vestal who had solemnly offered someone her virginity, only to realise that her beloved didn't give a damn about either it, or her.

20

Fennell did not linger in London. His case had been thrown out of court by Van Dusen, and he felt bruised all over. The Company having chosen to ignore him, both the Clubhouse and Whitehall had suddenly lost their appeal. The day after the meeting in Grosvenor Square that had officially never taken place, he fled to the country to lick his wounds and hide his disappointment. The Sharif's debriefing was due to begin that day. Frustrated by the American's unexpected rejection of his protégé, Fennell rang Catlow and had the opening ceremony postponed until he could get there.

They were all in the sitting room, Simon Blaker's pen at the ready and the recording equipment purring away in the background.

'Lucky Strike ...' The Sharif had just opened the bidding.

136

Lucky Strike, my foot, Fennell said to himself. His mind was still on his disastrous conversation with Tom Van Dusen. That strike had been anything but lucky.

'Lucky Strike,' repeated the Sharif. 'Does that mean anything to you?'

'Lucky Strike?' Fennell was perplexed.

'Yes, Lucky Strike.'

The Sharif held up his packet of cigarettes.

'Your brand of cigarettes ...'

'Yes, my cigarettes, but there's more to it than that. Some rumours I heard just before I left Beirut. Rumours about an operation that was being planned against a target called Lucky Strike.'

A puzzled Fennell looked at his assistants, but the name obviously meant nothing to any of them.

'Lucky Strike. Mean anything to you?' insisted the Sharif, waving his packet of cigarettes once more.

'Lucky Strike ... Sounds American, doesn't it?'

Fennell was beginning to have new hopes that his yearling might still run in the Kentucky Derby after all. He could already see himself in Tom Van Dusen's office, suavely giving him the details of a murderous terrorist attack on a US target.

'It might be American. I couldn't say.'

'And that's all you know?'

'I also know the name of the operation: The Domes of the Four Caliphs.'

'The four caliphs?' Fennell turned to Blaker.

'The Prophet had four successors,' the Rookie replied. 'Abu Bakr, Omar, Othman and Ali.'

'What about these domes?'

'I don't know,' admitted a contrite Blaker.

'Nor do I,' said the Sharif, drawing attention away from the Arabist's ignorance. 'All I can think of is the Dome of the Rock in Jerusalem. The dome of what is sometimes called the Mosque of Omar.'

'An operation in Jerusalem?'

Fennell pictured himself being demoted from doing the Americans a favour to doing the Israelis a favour.

'I doubt it,' said the Sharif. The reference to the domes of the caliphs must be purely symbolic.'

'Did you hear anything else?'

'I heard talk of a date. Friday the first.'

'Of February?'

'Yes.'

'But that's in a week's time. You might have told us earlier!'

'I thought you wanted to complete all the "administrative" formalities first ... To keep the bureaucrats happy ...'

'And you can't give us any more details?' Fennell ignored the sarcasm.

'All I know is the target's code name – Lucky Strike; the code name for the operation – The Domes of the Four Caliphs; and a date – Friday, 1 February.'

'What the hell could Lucky Strike mean?' Perplexed, Fennell got up and went to the corner of the room to call the Green Keeper on his secure mobile.

'Nico? It's Guy. Does "Lucky Strike" mean anything to you?'

'Lucky Strike, you say? Hmm, not on the face of it. Give me a minute, and I'll see if the name is in our data bank.'

'Might be American,' Fennell prompted him hopefully.

'Hang on ... Lucky Strike ... Come on, search engine, come on ... Lucky Strike ... You're right, Guy, it is American.'

Jackpot, Fennell said to himself.

'Lucky Strike is the name of an American base.'

A real lucky strike, thought Fennell. Tom Van Dusen could go and take a running jump. Before long, Fennell would have him eating out of his hand.

'Somewhere between Le Havre and Dieppe.'

'An American base in France?'

'An old, disused base.'

'Disused?' Fennell came down to earth with a bump.

'A base built in 1944, at the time of the Allied landings in Normandy.'

'A base with no one in it, you mean.' Fennell sounded mournful.

'Deserted, Guy.'

'Not much of a target for a terrorist attack.'

'Not unless they're targeting fields of beetroot, or trying to wipe out the local gull colonies.'

'Any domes on the base? Any spherical buildings?'

'Let me look at a map. Just a moment ... Hmm ... nothing that looks like a dome or a sphere.'

'You're sure?'

'Not on the base itself. But I can see some domes not too far away. Four domes, to be precise.'

'You can see four? Four domes?'

'At Paluel, near the old Lucky Strike base ... Paluel is a nuclear power station.'

'A nuclear power station!' Fennell was overjoyed. He glanced at the Sharif like a doting parent.

'There are four reactors, and four fine domes to protect them.'

'Fantastic!'

'As important as that?'

'More than important, more than important … primordial … How far is the power station from Paris?'

'A hundred miles, as the crow flies.'

'Just a hundred miles?' Fennell could already see himself being acclaimed as the saviour of Paris. He was going to be a second General Leclerc. 'And how far from our coast?' he asked a second later. He was beginning to hope he'd be able to kill two birds with one stone.

'Sixty miles or so from Eastbourne, I should think.'

'Brilliant.' Fennell almost shouted at the thought of this brace.

'Just tell me what's going on, Guy … Why all the questions?'

'No reason. I'll tell you later. I'm returning to London immediately. I have to see Dupond-Aignan as soon as possible.'

21

Fennell had the self-satisfied appearance of a man who was both looking forward to a weekend's shoot on a big estate and bringing his hosts a magnificent present. The magnificent present was Lucky Strike, and the big estate was a seventeenth-century manor in the middle of a forest near the Paluel nuclear power station in Normandy.

'The power station houses four units, each generating 1,300 megawatts,' his host was telling him. The lord of the manor was a reserve colonel in the Gendarmerie. He also happened to be related by marriage to Henri Dupond-Aignan. In short, he had married into the French secret service and become one of its *honorables correspondants*.

'The entire landward perimeter is surrounded by an electrified fence and is constantly patrolled,' said Dupond-Aignan while poking the logs in the great fireplace. Above it hung the portrait of an ancestor who had been in the slave trade between Saint-Louis-de-Juda and the West Indies.

'So we can rule out the possibility of a full frontal assault.' Fennell was delighted to be able to hold forth in French.

'Unless they use tanks. The patrols have been stepped up, haven't they, Hubert?'

'Of course,' confirmed the other man, patting the head of the golden retriever at his feet. 'And on the seaward side, a series of defences would make it difficult for anyone to launch an amphibious assault. We'd see them coming from a long way off. Besides, the Royale is always on the lookout.' His family having supplied France with many an admiral, Hubert Anne-François de Botreaux de Fauconberg habitually spoke of the French Navy as the Royale, rather as though the French Revolution had never happened.

'Which leaves the possibility of an attack from the air.' Fennell peered at the map they had spread out on a low beechwood table. One side of the table flirted dangerously with the fire. As it warmed up, the beech gave off a scent of roses. Fennell was in a state of bliss. This vigil-at-arms was everything he had ever dreamed of. This is how he imagined Robert Walker and Cecil Devereux spent their evenings in their country houses. First, a haunch of venison and a 1970 Pichon-Lalande served in the panelled dining room, and now this 1977 vintage port they were savouring in a library lit by firelight, with a rustic dog sprawled on the deep carpet.

'The air does pose a little problem,' said Botreaux, squatting beside the table in a military posture that suggested the campaign had already begun. 'The airspace over this area is extremely crowded. We call it "the railway in the sky." Most of the traffic between Paris and London, and Paris and Frankfurt, passes overhead.'

'Not to mention the transatlantic flights,' added Fennell, his mind still on Tom Van Dusen.

'True,' conceded his host. 'Obviously, overflying the power station is strictly forbidden, and the Air Force would be alerted. But if, by some mishap, a plane going from, say, Roissy to Gatwick was hijacked over the station, the fighter-aircraft really wouldn't have time to intervene. That's why the Direction de l'Aviation Civile modified all flight paths and allocated new ones that steer well clear of the area as soon as we received your intelligence.'

'And,' interjected Dupond-Aignan, 'security measures have been stepped up at check-in desks, and on all flights that might come within one hundred kilometres of the power station.'

'In any case,' said Fennell, 'the terrorists would have to take control of the plane. I mean physical control.'

'Of course,' said Botreaux. 'If the people in charge of security do their job properly, there is no danger of that happening. But if it did, the Air Force could intervene and either force the plane to land or shoot it out of the air.'

'We'd all like to avoid that happening, wouldn't we?' Fennell was enjoying playing the role of the English gentleman respectful of human lives, in front of an audience of Continentals.

'If we can...' His family having generously sacrificed at least one son in every armed conflict that had taken place since the Napoleonic Wars, Botreaux took the view that la patrie was more important than the sum of innocent people that made it.

'There are already antiaircraft batteries in place around the power station,' said Dupond-Aignan. 'Obviously, we can't do too much for fear of sowing panic amongst the locals. The nuclear station worries them enough as it is.'

'I presume,' said Fennell, 'that the reactor domes are capable of standing up to the impact of a small aircraft. But I doubt if anyone ever dreamed that an airliner might try to crash into them at the time they were built.'

'You're right,' Dupond-Aignan conceded. 'But even so, domes aren't such a good target. The terrorists who flew into the towers crashed into them horizontally. In relative terms, that's almost child's play. But with domes, which are points on the ground, they would have to put the plane into a tailspin to stand any chance of hitting them. It's not that simple.'

'Which minimises the risk but doesn't rule it out completely.'

'There is indeed a danger inherent in the new measures introduced in the United States. The Americans have developed a remote control system that allows them to regain control over a plane that has been hijacked while it is in the air and bring it down to the nearest airfield. All from a command post.'

'Are you saying that a terrorist who infiltrated a command post could hijack a plane and crash it into the target of his choice?' asked Botreaux, who used the formal *vous* whenever he addressed his relative.

'In theory, yes. But only in theory. The command posts are inside air force bases. There is no possibility of a terrorist getting into one and doing what he pleases.'

'To sum up,' said Fennell, taking charge, 'we all agree that the risk of a land attack is close to nil.'

'We agree,' acquiesced Dupond-Aignan.

'And we agree that a seaborne assault would stand even less chance of success.'

'We agree.' Botreaux's faith in the Royale remained unshakeable.

'And we agree that whilst an air attack is a theoretical possibility, it is highly improbable, mainly because of the security measures that have been introduced in light of the intelligence we provided.'

'We agree,' said Hubert de Botreaux, feeling uncomfortably grateful to this Englishman who was helping him save *la patrie* and his ancestral home. Uncomfortably, because he felt he was betraying the memory of his father – who had never forgiven the English for sinking the French fleet at Mers el-Kebir to prevent it falling into German hands.

'Which, by a process of elimination, leaves us with only one possibility,' concluded Fennell, sounding like Sherlock Holmes. 'Terrorists infiltrating the power station.' He almost added: 'Elementary, my dear Watson.'

'The security service already vets all employees,' replied Dupond-Aignan. 'I find it difficult to believe that a suspect could have slipped through the net and got a job there.'

'We must widen the search to include all occasional visitors, and especially subcontractors.'

'That would take forever.'

'We'll take care of that ourselves,' Botreaux volunteered. There had been few opportunities for him to serve his country since the end of the war in the Balkans, and this one was not to be missed.

'Perfect!' Fennell hastened to say. 'That way, we can save precious time.' He knew how to exploit men like Hubert de Botreaux. They were all loyal men who had an innate sense of sacrifice and public service, but also an unfortunate tendency to confuse great causes with the politicians and bureaucrats who used them while pretending to serve them. Yes, Guy Fennell was expert in the art of

145

using men like Hubert de Botreaux, and at squeezing them like lemons until dry and then throwing them away.

'We are in a better position than the security service,' boasted the lemon Fennell was squeezing. 'We know the area better than they do. I'll alert the Gendarmerie and call in the territorial brigade, and we'll go through the files of the local chamber of commerce and the employers' federation.' Hubert de Botreaux had obviously fallen for the romantic illusions about spies, and was delighted with this windfall. Hunting bearded Islamists in Normandy sounded much more exciting than hunting game. Which would normally have been his daily fare until the end of the season.

The following morning, armed not with his custom-made Holland & Holland shotgun but with his well-filled address book, his mobile phone and a flask of sloe gin, the aristocratic reserve colonel cheerfully embarked on the campaign accompanied by his new comrades-in-arms. Hubert Anne-François de Botreaux de Fauconberg liked to feel he was making himself useful, and he certainly felt useful that morning; very much so.

Fennell was equally delighted. This was fieldwork at its best: cars driving at full speed through the Norman countryside; halts punctuated with salutes; hush-hush meetings in village halls; tense briefings at the Gendarmerie; orders carried out with no questions asked; black coffee served in tin mugs; crunchy croissants swallowed in one mouthful; and greasy fingers wiped on well-cut trousers.

On the third day of the hunt, one of the beaters Hubert de Botreaux had dispatched to Le Havre finally came back to the command post with a name he had dredged up from the town's trade register: EGS, Entreprise Générale de Services.

'It's a family firm. Plumbing and central heating,' he explained as he handed Botreaux a sheet of paper. 'It was founded by the father of the present owner and some maintenance work at the Paluel power station has been subcontracted to it for years. What caught my attention is that, a year ago, forty-nine per cent of the shares were sold. The buyer is a French national, all right, but he also seems to be of North African stock.'

Taking the sheet of paper, Botreaux left the room to consult the Gendarmerie's files.

'The other thing that intrigued me,' continued the astute beater, 'is that the gentleman in question could easily have bought the whole firm for what he paid for a minority holding. He paid over the odds!'

'And whereas Gulf Arabs are famous for spending lavishly,' said Dupond-Aignan, 'North Africans tend to have a reputation for being careful businessmen.'

'Precisely. Strange.'

'Buying only a minority holding was obviously a way of making sure the takeover was discreet,' Dupond-Aignan said.

'There's been no change on the board. And the other interesting thing is that EGS has taken on five new men over the last six months. Four of them have foreign names.'

'Got them!' Botreaux interrupted, having found what he'd been looking for. 'The Gendarmerie's got them!' Botreaux was obviously a man who knew what *esprit de corps* meant.

'Got what?' asked Fennell, who wasn't much interested in *who* but *what* they had found.

'The gentleman is indeed French, but he's only been French for ten years or so. He was born in Blida, in Algeria, and made his fortune by importing pharmaceuticals. And listen to this, he financed the Islamists' election campaign, but then he changed sides and began to support the military when the Army moved against them.'

'What about the men he took on, the new recruits? Are they Arabs?'

'He's been more subtle than that, my friend. Two Bosnians, one Turk and an Albanian. Sure, they're Europeans of a sort, but they're still Muslims. Muslims, but not Arabs carrying the plague. A nice set-up. EGS's technicians have access to everything in the power station. And I do mean everything. There are pipes all over the place.'

'Terrifying!'

'None of them has a record, of course. But that won't stop us from searching their homes and EGS's premises.'

Fennell was truly delighted to be in France. On the other side of the Channel, and in the same circumstances, it would have taken ages to convince a magistrate to sign a search warrant. Europe did have its good points after all.

When Hubert de Botreaux returned later that afternoon, he was smiling the embarrassed smile of a beginner who has felled with his first shot the three-hundred pound wild boar that was charging him. In the home of one of the suspects – a Bosnian engineer who had become a plumber somewhat late in life – they had found a diabolically simple plan to sabotage the pumps so as to prevent the seawater reaching the reactors and cooling them. Starved of water, the temperature in the reactors would rise, leading to a meltdown.

'Banco!' cried Dupond-Aignan, for whom Mayfair's casinos held no secrets.

'Congratulations, Hubert,' said Fennell. He could already see himself being made a Chevalier in the Légion d'Honneur.

'We've been lucky,' was all Botreaux said. He was modest about his triumphs and happily attributed them to fate, if not his genes.

On the evening of their victory, the three just men went back to the manor house with a whole mob of hounds and beaters, some in uniform and some in plainclothes, that Botreaux had enlisted for the occasion. In keeping with the purest feudal tradition, the lord of the manor gave them all a drink in front of the fire in the kitchen. Fennell was over the moon again. This success more than made up for the way Van Dusen had let him down. The Atlanticist suddenly discovered that he had the soul of a European, and he took a solemn oath that he would vote for Britain's entry into the Euro zone in the coming referendum. He also began thinking of selling his farmhouse in Staffordshire and buying a small cottage in Kent or Hampshire. That would make it easier to visit his good friend Hubert de Botreaux de Fauconberg.

Afterwards he went to Paris, where he was greeted with full honours. He took the opportunity to tell his grateful listeners about his plan for a co-ordinating committee to prepare for the new European intelligence community. Delighted at the way the Entente Cordiale had been revived, they were only too happy to listen.

Fennell had good reason to be satisfied. He had succeeded in turning the Sharif's information into political capital – on behalf of Whitehall and the Clubhouse, of course, but mainly for his own benefit. His colleagues would not have been surprised to learn that he had invested a tidy sum in Eurotunnel shares.

22

Lucky Strike and its happy outcome had given Fennell a taste for travel and a new enthusiasm for Continental Europe. Scarcely a week after his triumph, he flew to Moscow at the invitation of Vladimir Dimitrivich Lukin, who was about to celebrate, in style, the first anniversary of his appointment as head of the Centre. The Sharif's intelligence about Islamists in the Transcaucasus, duly passed on by Guy, had enabled Lukin to uncover a terrorist group run by a Dagestanian called Gaïdar Azimov, who had sworn to put the Russian capital to fire and the sword – notably by targeting the big hotels in Moscow that hosted the country's foreign creditors, and were essential links between Russia and her new friends in the West. Lukin could have acted earlier on the basis of the intelligence supplied by the Brits but, being a typical New Russian, he was striving for effect and wanted the arrests to coincide with the anniversary of his appointment as Grand Spymaster. He had therefore done no more than put the suspects under close surveillance. Magnanimously, he had insisted on Guy sharing his triumph when the time came. Vladimir Dimitrivich Lukin was anything but ungrateful.

So Fennell was on his way to a sort of party when he boarded the regular London-to-Moscow flight that day. He flew British Airways, as his faith in the New Russia did not extend to Aeroflot. Far from it. He travelled light, his present (vintage Sharif) having gone to Moscow ahead of him. He was also feeling light-headed, becoming rather more so as the first-class stewardess (who reminded him of Joan, especially when seen from behind) plied him with glass after glass of Pol Roger 1988. Having at last got over the distress Tom Van Dusen had caused him, he was also feeling light-hearted – so much so that, once he was in Russian airspace, he began to feel the way Winston Churchill must have felt *en route* to visit the Little Father of the Peoples to consolidate the Anglo-Russian alliance against the Antichrist.

The welcome he was given at Sheremetyevo Airport seemed to him worthy of that great historical figure, and it was only the Teutonic origins of the black limousine that was taking him round the ring road that prevented him from believing that this was a remake of the memorable meeting of those two wartime leaders.

As they approached Yasenevo and the ash grove that gave it its name, he felt a twinge of nostalgia. Before becoming home to the friendly Russian Centre, Yasenevo had been the headquarters of the not-so-friendly Soviet Centre. True, Fennell had sat out the Cold War at the Department of Trade and Industry. But when he saw that interminable surrounding wall, the twenty-storey skyscraper that soared above it and the dachas in the distance, he had a feeling of *déjà vu*. It was as though he had by magic assimilated the memes, if not the genes, of all those British Cold Warriors who had spent (and sometimes sacrificed) their lives fighting yesterday's enemy. By the time the Mercedes entered the heavily guarded gate and drew to a halt at the entrance to the right wing of the complex, Fennell actually had turned into such a warrior.

Lukin received him in his second-floor den, which had a view over the wooded park and ornamental lake. The office was a rather successful mixture of monumental Soviet furniture from the 1930s and sophisticated modern equipment. Its occupant was just as syncretic. Small, stocky, with high cheekbones and slightly slanting eyes, he looked just like Fennell's image of the quintessential apparatchik. But unlike the typical Soviet high official, he was young – barely forty – and wore a grey striped suit that had obviously been made to measure. Fennell's expert eye could tell it was cashmere. Plus, Lukin spoke American.

'I wanted to thank you in person for all the intelligence you have supplied us with,' said Lukin, once they had settled comfortably into enormous leather chairs with wooden armrests.

'It was the least I could do.'

'In my view, this business is of particular importance. As you know, I spent years dealing with Islamic terrorists before I was appointed to this post.'

'Yes, I know. You're the great specialist.'

'A specialist who is always willing to learn. And I have to admit that I learned a great deal from your intelligence.'

'It's very kind of you to say so.'

'My appointment is obviously a reflection of the importance our President attaches to this subject. It is now our number-one priority.

And your intelligence has made us still more determined to fight terrorism with all the legal means at our disposal until we finally eradicate it.'

'What we need is a common front against the enemy.'

'It is a difficult task. As you know, the Soviet Empire has bequeathed to us a far from negligible number of Muslims. And now they are living amongst us, and they all hold Russian passports.'

'In the same way that the British Empire left us its Muslim Asians.'

'Indeed. Our experiences are comparable.'

'And whilst it is true that diversity is a source of wealth,' said Fennell (even though diversity left him rather cold) 'it has to be kept under control, and it can't be allowed to degenerate into being a cancer that could undermine our societies.'

'You put it very well. It really is a cancer, and unfortunately we are less well-equipped to deal with it than the doctors. There are serious legal restraints.'

'Mustn't kill the patient trying to kill the cancer.'

'The difficulty is all the greater in that we are fighting on two fronts at once. On the one hand, we are waging a merciless war on terrorism. On the other, we are trying to establish a constitutional state.'

Lukin sounded like a man who was getting ready to defend his service before a parliamentary committee.

'We mustn't use the same weapons they are using,' said Fennell, who believed just the opposite.

'Precisely,' lied Lukin. 'If they force us to set up a police state, they've won.'

'And a police state is the last thing Russia needs these days. It would be bad for trade.'

'Which is why we attach such importance to collaborating with services like yours. Quite apart from the precious intelligence you can supply, we are also interested in learning about your methods. The assignment the President gave me is as much an educational as it is an intelligence task. The Centre I am now running has nothing to do with the old Centre, the Cold War Centre.'

'I don't doubt it.'

'You might be surprised to learn that whilst jokes about the oligarchs, the Duma and sometimes even the President himself are still going around Moscow, no one tells jokes about the security services any more. Just goes to prove that some things at least have changed, doesn't it?'

'It certainly does.' Fennell didn't like jokes about men in power. Any men. Any power.

'To get back to the "object", this Gaïdar Azimov whose name you were kind enough to give us. We had no idea about his Islamist sympathies.'

'Really?' Fennell was delighted with his scoop.

'All we knew until we got your information is that he was a wholesaler who supplied some of the big hotels in Moscow with frozen sturgeon and fresh fruit from Dagestan.'

'A market trader?' Fennell was amused.

'So we began to take a close interest in the "object's" activities,' said Lukin, repeating a word in common use inside the Russian security services. 'And two days ago one of my men succeeded in getting inside the object's refrigerated warehouse, even though it is heavily guarded. It's not far from the Kursk railway station. He got close to a delivery weighing over a ton that was intended for the Metropole. When he looked inside the refrigerated van, he found to his surprise that it contained not only sturgeon, but also some semtex, Mr Fennell.'

'Incredible!' Fennell was delighted.

'The object's van usually parks in the underground car park alongside the hotel when it delivers its load to the kitchens. It will be parked there again this time. But while Mr Azimov and his staff are unloading the sturgeon in the Metropole's kitchens, his accomplices will be busy unloading the other stuff and planting it by the strategic pillars in the basement. '

'Terrifying!' Fennell was thrilled.

'I don't know if you are familiar with the area,' said Lukin, who made a point of pretending that he didn't have foreigners shadowed whenever they were in Moscow, 'but the new underground car park is next to the hotel's swimming pool, gym and night club.'

'That's terrible.' Fennell was overjoyed.

'And that's not all. The fact is that there is a warren of underground tunnels. People used to store wine there before the Revolution. It's like a Swiss cheese down there.'

'An explosion would be a real disaster.'

'A short distance from the Bolshoi and the Kremlin.'

'It would have a huge media impact.'

'To say nothing of the fact that the Metropole's main restaurant hosts special parties for various ministries and their foreign guests.'

'This could have repercussions far beyond Russian borders.'

'An explosion would indeed have international repercussions. But to get back to Gaïdar Azimov, when my man discovered this strange load, he took care not sound the alarm. He carefully locked the van, and just told me about it.'

'Fantastic!' Fennell liked this Lukin chap. The discovery of half a ton of explosives near an outlying railway station wouldn't have been anything more than evidence of a minor plot on the outskirts of the capital. It might just as well have been on another planet. But allowing the terrorists to deliver something that unpalatable to the Metropole, and to place it in the hotel's labyrinthine cellars beneath the walls of the Kremlin itself, gave the affair a whole new dimension.

'So we let them get on with it. And we are now waiting for the object, who should get unhindered to the hotel in the next couple of hours. I've made sure he reaches the hotel safely.'

'Well done.' Fennell was thinking not so much of this fine catch as of the way it was going to be caught.

'I should be saying "well done" to you. This fine haul is down to you. Just imagine the Metropole's foreign guests being served semtex explosives instead of the sturgeon they're expecting. It's not even on the menu. Imagine the disastrous effect that would have on our financial backers.'

Fennell could imagine it all too easily.

'We'll wait until the object has unloaded his cargo and goes to the manager's office to collect payment. That's when we will intervene.'

'Remarkable!' Fennell was taking a tremendous liking to Lukin.

'I'm telling you this,' said the object of his admiration, 'because I would like you to be at my side when we make the arrest.'

'With ... with pleasure,' stammered Fennell, who was somewhat taken aback.

'There'll be no trouble.' Lukin knew perfectly well what his guest was thinking. 'No shooting. The shooting – if there is any, and I very much doubt it – will take place in the cellars, well away from us ... So, what do you say?'

'It would be a great honour.' It was, in fact, a great relief for Fennell to learn that there would be no shooting.

156

'Perfect. I'll leave you to rest for a while, and pick you up to go to the Metropole. You'll be staying here in Yasenevo, in a dacha close to mine. I trust you will find it to your liking.'

Fennell was relieved that Lukin's self-confidence hadn't extended to putting him up in the Hotel Metropole.

A Russian dacha hidden away in the snowy forests of Yasenevo seemed to Fennell to be the perfect sequel to last week's Norman manor house.

Once he had washed and changed his shirt, he thought of phoning the office, or perhaps Edwin Trench, his man in Moscow. Just to kill time. But the Russian décor reminded him too much of old spy films. Of course, Lukin had told him that enormous changes had taken place at the Centre. Because he wanted to get closer to his host, he had of course agreed. But now that he was alone, he wasn't so sure. That fine mirror might, he said to himself, be a two-way glass, and the place might be full of microphones. So he simply lay on the bed and stared at the ceiling. He decided that anyone who might be watching him should receive the impression of a meditating yogi; it would look good in the file the Centre no doubt kept on him.

He was still meditating when Lukin rang an hour later. Putting on his heavy overcoat, gloves and fur hat, he went out into the snow and darkness and found his host waiting for him at the wheel of a pale grey Mercedes coupe. It was flanked by two black cars that looked much more sinister, much more in keeping with the task that awaited them.

It took them a good hour to get from Yasenevo to the Hotel Metropole, which was not far from Red Square. As they passed the Bolshoi on the left, drove around Karl Marx's statue and drew up outside the magnificent art nouveau building, with its Vroubel

157

mosaics and splendid wrought-iron work, Fennell's heart began to beat faster even though there was nothing to worry about. It was all so civilised: no guns that he could see, no sirens, no whistle blasts and no yelling into walkie-talkies. Much to his surprise, Lukin even waited patiently for the car valet to give him his ticket. As he led his guest into the cavernous lobby, he looked more like a prosperous businessman than the formidable head of the equally formidable Centre.

A little old man in his sixties, who was no more than five feet tall, was waiting for them, and came straight over. He shook Lukin's hand, nodded to Fennell and the minders and then led them in Indian file past reception and down a corridor to a drawing room where three secretaries were hard at work despite the late hour. Five young men who looked like bouncers kept them company.

The heavy door on the other side of the room was padded with leather and reminded Fennell of the door to Devereux's office. The little old man opened it without knocking, pushed open another that looked just the same, went through the 'airlock' between the two and led them into a room. A fifty-year-old colossus was sitting behind a desk and staring at a much younger and much less imposing man, who looked lost in his big leather armchair. The younger man jumped to his feet as they came in: Gaïdar Azimov, said Fennell to himself.

Lukin said something in Russian that Fennell didn't understand. The Centre's boss spoke softly and calmly, but there was an increasing look of panic in the other man's eyes as he watched the henchmen crowd into the room. One of Lukin's men handcuffed him, another covered his hands with a scarf so as not to frighten the hotel guests and a third threw an overcoat over his shoulders. Then they escorted him away without a word. The whole operation, beginning with their arrival at the Metropole, had taken no more than three minutes. Fennell couldn't get over it. Was all fieldwork as simple as this? The Rough was not that rough, he thought to himself.

Once the Dagestanian had left with his new friends, they reverted to English. Lukin introduced the colossus and the little old man who had been their guide to Fennell. They were, respectively, the hotel manager and his head of security.

'Azimov's accomplices have just been taken away,' he said after taking a call on his Nokia. 'And so have the explosives.'

'I hope you haven't taken the sturgeon,' said the manager as he lit a cigar that was a good ten inches long.

'Of course we have,' joked Lukin. 'It's an exhibit.'

'It's a real pity about Azimov,' complained the colossus. 'I'll miss him.'

'We'd have missed you if we had let him make this last delivery,' laughed Lukin.

Fennell laughed too, and his laughter was genuine; winning always put him in a good mood, and today he found everyone extremely congenial.

To celebrate their victory, the survival of the Metropole and the first anniversary of Lukin's appointment as intelligence Supremo, the hotel manager was giving a party. Lukin's old friends and all the new ones he had bought himself over the last year had been invited. Far from being an impromptu affair, the evening appeared to have been planned well in advance. Fennell could not help but admire Lukin's nerve. The Russian had never had any doubts as to the operation's happy ending.

The huge restaurant had been closed to the public for the occasion, and the tables arranged in a circle around the central

159

fountain, which was straining to spit its water at the twenty-foot-high ceiling. Lukin insisted that Fennell sit on his right, and to the left of an English-speaking *consigliere* who, so Fennell had been told, had the ear of the President.

They ate well that evening, including Azimov's top quality sturgeon. A lot of toasts were proposed: to Vladimir Dimitrivich, to his son, to his wife, to his numerous mistresses, to his success, to the past, present and future, to the President, to Fennell and, of course, to Anglo-Russian co-operation. Fennell could already see the two-headed eagle keeping company with the Légion d'Honneur on his lapel.

23

'Have you seen the papers, Harry?' asked Briggs as they left the great vaulted salon to go out on the terrace.

'You mean the warlords in Kabul?'

'Actually, I was thinking of the meeting in Madrid.'

'Madrid?'

Boone followed him over to the balustrade. It was a fine winter's day in the mountains and from where they were standing, no more than an hour's drive from Beirut, they had a magnificent view over the whole of the coast. Seen from this vantage point the shore looked deceptively unspoilt, and the heavily polluted sea looked idyllic.

'The latest meeting of European foreign ministers, Harry.'

'There's talk of reprisals, isn't there? There's even talk of boycotting Arab oil to cut off the terrorists' sources of revenue.'

'And there are serious differences of opinion between Germany, Belgium and their European partners ... I really thought you'd have been taking a closer interest, Harry.'

'Why?'

'Because of the Sharif, that's why. He's the one behind all this sabre-rattling. He's named names.. The Germans and the Belgians are in an awkward position, and the French are overjoyed. They can just see Brussels falling from favour, and Strasbourg becoming the new capital of Europe.'

'What about terrorist attacks against the Americans?'

'No, nothing on that, unfortunately. The Sharif says they've never used him to gather intelligence about the Americans.'

'You think he's telling the truth?'

'I don't see why he should lie to us about that when he's dissecting all the Islamists' European operations before our very eyes.'

'Too bad for the Americans. But you can't have everything.'

'That's true. But thanks to the Sharif, we do know everything about the Apparatus. Its structure, the personality of its leaders, internal struggles, cells in Europe, channels, safe houses, the first, second and third circles, financiers, bank accounts. The whole lot. Never seen anything like it. Every door in Whitehall is open to us, and the Treasury is loosening its purse strings. Our European friends are falling at our feet and combing their archives for our benefit, and the Bunkers are green with envy.'

'You make this sound like a real Birdie.'

'Yes, it is a Birdie, as you put it. And it's not over yet. Every day brings its draught of fishes. The Guy-Sharif duet is performing miracles.'

So that's it, said Boone to himself. Archie has come all this way to talk to me about Guy. Starved of funds by the Exchequer, the Foreign Secretary had decided to refill his coffers by selling the Ambassador's summer residence in Lebanon, and Archie had taken the opportunity to come over, using the diplomatic service as cover. The official purpose of his visit was to take an inventory of the fine eighteenth-century house, survey its three acres of land and count its hundred-year-old oaks and walnut trees.

'Guy and the Sharif!' said the old spy-turned-estate agent. 'The couple of the year! Guy apparently can't do without the Sharif. When I think he used to get homesick once he put his foot outside Whitehall. He is literally camping out in Cornwall, now. His star is in the ascendant.'

'What are you getting at?'

'Something bothers me,' said Briggs once they were out in the garden and amongst the roses and cyclamens. 'The Americans ... Guy's friends ... When all this started, I mean when intelligence from source Tiger Woods was just starting to come in, Tom Van Dusen got very excited. Langley was always pestering him. And now, nothing. He's lost interest all at once. I wonder why ... In a sense, it's a shame for Guy. He's never really happy unless the Americans are at his side.'

'You were saying just a moment ago that the Sharif has nothing to give them.'

'I know, I know,' conceded a distracted Briggs. He had just caught sight of a shrub with shiny green leaves and little yellow flowers: *azara microphylla*. He noticed with satisfaction that it had been planted facing west, not south. That spared it the shock of the sudden shift to the morning sun after the cold frosty night. Very wise, he said

163

to himself. Very wise. The Ambassador's gardener had gone to the right school.

As Briggs still said nothing, Boone went over to the shrub that seemed to fascinate his boss so much, and was greeted by a strong smell of vanilla.

'Even so ...' Briggs finally said, walking away from the shrub with obvious reluctance. 'Not one serious request for intelligence from the Americans in all the time the Sharif's been with us. That's not like them. Usually, it's all grist for their mill. It's really not like them. As soon as the Sharif turned up, they lost interest in him. Why, Harry? What did Van Dusen learn in Langley? Why are the Americans avoiding the Sharif? You see what I mean?'

'What I can see is that you've found the chink in Guy's armour. You want to use Langley's half-heartedness to get at him.'

'There's something going on. I can smell it. My instincts tell me there's something going on.'

'Your instincts! You never stop talking about the Sharif. The Sharif this and the Sharif that. You'd be the first to agree that he's giving us four-star intelligence. What you do want, Archie? Are you trying to sabotage the operation just to piss off Guy? To stop him putting one over on you?'

'And you! If Guy gets the upper hand, you won't be in Beirut for much longer. You can count on that.'

He's right, said Boone to himself. Guy won't let me off the hook.

They had reached the spot where Lady Hester Stanhope had been lying at rest for over one hundred years. Boone was wondering what would happen when some wealthy Lebanese eventually bought this fine property for the million-dollar asking price. What would he make of the tomb, and of the remains of the noble adventuress who had turned her back on life at Number Ten for the love of Arab studs

– some with four legs and some with two? Would he let her rest in peace? He told himself that a Druze would. The Brits and the Druze had always got on like a house on fire. It was said that the FCO still drew up an annual report on the state of the Druze community – a tradition that went back to the nineteenth century. But Boone thought it highly unlikely that the Ambassador's summer residence would end up in the hands of a Druze. They no longer had that kind of money. All the money in Lebanon was now in the hands of Sunnis and Shiites, and they owed Britain and Lady Hester nothing.

'What do you expect me to do?' he asked after the moment's silence.

'Start digging into the Sharif's past. Get to know him better. Give me ammo. Stop Guy taking control of him. Stop him taking control of the Service.'

Boone told himself that he would be mad to play along with Briggs and put his system in danger. Maria would never forgive him for taking such a risk. On the other hand, he couldn't stand there with his arms folded until Guy Fennell found someone to replace him in Beirut.

'OK,' he said, thinking to himself that he belonged to a race that always ended up fighting other people's wars for them. The Aussies, the Kiwis, and the Paddies of the Empire. Cannon-fodder, all of them.

24

As Boone got out of the car, the door slammed shut behind him, filling the empty sonic space. There were no competing noises in the Jesuit Quarter. Not even the noise of children playing. It was as though the entire neighbourhood, taking its cue from the religious order that had given it its name, had taken a vow of chastity. The old front line that had divided the capital for so long had eventually run through the whole neighbourhood, killing off small trade and driving away the active population. Only those too old to make new lives for themselves elsewhere remained. Cloistered away behind their closed shutters, they were dying the same slow, painless death as the buildings themselves.

Boone was walking beside some railings outside a disused church which the Jesuits had leased it to a property developer only a few months before the Lebanese started to kill each other. Everyone knows that Jesuits are shrewd businessmen. As for the developer, he must have been more of a sucker than a shark.

Boone came across a poxy old container that had once been used as a barricade, a wartime relic no one had bothered to clear away. A little further on, a gothic arch sheltered the small oak door to what seemed to be an annex of the nearby Oriental Library. Although it could just as well have been an annex of the container, depending on how one looked at it. A newly engraved copper plate informed visitors that they were at the ERA.

The door was embellished with a monastic-looking bell. Boone pulled the chain. A spy hole protected by a grill finally half-opened. It was then slammed shut and the door opened to reveal Theo Damiano in a dark grey suit and a black turtleneck sweater, wearing a little silver cross in his button hole.

'Harry! Good to see you again. Come in, come in.'

Entering, Boone found himself in a hallway. It was the scene of intense activity. A dozen or so cubs and brownies were sorting, weighing and packing parcels under the watchful gaze of a middle-aged woman wearing the strict uniform of social workers. Giving them a word of encouragement, Damiano led the way into a room dominated by an enormous strongbox: a real antique that impressed no one any longer, barring the cleaning lady who clearly avoided dusting it and treated it with the respect and aloofness that people with little education reserve for symbols of wealth and authority. The rest of the room was taken up with a walnut table flanked by two venerable smoking chairs that wouldn't have looked out of place in Brooks's. The Padre was obviously in the money. The Sharif had, it seemed, brought him luck.

'So, you've moved,' said Boone as he took a chair.

167

'It's more cosy here, don't you think? More central.' Damiano was being modest.

He took a bottle and two whisky glasses out of the cupboard. Boone's trained eye could tell from the squat shape that it was Dalwhinnie.

'The Clubhouse's money has been well spent from what I can see,' he said, as he admired the Bokhara carpets and damascene hangings.

'Reputations shape reactions, Harry.' Damiano sat in the other chair. 'It wasn't easy, receiving visitors in the slum I used to have.'

'You got the balance?' Boone savoured the heathery smell of the malt Damiano had just poured.

'For the Cité Sportive job, you mean. Yes, I got it. I didn't expect to get it so soon. As a matter of fact, I was expecting you before the money.'

'Why's that?'

'To be quite honest, I thought that ... I thought that, given the way things worked out, London might delay payment. That's why you are here today, isn't it? To preach to me. London must have a guilty conscience.'

'Theo ...' Boone stopped him. To his relief, the Padre didn't seem to suspect anything.

'The clean kill we promised them wasn't that clean after all, was it? I suppose they've set up a committee to investigate.'

'Theo ...'

'Fifty dead ... A bit too much for the bean-counters, I suppose. Tell me, Harry, how many deaths make a clean kill in London these days? Can I count them on the fingers of one hand? The fingers of both hands? How much is a dead old man worth nowadays, Harry? Half a dead woman? And killing a child? How many adults does that count as? Ten? More?'

168

'I'm not here to preach, Theo. The thing is, there are some at the office trying to use this thing to recall me to London.'

'I see ...'

'Maria would never agree to follow me there.' Boone poured himself another malt. 'And I certainly don't want to leave Maria, or Lebanon. I like it here. We were even thinking of buying a little place ... over by Dlebta. I have to do something to get out of this spot of bother. The chop could fall at any moment.'

'Listen to me, Harry. The operation was planned – and it was well-planned, believe me – to claim no more than ten victims, give or take one or two ... On my express orders, no more than two hundred kilos of explosives were used; there were no more than six twelve-millimetre mortar shells in the back seat; and only ten antitank mines in the boot. Ten little mines, Harry! And the car was parked over fifty metres away from the gates. Over fifty metres! I do have a heart, you know. I spoke to my man. He was there on the spot.'

A thousand dollars saved, Boone thought to himself. The thousand dollars that should have been paid to the lookout. Damiano had haggled over the lookout, and used the money to buy his hangings.

'My man, Harry,' said the bargain-hunter, 'a man in whom I have complete trust – he's a professional – assured me that even with a population density as high as ten people per square metre – per square metre, Harry! – the charge he used could not have claimed that many victims.'

'Your man got his sums wrong. It was an overkill ...'

'An overkill! I like your sense of humour, Harry. He saw the car and its passengers. There was nothing left. Just bits of flesh and metal. An armour-plated Mercedes! Blown to smithereens! Just like the old banger we used.'

169

Old banger! Damiano had talked about a car in good running order and costing two thousand dollars. So that was another fifteen hundred saved. That would have paid for the carpet.

'You'd almost think there was another bomb that day.'

'Nonesense.' Boone was beginning to worry about the implications of another explosion.

'Maybe, Harry, maybe. The only thing is, you see, that there was Sheikh Hammud as well. Because only a few minutes after we had sent the Sharif *ad padres* – always assuming that a man like that will ever find himself in the presence of the Lord – someone saw fit to send Sheikh Hammud to join him ... Pure coincidence, I suppose.'

'Pure coincidence.'

'I don't think so. You know what I think, Harry? I think my man was right to say there was another bomb that day. Probably in the Sharif's Mercedes. You know what else I think? I think – and this makes me terribly sad – that the pathetic little operation you entrusted me with was just a diversion. Congratulations, Harry! I'd never have believed that London had the balls for that kind of setup!'

'You're talking nonsense. Why the hell should we do that?'

'Why? For the sake of your source. That's why.'

'Source? What source?'

'If memory serves, when you first came to see me you told me you had a reliable source who'd assured you that the Sharif had a hand in Cholmondeley's death.'

'So what?'

'If memory serves, and correct me if I'm wrong – I'm getting old and my memory's not what it used to be – it was you who decided where, when and how. Down to the last detail.'

Our lies catch up with us, said Boone to himself.

'Which suggests to me that the operation you got me to mount was simply intended to protect your source. A smokescreen, if you'll pardon the expression. To throw everyone off the trail and to allay suspicion. To convince the Apparatus that killing the Sharif was not an inside job. And you had Sheikh Hammud killed to muddy the waters still further. Well done, Harry!'

'Theo ...'

'I now have a better understanding of why you haggled over the cost of the operation. London wanted its smokescreen all right, but not at any price. The real investment was going somewhere else, wasn't it? The jackpot was going to the mole. And as is so often the case, the lucky winner wished to remain anonymous. So you call in old Theo to play second fiddle ... I suppose I should be glad you didn't just sacrifice me to protect your source. Or is that still in the cards?'

'Theo ...'

'Theo, Theo, Theo, what?' Those humanists in London saw fit to sacrifice fifty or so poor sods and mutilate another hundred and fifty to protect the source who betrayed the Sharif and allowed them to eliminate him. So tell me, why should they have any qualms about sacrificing old Theo?'

'This is madness.'

'Madness? You expect me to believe that two different outfits decided to eliminate the Sharif on the same day, at the same time, in the same place and in the same way? Come on, Harry... Unless we're dealing with a crime of passion and not a political assassination, of course!'

'Please be serious!'

'I am being serious, Harry. Couldn't be more serious. The Sharif had a woman in his life.'

171

Boone was relieved to hear Damiano still speaking of the Sharif in the past tense, as though he was dead. 'A woman? His wife, Fatima Kronfol!'

'Who said anything about a wife, Harry? I'm talking about a *woman*. One he kept hidden away. He may well have been a descendant of the Prophet, but the Sharif was keeping a mistress!'

'Where did you get this information?'

'Charity,' replied Damiano in humble tones. 'Charity. Give, and God will repay you hundredfold. So I gave, and the Good Lord repaid. Perhaps not in coin of the realm, but with information. In our business, it all comes to the same, right?'

'Go on.'

'Would you believe that, just a week after the Sharif's tragic death, a bearded man turned up at the Baptist College of Beirut to see the headmistress? She's a friend of mine, Harry. A very dear friend. The bearded man introduces himself: Abul Abbas, no less. Does the name mean anything to you?'

'The man who took over from the Sharif?'

'The very same, Harry. No sooner had he sat down than he launches into a diatribe about – and I quote – "the murderers who, by targeting the Sharif, have also targeted the spirit of tolerance he represented". End of quotation. Needless to say, this speech left my headmistress deeply perplexed. She really couldn't see what her unexpected visitor was driving at. But she was wary enough not to ask him to be more explicit. Once he had finished his tea, Abul Abbas stood up to take his leave and on the doorstep he assured her that the protection her school had enjoyed while the Sharif was still alive would of course continue to be provided. She still had no idea what he was talking about. When he had gone, she did, however, recall that in the past a female member of her staff by the name of Randa Bsat used to take care of all the problems a Christian establishment can run into in an increasingly Islamised country. On one occasion, some militiamen saw fit to take up position in the college chapel; on another, a Christian teacher was kidnapped. My headmistress found the idea that one of her colleagues could be linked – either directly or indirectly – to someone dangerous and powerful enough to get himself blown to bits by a car-bomb so deeply upsetting that she ran to me for advice.'

'An interesting tale. But what makes you think this Randa was his mistress? She might have been a source.'

'A source? You must be joking. I can't see the Sharif having personal dealings with a marginal source. And I certainly can't see him giving away a source by doing it minor favours. We are talking about the Sharif, Harry, not Colonel Kamel. About someone who does things properly. No, I've thought about it a lot. There's only one explanation for this long-term relationship between him and a beautiful young woman, and a single woman at that. They must have been lovers.'

'If he was really interested in her, why didn't he marry her?'

'Marry her? A psychology degree from the American University, a penthouse flat with a sea view, a fancy car, and even fancier clothes? I can't see her marrying the Sharif, being buried alive along with Fatima in some harem in Beirut, and only being let out in a veil to shout "Death to the American Satan" for some spontaneous women's demonstration. No, I think a bit of love in the afternoon was as convenient for her as it was for him.'

So, said Boone to himself, there was a woman in his life. That would explain his evasive tone, and his irritation, when Guy suggested exfiltrating his wife Fatima. Fatima was the last person he wanted by his side.

'What you do think of that, Harry?'

Harry thought that all this would be music to Archie's ears.

25

'So, Boone the gossip sent you this ... "information" ... Still in Beirut, is he?' Fennell was in a bad mood. Devereux had recalled him from Cornwall that very morning, and when he got to the Clubhouse, he was surprised to see that Briggs was in the director's office, an empty teacup proof that he had been there for a good while. Fennell excelled at interpreting bureaucratic signs, and he did not like this one a bit. The courtier who slumbered inside him bitterly regretted having left the court, leaving Devereux to fall under the influence of his rival. He felt excluded, and what Briggs had said had done nothing to raise his spirits.

'So, according to your man Boone, the word in Beirut is that the Sharif has a mistress?'

'That's right.'

'And, still according to Boone, there are persistent rumours that it was a so-called double explosion that caused the Sharif's "death"?'

'That's right.' Briggs was exaggerating.

'But they are just rumours, aren't they?'

'I didn't want to check any further without having talked it through with you.'

'Rumours,' Fennell insisted. 'Just rumours.'

'True,' Biggs conceded.

'And you're weighing the intelligence the Sharif is giving us against the gossip peddled by some Levantine outfit that's clearing out its drawers to make ends meet? Gossip that Boone picks up third-hand at the local marina?'

'Gossip it may be, but it's still a good idea to check it out with the Sharif.'

'He is co-operating fully, and I don't wish to upset him.' Fennell had guessed that Briggs would try to take over the debriefing, and he was determined not to let him.

'The fact remains that, if the Sharif does have a mistress, he may have told her about his plans.'

'Pure speculation. Nothing that justifies an interrogation. It's hard enough to get him to forget about the flutterer episode.'

Briggs never failed to be amazed at Fennell's ability to quickly distance himself from a bad idea that had been his in the first place.

'The fact remains,' he said, 'that if there were two explosions, if the Sharif had his own car blown up to make sure that the bodies would be unrecognisable – a sort of insurance policy, so to speak, in case we messed up – it would mean that he had accomplices. I don't see how he could have succeeded in packing his own car with explosives, blowing it up at just the right moment, and at the same time booby-trap the attaché case that killed Hammud and Shartuni. If

175

he did have an accomplice, we have to assume that someone knows that he didn't die in the explosion. And that that someone also knows he is here. With us.'

'Archie is right,' Devereux intervened. 'If Boone's information proves to be accurate, if the Sharif does have a mistress, and if there really were two explosions, it is possible that at least two people are in the know. It's worrying ...'

'Harry could come over and talk to him.' Briggs was pressing home his advantage. 'The two of them seem to get on fairly well together.'

'Upsetting the routine is out of the question.' Fennell protested. 'The Sharif is used to Catlow and his team. He's been well broken in. Boone's interference would disturb the rhythm and his production would suffer.'

Being a good tactician, Briggs had struck at the very spot where he didn't expect to score any points. He was merely trying to unsettle his adversary.

'So the only thing left to do is to keep on looking in Beirut,' he sighed.

'That would make waves.' Fennell still wouldn't give in.

'There are enough waves already. If these rumours about the Sharif have reached us, they must have reached other people too. That's the way it is with rumours. We can't just put our heads in the sand. We have to know what everyone else is up to. We can't keep our distance. Not if we want to protect our source.'

Devereux turned to Fennell, who still kept silent, as though to indicate that he wasn't entirely unconvinced. But they were both coming round to accepting Briggs's logic.

Briggs congratulated himself on his strategy, on having judged his colleagues so well and on having understood – presumably by extrapolating from his own experience – the tortuous way their bureaucratic minds worked. Ultimately, whether or not the Sharif had a mistress or an accomplice was neither here nor there. The fact of the matter was that it was nothing to do with them. What did matter, on the other hand, was what others knew or might know, be it true or false. The absolute truth was of no interest to them. Relative truth was all that mattered. Comparative truth. Competitive truth. That was where the potential threat lay. Not in some lie or omission on the part of the Sharif who, as it happened, was laying golden eggs with the regularity of an astonishingly fertile cuckoo clock.

'No needless waves, eh, Archie?' That was Devereux's way of saying: You can go ahead.

'Trust me,' said Briggs as he got up to leave before they changed their minds.

Back in his own office, he gave himself full marks. Now that Devereux had given him the green light, he could go on taking an interest in the Sharif. He was back in the saddle, whether Guy liked it or not. Guy could hide behind his debriefing committee if he wanted to. He could even turn it into a barricade if he had a mind to. Briggs was going to the Rough instead, using the field to sow doubts in their minds, and if need be to reassure them when the going got too bad. He would blow hot and cold, and they would be on the lookout for any scrap of information he might care to throw their way. All he had to do now was to recall Harry to London, brief him and then let him loose in Beirut – but on a leash. Not too short a leash, so as to allow him to do the job he was expected to do; but not too long a leash either. Otherwise he would do just what he liked, as usual. Striking the right balance and picking the right time – that's the secret, he said to himself.

26

Briggs left the Clubhouse and walked across the square to the tube station. At that time of day, the station lift was crowded to bursting, and when he did succeed in getting on a train, it was packed too. Briggs was not an imposing presence, and at sixty he was neither young enough to elbow his way through the crowd nor old enough to be treated with deference. Besides, he was fairly shy by nature and the job he had always done, first in the Security Service and then at the Clubhouse, had taught him to keep a low profile. Not a good recipe to survive the London tube at rush hour.

He held out for a good ten minutes, but by the time he got to Leicester Square the crowd had gained the upper hand and he decided to give up and go the rest of the way on foot.

The West End's pavements were as crowded and chaotic as the subterranean world he had just left, with workers anxious to get to the station on time for a suburban train that might or might not come, trendy young men jostling to get into the pubs for the Happy Hour ritual and swarms of Asian tourists flying the golden green Harrods logo. Everyone was pushing and shoving on either side of a stationary line of traffic, belching exhausts proof that, quite aside from its doubtful ecological virtues, unleaded petrol at least gave drivers a clear conscience. Briggs was already regretting having given up on the tube. To make matters worse, it had started to rain. Not the fine, gentle rain he and all his generation had grown up with, but heavy warm rain not even the most elusive of Englishmen could escape.

In Piccadilly, he tried to shelter from the deluge by ducking into one of the shopping arcades property developers were constantly excavating inside old imperial buildings. In one booth, the sort that sprouts up like a mushroom and lasts only as long as the latest fad, a young couple were having their photograph taken in full Victorian dress. Briggs decided arbitrarily that they were Italian. The girl was doing her best to keep a straight face, but she was also smiling shyly as if to say she wasn't taking all that seriously. When Briggs's eye caught hers she blushed slightly, like a rosebud before coming into flower, and then looked down. An equally embarrassed Briggs turned away and stared through the glass door giving on to the street.

It was still raining. He had wanted to take shelter from the shower, but this was more like a monsoon. This was colonial rain: the Crown's former overseas possessions were sending the metropolis a climatic reminder of their existence. On the opposite pavement, an overworked postman crouched in front of a letterbox was hastily picking up the letters he had been clumsy enough to drop in a puddle. Briggs spared a thought for the Royal Mail's loyal fans who had never got used to the idea that the post had been privatised. The pretty Italian girl came out of the photographer's holding an artificially aged photo in an artificially aged chipboard frame. Her boyfriend caught up with her, and, twenty pounds the poorer, they happily set off in search of other souvenirs of London.

The rain was still falling, and Briggs did not carry an umbrella. Briggs never carried an umbrella; it was his only vanity. He had always refused to get one so as not to be the victim of all those puns. 'Briggs and his Brigg's,' someone would have said. 'Briggs has lost his Brigg's.' 'Is that a Brigg you have there, Briggs?' He would have been tempted to reply: 'It's a Smith's, as a matter of fact.' Not that that would have helped matters.

Umbrella or no umbrella, he wasn't going to stay forever in this clinical arcade where neon lights reigned supreme. Turning up his coat collar and pulling down his hat, he made himself very small and ventured out into the street where he was greeted by the hideous transatlantic siren police cars now use. It was a reminder that American influence in Britain extended far beyond Guy and his Whitehall friends.

It was still raining when he pushed open the door of his Pall Mall club. This was where an aging Talleyrand had cheated at whist and told his long-suffering partners about the countless diplomatic dirty tricks he had pulled. Seeing a couple in evening dress making for the door, Briggs politely held it open for them, thus forcing the lady and gentleman, who didn't quite know what to make of such courtesy, to run in their shiny evening shoes. It completely ruined the solemnity of their ceremonial dress.

'Your guest is waiting for you in the library, sir,' the porter told him.

He hung up his dripping coat and hat in the cloakroom before joining Boone and taking him into the smoke-room.

'You can sleep the sleep of the just, Harry,' he said as soon as they had been served tea. 'Your two scoops about the Sharif have bought you some time. Guy won't be pulling you out of Beirut in the foreseeable future.'

'Thanks for the respite.' Boone made a face as he took a sip of tea. He'd never liked the Earl Grey that Briggs was so fond of. 'But don't expect any miracles. For the moment, all we have are rumours. Just rumours.'

'Rumours, you say?' Briggs bit into a fat-free biscuit. 'Never underestimate rumours. Rumours make men rich and bankrupt them. They bring down governments. What you call rumours have got Cecil Devereux worried, and left Guy shaken. So you have *carte blanche.*'

'About the two explosions ...'

'Forget about that.' Briggs brushed off the crumbs that had fallen on to his jacket. 'Forget the two explosions. Concentrate on the Sharif. On him and this girl.'

'But what if the Padre is right? What if there really was a second explosion?'

'Your Padre is lying. Lying through his teeth. He'll say anything to justify himself and find an excuse for all those deaths. Forget it, Harry. Concentrate on the Sharif and his mistress.'

'But what if he is telling the truth?'

'The rumour about the two explosions has more than served its purpose. It's sown doubts in their minds. We don't need it any more. We've already exploited it to the hilt. They're already worried. Do

181

you want to panic them, or what? Do you want to frighten them so much that they let the Sharif go and then close down Beirut Station? Is that what you want? If you go on poking your nose into the alleged two-explosions business, and into these supposed accomplices, that's precisely what they will do. They'll take fright and put your Sharif on the first plane to Beirut. Then they'll recall you to London and carry on as though nothing had happened. Is that what you want? No ... Of course it isn't ... All I am asking is that you give me enough information to keep them guessing, and to reassure them from time to time. Let me decide on the dosage. Just send me scraps of information about the Sharif's past, the girl, and what the other outfits know about this business. I'll look after the rest. Your job is to gather information. Interpreting it for their benefit is my job ... Well? What do you say?'

For the moment, Harry Boone was saying nothing. He was too busy trying to get back into focus, trying to get rid of the squint his boss's twisted logic had forced onto him. What Briggs was saying seemed almost as bitter as his tea.

Briggs seemed to sense his dilemma, because he went on without waiting for an answer: 'Believe me, we'll get nowhere with those two by telling them the truth. I know them better than you do.'

I'll bet you do, thought Boone.

'If you turn up tomorrow with hard evidence about one of the Sharif's so-called accomplices, someone who might know he's not dead, that would be the end of it. They would wash their hands of him and leave you to carry the can, believe you me. After all, it's you who brought him along ... But if you start gathering information in roundabout ways, shedding indirect light on this whole business – and I do mean indirect – then you and I will have time to strengthen our hand, and we'll wear them down. We'll proceed at the same pace

182

as the truth. Whereas if we do what you suggest, the truth would quickly outstrip us, and we'd be left in the lurch. Is that what you want? No. So we'll do it my way, Harry: crabwise.' Briggs sounded more like Talleyrand than ever.

'Very well,' said Boone, defeated but by no means convinced.

'Spoken like a man.' Briggs helped himself to a chocolate biscuit to celebrate his victory. 'You give me the ammo I need, and I will decide the rate of fire. Who are you going to use? The Padre again?'

'Who else is there? He's already in it up to his neck.'

'The Padre it is, then. But above all don't take him into your confidence. As far as he's concerned, the Sharif is dead and buried. And he's going to stay that way, isn't he?'

27

'Pass me the soap, will you, Harry?' Damiano sniffed his fingers yet again. 'Fried red mullet is succulent, but to really appreciate it you have to dive in. No knives and forks ...'

The two men had just finished a copious lunch washed down with *arak* in a little fish restaurant in Barbara, about twenty-five miles north of Beirut. Now they were washing their hands – and forearms too, in Damiano's case – to get rid of the smell.

'There!' Damiano said at last, energetically crumpling the checked towel. 'What about a walk? I think that after that feast, a walk is a must. I have to think of my figure.'

Damiano had always been conscious of his appearance. It must be the company of all those charitable middle-class women he had to deal with, thought Boone.

'So, my intelligence has caused a wave of panic in London,' Damiano said with pride once they were on the beach. He seemed to be very pleased with himself. He was walking with a very straight back and taking regular deep breaths, as though to let everyone know that this was exercise.

'I wouldn't go so far as to say that. But they'd still like to keep an eye on things.'

'The story about the two explosions has them worried, has it? Just goes to prove I was right.'

'Right? Right about what?'

'About the second explosion, of course. The second explosion was you!'

'That's what you say, Theo. In London, they're convinced that you're telling a pack of lies to cover your blunder. What they are really interested in is what people are saying about this business.'

'The mole, eh? London wants to protect its precious source. London wants to know if its source inside the Apparatus is in danger.'

Boone said nothing. Better to let the Padre believe that the Clubhouse had succeeded in infiltrating the Apparatus, than having him beginning to wonder why the hell the Brits were so keen on a man they were supposed to have already killed.

Each trying to outwit the other, the two men reached a small inlet where a few fishing boats bobbed peacefully up and down after their morning's work. The entrance to the inlet was guarded by a heteroclite building: a medley of terracotta, wood planks, canvas and concrete. A ladder led to a terrace that was home to a stunted vine and a cage whose purpose was far from obvious – a pathetic harbourmaster's office for a forgotten port.

185

'George!' shouted Damiano. He had noticed a man making makeshift repairs to a boat.

Leaving his work, the man came towards them, wiping his hands on his rolled-up trousers. Moving away, Boone left them alone. He noticed the fisherman's tone and posture. He looked deferential, even obsequious. Damiano obviously had some kind of hold over him. Or perhaps he couldn't make a living out of fishing. Perhaps the Padre took care of that for him.

'George is a pigeon fancier,' Damiano said when he had dismissed the fisherman. He pointed to the terrace. 'That's a pigeon loft you can see up there. George keeps carrier pigeons. All this might not look much to you, but throughout the civil war it was the centre of our communications system.'

'You must be joking, Theo! Carrier pigeons!'

'And why not, Harry? Why not? Can you think of anything safer? I suppose you think I had diplomatic pouches at my disposal? Coded faxes? Encrypted radio signals transmitted at very high frequencies? During the war years, when we had no telecommunications and when couriers couldn't move from one region to the next without getting themselves killed, I kept in touch by using carrier pigeons. As it happens, I'm thinking about going back to that system, because with phones, faxes and e-mail every American, Brit, Russian, German, Frenchman and Chinaman knows what everyone else is doing.'

'Pigeons! Really, Theo!'

'Pigeons, yes, pigeons ... A good carrier pigeon, a one-time pad and a coded message. It's still the best way. More reliable. And cheaper, of course ... I didn't invent the system, you know. It's been in existence since the eighth century in this part of the world. Whenever there was trouble in the lands of the Caliph, the horse post was disrupted, but not the pigeon post. The pigeon post went on working as normal, precisely because it wasn't affected by the upheavals that were taking place at ground level. Sultan Baybars understood that. He was a great man, Sultan Baybars. Do you know who was in charge of the pigeon post? The head of the intelligence service. Like I say, a great man, Baybars. The letters were written in very small writing – "dust writing", they called it – on very thin "bird paper". Then they were attached to the birds' main flight feathers. Some carrier pigeons had a cruising speed of a hundred kilometres an hour, and they could do five to six hundred kilometres without stopping. My winged couriers could do Beirut-Larnaka in less than two hours. With a calm sea, obviously. Not bad, eh?'

'I find your low-tech system a bit too hazardous, Theo.'

'You're wrong, Harry, you're wrong … But I promise I won't introduce pigeons into our system, so as not to offend your technological bias.'

'That's reassuring.'

'Don't be sarcastic. To get back to business … If London really isn't interested in the two explosions, the girl – this Randa Bsat – is our best bet.'

'Perhaps your headmistress friend could grill her on our behalf?'

'That would take months, Harry. And there's no guarantee she would crack. No, we'd be better off removing her from her usual environment to soften her up, make her more receptive … Condition her, so to speak.'

'Condition her? Don't you mean "abducting her"?'

'Don't be so melodramatic. Who said anything about abducting her?'

'Explain what you do mean, then.'

187

'This is what I suggest. In a few weeks' time – at Easter, to be precise – the Eastern Council of Churches is organising a conference on education in the countries of the Mediterranean. A praiseworthy undertaking, I'm sure you'll agree. The conference will be held at the Ayia Napa monastery in Cyprus. We could arrange for Miss Bsat to be invited, couldn't we? And once she is on the island ...'

'It's too dangerous, Theo.'

'Do you want to talk to her or not?'

Boone did want to talk to her. He would do anything to keep his system afloat.

'If you want to talk to her, we'll do as I say.'

'No, Theo ...'

'Do you want to stay in Beirut or don't you?'

'But ... kidnapping!'

'Who said anything about kidnapping?' Damiano shook the sand off his brand new Italian moccasins. 'We invite Miss Bsat to the conference, she goes to Cyprus of her own free will, we send a car to pick her up at the airport, and rather than leaving her to be bored to death listening to academics talking learned nonsense all day, we arrange for her to spend a couple of pleasant hours in your company.'

'She could bring charges.' Boone was asking for reassurance.

'You must be joking, Harry. If this girl is what I think she is – and she is – she'll leave the island without making any fuss. So, what do you say?'

Boone had nothing say. He would rather have been somewhere else. Far away from this loose cannon. The old man's audacity made him shudder. Theo Damiano had been out of it for too long. Then Boone came along and had given him two chances to prove himself, in his own eyes and in the eyes of his people: first the car bomb, now this 'conditioning', as he so nicely put it. It had brought it all back: slush funds, secret compartments, adrenaline and coded messages. Why not carrier pigeons, while he was at it? Theo Damiano had reverted to being the Padre once more, and that's what frightened Boone. The Padre would eventually bring him down. One false move and it was all over. No more Maria, no more Lebanon, no more house in the mountains and no more retirement in the sun. But on the other hand there was Guy Fennell. If he did nothing, Guy would end up chopping his head off. Boone was between the devil and the deep blue sea. He had to choose between the wild field agent and the wily espiocrat. It didn't take him long to decide.

'How much, Theo?'

'How much?' Damiano smiled. 'Forty thousand dollars should do it.'

'Twenty. My boss won't pay more than twenty thousand.'

'A measly twenty thousand dollars? It's not a lot ... But I suppose I'll have to make do with that.'

'Do you have a plan?'

'I'll need four or five people ...' For the Padre, any operation was an excuse to provide jobs for the tribe. 'I'll talk to a friend who's on the conference organising committee, and I'll arrange for Randa Bsat to be invited. I'll also speak to her headmistress, who will encourage her to go. Then, a few days before the conference begins, one of my men will go to Cyprus to rent a car and a villa, and he'll disappear. The day before she arrives, two other men will take possession of the villa and the car, Joseph and Carlos. I'll introduce you to them, Harry. I'm sure you'll like them. Particularly Joseph. I found him in a seminary. He'd got it into his head that he should devote his life to studying the liturgy of the Eastern Uniate Churches. I had a hard time of it convincing him that his gifts could be put to better use elsewhere. Though he'd have made an excellent father confessor. Sinners are drawn to him as flies to honey. I'm sure the two of you will get on well together ... To get back to the plan, another of my men will then rent a second car. A limousine, something sober and ecclesiastical, you know the kind of thing I mean. When the time comes, he'll go to the airport to pick up the girl, carrying a sign so that she can identify him. That's important, don't you think? It will be up to her to make the first step. She mustn't think she'd already been spotted and was being picked up ... You agree?'

Boone agreed.

'Once she sees the sign carrying her name, she will approach him and he will drive her off. On the way he will tell her that not everybody will be staying at the monastery and that she will be put up nearby. Hence the villa. Once he has handed her over to Joseph and Carlos, he will return the limousine and leave the island. What do you think, Harry?'

'It's a good plan. But I fear that Miss Bsat will still be on her guard, alone in a car with a strange man. She might even object when he tells her they're not going directly to the monastery. After all, she won't know him from Adam. Just because he is perfectly charming, and has the courtesy to carry her bag and open the car door for her, she won't necessarily quietly go with him to an isolated house.'

'Hmm ...' Damiano had stopped and was stroking his chin. 'You're probably right. We need something to make her trust us from the start. Something, or someone ... A third party ... Another woman, perhaps. Yes, a woman. Why not Maria, Harry?'

'Leave Maria out of this, Theo.'

'Hmm ... A nun, then. An old maid. Not wearing a habit, of course – that would be overdoing it – but with a prominent cross,

190

and wearing those black shoes with the squatty heels that nuns like so much. What do you say?'

'Should do the trick.'

'Then we're agreed. I'll arrange for a woman to be on the same flight as Randa Bsat, and when they reach Larnaka our man will be carrying a sign with two names on it instead of one. Miss Bsat won't suspect a thing.'

'Good plan.'

'Introducing this new element – I mean the "sister" – will obviously mean more expenses. But don't worry. I'll stick to my original estimate.'

With a holy picture in lieu of a gift voucher, Boone said to himself.

28

Perched on his swivel chair, the Cypriot policeman examined the crested passport with the disdain that Third World officials habitually reserve for their former colonial masters. Small countries, small acts of revenge. Taking his time about it, he half-heartedly consulted his files and, eventually and with bad grace, granted Harry Boone the right to spend his money on the island for three months. As soon as he was released, Boone obliged by going to change money at the nearby bureau de change: a sign of good faith. He collected his luggage from the squeaky baggage reclaim and, ignoring the customs officers, went through to the arrivals hall.

In the car hire souk, an eager-beaver young lad tried to foist on him a big Mercedes and a life insurance policy, but finally handed him the keys to a bottom-of-the-range Vauxhall. Boone found the car on a patch of waste ground that apparently served as a car park. As he might have expected, the tank was half-empty. Small countries, small profits.

Driving away, he turned right and drove for a couple of miles along a road that wound across a salty landscape. As he approached Larnaka, he slowed down several times, drove round a roundabout twice, hesitated a bit like a good tourist and then headed east. No one had followed him.

Ten miles further on, the main road headed north – but Boone and the flow of traffic he had joined turned their backs on it and took a minor road leading to Dekhelia, and from there to Ayia Napa. The main road, which everyone turned its back to, led to Famagusta and the Turkish part of the island. It had fallen into disuse since Ankara's troops had invaded Cyprus. When they lost the north, the Cypriots had also lost all latitude. They could no longer find their bearings.

On the way into Dekhelia, he slowed down to give the British sentries time to size him up. Dekhelia looked nothing like a Cypriot village. It was a royalist base in a republican land. As he gained speed again, he looked through his windscreen at the neat little bungalows that lined streets with familiar names. The space was unmistakably English, and so was its semiology.

He saw the villa as he came round a bend. Theo Damiano had chosen well. Standing at the water's edge and close to a landing stage, it stood isolated and seemed to date from the days when building regulations didn't apply to developments along the coast.

Leaving the villa behind him, he headed towards Ayia Napa. As he drove, he remarked to himself that Theo Damiano had chosen well there, too. The villa he had picked was in the ill-defined area that lay between the Cypriot and British zones. Naturally, both sides conscientiously avoided it. It was a sort of tacit no-man's-land where the threshold of impunity was relatively high – which suited Boone perfectly.

Twenty minutes later, the car made a chaotic entrance into Ayia Napa, slipping past concrete skeletons that were mercilessly tightening their grip on the old fishing port: drained of its lifeblood, but a willing victim. Bearing left, Boone plunged into a labyrinth of one-way alleys and found himself nose to nose with a local van that didn't seem at all embarrassed at being in the wrong. The Highway Code obviously didn't apply this early in the season. Having learned his lesson, Boone kept even further to the left, climbed winding alleys lined with terraces littered with folded parasols, and came to a halt in front of the monastery. He stopped for a moment to have a closer look at the Padre's Easter retreat, then hurtled down the hill and parked outside the Grecian Bay Hotel.

Inside the bar, two fat tarts whose Athenian pimps had dumped there were trying to keep up the fake party mood. The best they could do was to hang around watching the barman energetically shaking cocktails for non-existent customers. This was a dress rehearsal. Everybody was waiting for the Easter tourists to arrive. Picking a corner seat, Boone made a phone call.

'Mr Damiano, please,' he said in English to a Greek voice that kept saying '*parakalo, parakalo*'.

The request sparked off a series of noises from the switchboard's digestive system. After a lot of gargling sounds and mechanical eructation, he heard the Padre saying '*parakolo*' in his turn.

'Theo, it's me ...'

'Where are you phoning from?'

'The Grecian Bay. I'm in the bar.'

'Give me ten minutes.'

Boone had just ordered a drink – 'no, not "a Black Label of course", just a Ballantine's' – when the Padre made his entrance. He was wearing cream trousers and a black polo shirt that went well with his spotless white beard.

'Theo,' he called.

'So there you are!' Damiano came over to him with outstretched arms, not quite sure whether he should give him a hug or just a handshake. Boone, who could have done without either, offered him his hand. At first that seemed enough for Damiano, but then he changed his mind, drew Boone to him and gave him little pats on the back. Boone made a note of the Sea Island cotton polo shirt, a Smedley that must have cost him a hundred quid.

'Are you staying here?' asked Damiano when he had ordered his drink.

'No, at the Palm Beach in Larnaka.'

'Very wise. More anonymous.'

'No last-minute hiccups?'

'None at all, Harry. Joseph and Carlos got to the villa this morning, and Miss Bsat should be on tomorrow morning's flight.'

'With the good sister?'

'With the good sister … I've even arranged for them to sit next to each other on the plane.'

'Perfect. The more they get to know each other before they reach Larnaka, the better it is.'

'The devil is in the detail, as you people put it. And you have to admit that I've taken care of every detail. This isn't one of Colonel Kamel's operations!'

'Then let's drink to it,' said Boone, hurriedly emptying his glass and rising to leave before the Padre had time to launch into yet another diatribe about the Sûreté and the Clubhouse.

195

29

Sitting on his balcony, Boone was enjoying his first cigar of the day. Cyprus's hybrid cuisine did not appeal to him, and this was his breakfast.

It was the start of the Easter holidays, and the hotel was beginning to fill up with its seasonal cargo of pale-skinned anatomies. They came to the island in the hope of getting a tan and went home looking like boiled lobsters. The day's quota of women had already attracted a swarm of local guides, coaches and assorted gigolos. They had taken over the poolside, occupied strategic positions and, with the same unfinished drink in their hands, were lying in wait for their prey. Boone was spying on them through the arabesques of the balustrade, but the ringing of his mobile soon put an end to his professional voyeurism.

'Harry?' Damiano's voice said as soon as he answered. 'The bird has landed and is in the cage.'

Bird? Cage? It made Randa Bsat sound like one of the Padre's carrier pigeons.

Boone rang off, slipped on his jacket, left the hotel and went as far as the main road. A pedestrian crossing had been painted there for the benefit of the travel brochures, but it seemed that no one had got around to informing the Cypriot motorists of its existence. At one point, he tried to step off the pavement. In Britain, that would have been more than enough to make the most aggressive of drivers step on the brake pedal. But the Cypriots had apparently decided to make this a sovereignty issue, and had obviously got rid of the British Highway Code when they shook off the English yoke. He waited for a good two minutes for a gap in the traffic. Then he put his faith in God, dodged between two angry horn blasts and miraculously succeeded in reaching the other side in one piece.

There, someone had had the bright idea of building a shopping centre that looked like a Mexican's vision of a North American mall. A sports shop and a fashion boutique selling fake Lacostes, Reeboks and Nikes vied for pride of place with an Island Burger and a Larnaka Fried Chicken, where Western stomachs suffering from *la turista* came from time to time in the forlorn hope of making a full recovery. Sitting in the shade of a parasol on the Island Burger's terrace, Boone ordered a Nescafé. What he got was a cup of hot water, a ragged sachet of chicory, another of sugar and a little plastic receptacle containing milk guaranteed never to have been anywhere near a cow. He was still wondering what to do with it all when a white 4x4, a Toyota, drove into the parking area that had been put at the disposal of the shopping centre's customers. The driver paused to give him time to notice him, then parked behind an empty bus.

Leaving his untouched Nescafé and some small change on the table, Boone went to meet him.

'Everything went exactly as planned,' said Joseph, taking off at top speed. The respect men like him had for their bosses was always proportional to the match between their theoretical plans and practical applications. Harry Boone thought to himself that Joseph must have been feeling very proud to be working for the Padre.

'Is she already at the villa?' He asked.

'They're both there. I left them with Carlos.'

'As soon as we get there, bring her to me, and tell Carlos to take the other woman back.'

'She's in her room. It overlooks the sea, so she won't see the "sister" leave.'

'Does she suspect anything?'

'Not for the moment. The presence of another woman must be reassuring to her. But there are limits, and Carlos doesn't speak much English – his Greek is even worse.'

Boone had made Carlos's acquaintance, in a manner of speaking, and thought that even the man's Arabic vocabulary had to be very restricted.

'I've asked him to make himself scarce,' went on Joseph, 'and to keep quiet. But she might still bump into him.'

A short while later, he stopped the car outside the villa's porch. The door was opened immediately; Carlos seemed relieved to see them. When Boone spoke to him, he remained silent and looked puzzled, as though he wasn't too sure that he was now allowed to break his vow of silence. He had obviously taken Joseph's orders very seriously. Then, to mask his lack of composure, he unconsciously put his hand on a bulge that was pulling his jacket out of shape at waist level. The gesture reminded Boone – as though he might have been tempted to forget – that this woman was being held against her will, no matter what Theo Damiano might say.

Leaving Joseph to deal with Carlos, Boone went inside the villa and into the dining room. He had decided that his was where he would interrogate her. Joseph had carefully closed the shutters and drawn the curtains. Boone flipped a switch and a ceiling lamp in a wicker shade revealed a motley collection of furniture, a combination of cold rusticity and washable surfaces. Someone had placed an ashtray at the opposite end of the table that divided the room lengthways. Joseph, noted Boone; Joseph was proving to be attentive to his every need, and was suggesting that he sit at the far end of the room for effect, facing the door so that they had the girl sandwiched between them. Boone appreciated the attention, but the suggestion irritated him. He took out a small cigar and lit it without thinking. A few minutes later, he heard the Toyota start up and drive off. Carlos and the 'sister' have gone, he said to himself, as he made for the ashtray and the place Joseph had chosen for him. He was sitting there when she came into the room.

'Oh! I'm sorry ... I thought Sister Marie-Thérèse was waiting for me here ...'

She spoke good English, with a strong American accent. Every state in the Union was there. So this was the Sharif's mistress. Boone figured the Sharif must have learned his English from her. Pillow English, just like the Arabic Maria had taught him. Her strict beige suit and her urchin cut made her look quite severe, but her mouth and big dark eyes made it perfectly clear that she was no prim schoolmarm. She really was beautiful.

'I was told ...' She stared at Joseph, who was blocking her way and preventing her from leaving the room.

'Sister Marie-Thérèse won't be long,' Boone lied in English.

199

Not at all put out, she leaned forward over the table with a smile on her lips and offered him her hand. He caught the full blast of her perfume: Shalimar. A Western perfume with an Eastern name, just like her.

'Randa Bsat,' she announced. Another sign of American influence: this was a woman who was used to mixing with people, who was sure of herself and of her charms.

'Please take a seat,' Boone said in Arabic. He wanted to re-establish the distance that her beauty and fragrance had just abolished. 'Please take a seat,' he said once more, without letting go of her hand.

Those few words of Arabic – pronounced with an obviously foreign accent – had the desired effect. She quickly withdrew her hand, and became tense.

'Please sit down,' insisted Boone, as Joseph closed the door and leaned against it.

'Where is Sister Marie-Thérèse?' She was visibly worried.

'I have a few questions to ask you,' said Boone, who had been rehearsing his Arabic.

'Who are you? Where is Sister Marie-Thérèse?'

'I'm a friend of the Sharif's.'

'I don't know who you are talking about. I would like to leave now, please,' she said, looking to get past Joseph.

'Not until you've answered my questions.'

'What questions? What do you want from me? I don't understand. I demand that you let me go. Immediately!'

She insisted on speaking in English, as though it offered her some sort of lifeline. Boone stuck to Arabic, even though it cost him.

'You can leave as soon as you've answered my questions.'

'Who are you?'

200

'I've already told you. I'm a friend of the Sharif's.'

'But I don't know any Sharif!'

'Don't play games with me. We know all about you.'

'You're Israelis!'

Boone shook his head and smiled sadly. Why on earth did Arabs always think of the Israelis when anyone said they knew everything?

'We're not going to hurt you,' he said, switching to English in the hope that she would realise that he didn't have the guttural accent of an Israeli. He'd unsettled her, and now he had to reassure her. He walked round the table to get closer to her. 'But you'll have to co-operate,' he said.

'Co-operate? Co-operate with what? Let me go!'

'As we speak, a Miss Randa Bsat has reached the monastery in Ayia Napa, where she's been given a room with a view of the dome of the church. This Miss Bsat will take part in the conference and read a paper. It will go down well. On Sunday she will take a plane to Athens for a few days' well-earned rest. She will, of course, be travelling on your passport, which has been slightly doctored for the occasion. This Miss Bsat certainly doesn't have your looks, but I had to make do with what I could find. All this is just my way of saying that I have all the time in the world. So, sit down. Please. The sooner we get it over with, the sooner you can go.'

Gripping the back of her chair with both hands, she looked around the room. The curtains were drawn and Joseph was blocking the doorway. She began to see reason and sat down, but at an angle to him, with one elbow on the table and her chin in her hand. Sulking.

'Your name is Randa Bsat,' said Boone. He too had sat down, and was addressing her left profile. 'You were born in Sidon, and you are twenty-five. You have a degree in psychology from the American

University in Beirut, and you work for the Baptist College as an educational adviser. You also teach in the Lebanese University's Department of Psychology. You are single, and you live in the Rue d'Australie. Your rent is eighteen hundred dollars a month and you own a car. You go out and you travel. Now, given the state of the Lebanese pound, your monthly income amounts to no more than two thousand dollars. You have no other visible source of income, and you are obviously living beyond your means.'

'Are you a tax inspector?'

'I was saying that you are single. Yet there is a man in your life.'

'Oh, I see.' She turned to face him with an ironic look. 'You're from the vice squad.'

'A man who pays your rent, and who pays for your car, your holidays and your clothes.'

She'd responded to the provocation. She was becoming involved. Boone, who had been afraid she would retreat into silence, now believed she would be easy to break, for all her haughty airs.

'Your private life is of no interest whatsoever to me. What does interest me is the man who used to pay your bills. The Sharif. I'm very interested in him.'

'I don't know who you're talking about.'

'The Sharif. Abu Hasan Al-Husayni. Or Ali Al-Husayni, if you prefer. That's who I'm talking about. Do you deny knowing him?'

She said nothing. She was trying to work out what he really did know. Boone decided not to help her. He remained silent.

'He ... That's the man who was killed two or three months ago, isn't it?'

'Oh, Come on, Miss!' Boone relit his cigar. 'You know him better than that. He used to pay your bills. He took care of your colleague's problems. You'd known him for years, you were having an affair

202

with him. Until his accident. Until he died in a car-bomb attack at the Cité Sportive.'

'I read about it in the papers. What's it got to do with me?'

'There were a lot of victims that day. More than fifty dead, in fact.'

'And I suppose you think I'm responsible?'

She knows, Boone said to himself. She knows he isn't dead. That's why she's being so high and mighty. He decided to use his secret weapon.

'You might not know it, Miss, but those who planned the attack had a little surprise coming.'

She didn't move. She didn't even bat an eyelid.

'You see, there was a second explosion at the Cité Sportive that day, a few moments after the first; a second explosion that claimed more victims than expected. You follow me?'

She said nothing, but she did stiffen. He went back on the attack.

'This second explosion ... How shall I put it? ... It upset the original plan.'

She was obviously worried now. He'd succeeded in sowing doubts in her mind. She hadn't known about the second explosion, and now she was afraid that he really was dead. Boone didn't leave her any breathing space.

'I know you were very close to the Sharif. I know he loved you.'

His use of the past tense acted as a whiplash. She suddenly couldn't bear hearing this stranger talk about her lover in the past tense in such a matter-of-fact way. Jumping to her feet, she took a deep breath, looked in desperation at the closed window and sat down again. Got her, thought Boone. I've found her weak spot. I know she knows the Sharif didn't die that day, and now she thinks that he might have been killed after all. For the last few months she's been convinced that her lover was alive and safe, and now she

203

realises that he might have been blown to bits in the explosion. He had her pinned. He could have pressed home his advantage. He could have cornered her. But he didn't. It was enough for one day. He'd unsettled her, now he had to let her stew.

That evening, Boone met Theo Damiano at a bar in Ayia Napa. The room was stuffy, the décor tacky, and the music reggae. The middle-aged English couple at the next table looked as though they'd rather have been at the Reid's, on Madeira, and were making the best of it by sipping cheap port.

'Just a few more hours, and she'll agree to fly to London with me. But I mustn't let her out of my sight.' Boone looked at his watch. 'I'll spend the night at the villa.'

'I don't recommend it,' said Damiano, who had stayed well away from the house. 'Go to the hotel. Joseph will pick you up in the morning.'

'No. She might decide to talk tonight.'

'As you wish, Harry, as you wish ... Another of my men has just got here; Grégoire. I don't think you know him. I wasn't expecting him, but it seems the source he went to meet in Athens didn't show up. I'll send him to the villa. It won't do any harm to have the three of them guarding Miss Bsat and you.'

'You're the boss.' Boone wasn't at all interested in this detail.

'No charge, of course.'

'Very generous of you,' said Boone, picking up the bill.

'Have to stick to the estimate, don't we, Harry?'

Particularly as putting up Grégoire at the villa meant one less hotel bill for Theo to pay, Boone thought to himself. No such thing as small savings.

30

She kept to her room the next morning. What with Radio Lebanon and the more spontaneous broadcasts of Carlos, who seemed determined to break the previous day's enforced silence, the house was full of Oriental music and gossip. Around midday, Grégoire, the newcomer, went into town to see Damiano and brought the newspapers back. Boone spent the afternoon reading the press and counting the hours. He'd decided to give her until the evening. As it began to get dark, she would realise that she was facing another night with her kidnappers. Shortly before six, she asked to see him.

'You wanted to speak to me?' he said when Joseph had brought her to him.

Boone's English was in sharp contrast with the Arabic she'd been hearing all day. She seemed to relax.

'What exactly do you want from me?' she asked as she sat down.

'Tell me about him.' Boone lit a cigar.

'Yesterday, you told me you were a friend of his.'

'Did he mention me to you?'

'Yesterday, you also told me that the plan had gone wrong.'

'Did he tell you about it?'

...

'Did he tell you about his plan?'

...

'Who else knew about it?'

'What went wrong? What really happened?'

'Listen ... We'll get nowhere like this. Let's make a deal. I'll answer your questions if you answer mine ... Did he tell you about his plan?'

'I want to know what happened.'

'Did he tell you about his plan?'

'I want to know!' she screamed, jumping to her feet.

'Did he tell you about it?'

'He ...' She sat down again. 'He told me that I would hear that he was dead ... That I shouldn't believe it ... That he needed ... to disappear.'

So, the Sharif had been lying.

'When did he tell you that?'

'Can't remember ... last summer.'

'When, exactly?'

'Can't remember. Mid-September, something like that.'

Before he went to Quetta, Boone said to himself. Before the first meeting with Shartuni, and long before he made contact with us. So he'd had it all planned from the start.

'Did he ever speak to you about it again?'

206

'Once ... Just before the bomb at the Cité Sportive. He left me some money that day. A lot of money ...'

The Clubhouse's money, Boone said to himself.

'He told me again that I would hear he was dead ... That it wasn't true ... That he had to go away ... That someone would contact me on his behalf ...'

'Who?'

...

'Who?'

'Tareq Ghazzawi.'

Another Tareq. The Sharif had already mentioned a Tareq. Tareq Bizri. The man with the limp, the man Shartuni saw when he went to see Hammud.

'Tareq ... he's the one with the limp, isn't he,' Boone asked on a hunch.

'Yes. He had polio when he was a child.'

So, the Sharif had been telling more lies.

'Is ... is he dead?'

Joseph, Carlos, Grégoire and Radio Lebanon no longer existed. They were alone now. Alone with the Sharif. Boone relit his cigar. Slowly. Very slowly. He knew he was treading the fine line between good handling and gratuitous cruelty.

'No,' he said at last. 'No, he isn't dead.'

Closing her eyes and bowing her head, she ran her fingers through her hair.

'Does he really mean that much to you?' asked Boone.

'It's ... It's not what you think it is.'

And just what do I think? Boone asked himself. That you're a kept woman? And what are you trying to tell me? That you really love him? That you're not with him because he's got power? Because he's

207

rich? For the sake of the penthouse in the Rue d'Australie? That he's your bit of rough? Is that what you're trying to tell me?

'Where is he?' she asked.

'Somewhere safe.'

'But you told me the plan went wrong?'

'Well, there was a second bomb, but it didn't kill him.'

'You're sure?'

'I'm the one who helped him get away. You can trust me.'

'Why should I trust you? It's Tareq who was supposed to contact me, not you.'

'That doesn't really matter, because I can take you to him.'

'He's here?' Her face lit up. 'He's in Cyprus?'

'No, he's not here.'

'I want to talk to him!'

'That's not possible. But I can take you to him.'

'When? Now?'

Boone could just see himself arriving in England with her. They would be forced to take him seriously. Guy would have to pipe down. He woldn't be able to exclude him from the debriefing. He couldn't stop him from having a face-to-face meeting with the Sharif. The Boone system was back with a vengeance.

31

Boone glanced sleepily at his watch. Four-twenty in the morning. Something had woken him up – a noise, maybe. No, not a noise; rather, the fact that there was no noise. No noise from the television downstairs; no noise from Carlos's footsteps on the gravel outside. Dragging himself out of bed, he went to the window and pulled back the curtain. Everything seemed to be where it should be in the moonlight. Everything, that is, except for the dinghy moored at the landing stage. That hadn't been there yesterday. Pulling on his trousers, Boone went out onto the landing. Not a sound. The entire household seemed to be asleep. He was rushing towards Randa Bsat's room at the end of the corridor when he realised that the front door was open. What looked like a large sleeping dog was blocking the exit. Turning back, he went down the stairs, keeping close to the wall. Once he was downstairs, he flattened himself against the cold stone and listened. Nothing. He began to walk across the bare tiles. Still nothing. He was only a few feet from the door now, and he could see that the big dog was Carlos, bound, gagged and asleep. Silent at last. Someone had apparently decided to use him as a doorstop. Boone approached him cautiously. Someone had relieved him of the bump in his waistband and had given him a new one in exchange, at the base of the skull this time. Leaving him where he was, Boone went into the kitchen, fumbled around for a moment, and then re-emerged with a wooden-handled knife. He was just about to go back upstairs when a noise made him jump back into the doorway. From where he was standing, he could see shadows moving furtively across the landing. A man – at first Boone mistook him for a child – came first, holding onto the banister to feel his way. Randa was two steps behind him. Two armed men brought up the rear. Boone held his breath. He had to do something, fast. Shout? Sound the alarm? Wake Joseph and Grégoire, who were sleeping at the back of the house? No, not while she was still with them. They were going down the stairs now, and the man in the lead was making them walk at an unbearably slow pace. One hand on the banister, one foot feeling its way, a scraping noise, and then a dull thud. The man was putting one foot on each stair before feeling for the next. He was very close now. Still the same irregular pace. He passed within inches of Boone, dragging one atrophied leg behind him. Polio, said Boone to himself. A man with a limp. *The* man with a limp. Randa's Tareq Ghazzawi; the Sharif's Tareq Bizri. When he finally saw Randa's silhouette, he leaped out, grabbed her by the arm, dragged her violently to him and took shelter behind the kitchen door. Holding her with one hand and his knife in the other, he called for help. On the other side of the door, someone was blazing away at the lock with a handgun fitted with a silencer. The lock soon gave way, and Boone bitterly regretted his lack of exercise and his pronounced liking for liquor, tobacco and good food. He began to shout even louder, and his screams seemed to cause a commotion in the hall. He heard someone say something in a low voice. Then he heard footsteps drawing near. A shadow appeared. He got ready to sell his life dearly.

'It's me,' whispered the shadow. 'Me, Grégoire.'

Grégoire! So Joseph and Grégoire had come to the rescue, and the attackers were retreating. A relieved Boone loosened his grip on Randa, who struggled free and flung herself into Grégoire's arms. Boone didn't understand. Then he saw the gun Grégoire was holding. A long-barrelled .357 Magnum. He'd seen that Magnum somewhere before: yes, it belonged to Carlos. Suddenly, all was clear. He understood why Carlos had been neutralised, and why no one had sounded the alarm.

He hurled himself at Grégoire. But he was reluctant to use his knife for fear of hurting the girl, and his adversary took advantage of his hesitation to hit him over the head with the gun. Boone staggered but managed to grab Randa's hand. She was still clinging to Grégoire. With great difficulty, Grégoire began to drag his heavy burden out of the kitchen and into the hall. Someone came to his aid and gave Randa his hand. That seemed to give her a second wind. She was grunting fiercely, struggling like mad and kicking Boone in the stomach with her heels. Boone was at the point of letting go when he heard a shot. Grégoire's accomplice let go of Randa and they both fell to the ground in a heap. The man had obviously been an easy target for Joseph. Randa flung herself at Grégoire, screaming in horror. With his face buried between her hot thighs and his belly on the icy tiles, Boone held on to her with one hand. With the other, he

211

plunged his knife into Grégoire's calf with all the strength he could muster. Grégoire screamed in pain. Eyes blazing, face contorted, he aimed his gun at Boone. Suddenly, someone shouted something in Arabic. Grégoire hesitated and turned. The shout had come from the man with the limp. It was him who had stopped the execution. He stared at Boone, and Boone – who was letting go, letting go of the Sharif's woman – stared back at him. Another shot broke the spell: Joseph again. Boone saw Grégoire go still, stagger like a broken puppet, lower his gun and press the trigger with the reflex of a dying man. The Magnum barked again as he collapsed.

Boone heard the sound of footsteps on the gravel. The man with the limp was running towards the beach as fast as his game leg would let him. Moments later, Boone heard the sound of a two-stroke engine moving away – the dinghy. Everything went silent.

Boone felt nauseous. He was hot and sticky. He was covered in blood. Grégoire must have nicked him. He felt himself for injuries. Nothing. Where had all the blood come from? Then he realised. Randa. She'd stopped kicking, stopped screaming. It was her blood.

Struggling to his feet, he shook her and heard her groan. A dark stain was quickly spreading across the front of her blouse. The bullet had gone right through her. A bullet fired by the dying man to whom she had clung to the end. A foetid smell filled Boone's lungs. He felt he was about to faint. Prostrating himself in front of her, he took her head in both his hands and gently cradled it on his knees. Don't go, he begged her. Don't leave me. She stared at him. She was clinging to him in desperation, just as she had clung to Grégoire. But the light in her eyes was fading fast. Boone knew he was losing her. He knew he was losing the Sharif. He knew he was losing Maria. He was still holding her with both hands when she shuddered, coughed blood and more blood, and then died in his powerless arms.

32

'So, Boone. We've been playing the hard man, have we? Kidnapping, illegal confinement, and a proper bloodbath into the bargain! You've been spending a bit too much time with your Lebanese friends. You've gone native.'

Boone stared stoically at Fennell. The others said nothing. Five minutes earlier, he had been brought into the meeting room next to the director's office. The room was all wood panelling and copper, all finely worked and aged to give it an air of Admiralty. Boone had found his superiors sitting in an almost religious silence around a cherry wood table. When the door was piously closed behind him, he walked quietly across the gleaming parquet and sat next to Briggs. But it was so obvious that Briggs wanted to distance himself from his subordinate that he might as well have been miles away. To meet some formalist desire for collegiality, the table was round. But that day, it seemed to Boone to be extraordinarily oblong, with him on one side and the rest of them on the other. He noticed that they all had the same red file in front of them. He hadn't been given one. All signs of the coming storm which Fennell was whipping up.

'Tell me, are you working for the other side, or what? If you were, you couldn't have made a better job of buggering everything up for the Service. What possessed you?'

What possessed me, said Boone to himself, was the fact that you were out to get me, Guy. And I wasn't going to let you.

'Quite frankly, Boone, I liked you better when you were playing your usual self and dozing in the Mediterranean sunshine.'

Boone shrugged his shoulders. He had a terrible headache, and he was angry with himself.

'What possessed you to do it?' asked Devereux.

'An opportunity arose. The opportunity to talk to Randa Bsat.'

'Are you taking the piss, or what?' shouted Fennell, getting to his feet. Boone's passivity seemed only to encourage him. 'An opportunity arose! An opportunity to kidnap her, you mean!' He leaned heavily on the table with both hands, as though to give more weight to the accusation.

'I didn't kidnap anyone,' said Boone in a neutral voice, partly to defend himself and partly because he was trying not to feel guilty about the young woman's death.

'Are you saying that Damiano didn't tell you about his plans? Or that you didn't want to hear about them?'

Boone didn't answer. After all, he had every right to pretend, as they all did, to know nothing about what the men in the field were doing.

'And, not content with being an accessory to a kidnapping, you take an active role in an illegal confinement.'

'I did not.'

'So I suppose she was in the villa of her own free will?' Slipping his right index finger under the red file, Fennell made it jump: a judge calling a witness to the box. 'According to the report I have here, the window of one of the first-floor rooms had bars on it.'

'I wasn't aware of that,' Boone lied once more.

'Not aware, not aware … the things you aren't aware of!'

'But what I do know,' Boone interrupted him and tried to catch Briggs's eye, 'is that she'd agreed to come to England with me.'

'Is that so? Is that true, Archie?'

So that's it, Boone said to himself. It's not me he's after. He's trying to implicate Archie.

Briggs dodged the question by muttering something inaudible, while making a vague gesture with his chin in Devereux's direction, as though to say – without really saying it – that the director had been informed. The manoeuvre worked. Fearing he was getting too close to the boss, Fennell again turned his guns on Boone.

'So she agreed to come to England, did she? Unfortunately for you, she's not here to confirm your version of events, is she? She's dead, Boone. Dead.'

Boone said nothing. Randa's death still stuck in his throat.

'To say nothing of all the trouble we're having with the Cypriots as a result,' said Rose, who sounded personally offended.

The Cypriots? Since when had anyone cared about them? Boone couldn't understand why the Caddy Master was so bothered about not offending the Cypriots. Perhaps he and Mrs Rose were planning a holiday on the island.

'Three dead!' Fennell was saying.

215

Boone made no attempt to defend himself. His mind was elsewhere. He was thinking of Randa.

'Including the woman he loves!' added Fennell. 'I wonder how he'll react to that news. Telling him now is obviously out of the question, but we can't keep it from him forever.'

'Yes, that might pose a few problems when it comes to his reinsertion,' admitted the director.

'But the fact of the matter is that he lied to us,' ventured Nico Mowbray-Smyth, adjusting the Indian print scarf he was wearing around his neck.

'Lied?' asked Fennell. 'What did he lie to us about?'

'Well, he didn't tell us about this Randa Bsat.'

'Why should he have told us about her?'

'And he concealed the fact that he had accomplices who helped him to blow up his own car and eliminate Hammud and Shartuni,' insisted Mowbray-Smyth, running his fingers through his hair, which he wore long and brushed back.

'You've only got Damiano's word for it, and he's crazy!'

Snapping out of his lethargy, Boone wondered why Nico had gone on the offensive. Was he rushing to the aid of a fellow Old Oxonian? Probably not. Nico was a Magdalen man first, and only an Oxford man second. Whereas Boone was 'redbrick'. Nico was simply going against the grain. Even at school, or so they said, he'd obstinately stuck to bum-freezers when his peers were proudly wearing tails.

'He concealed the fact that he had it all planned long before he contacted us,' Boone said.

'That's what you say!'

'But Randa –'

'She's dead!' Fennell interrupted. 'Dead!'

216

'What about the man with the limp?' asked Mowbray-Smyth.

'What man with a limp?'

'The one at the villa. The one who got away. He didn't say anything about him. And it seems to be that it was the same man with a limp who acted as go-between for the Sharif and Sheikh Hammud. The man who ferried the briefcase and the documents backwards and forwards.'

'He didn't just say nothing about him,' added Boone. 'He lied to us about his name.'

'What do you mean?' asked Fennell, with obvious bad faith.

'He told us that the man with the limp was called Tareq Bizri, but Randa Bsat told me that the man who was to contact her on his behalf when the time came was called Tareq Ghazzawi.'

'And who's to say it's the same man? After all, Tareqs must be ten a penny. You've never seen this Tareq Bizri, and all we've got is the rough description given by the courier. That Shartuni. The fact that you think you saw a man with a limp at the villa doesn't mean it was the same man.'

'Really Guy,' protested Mowbray-Smyth. 'What a coincidence! We know there's a man with a limp in the Sharif's entourage, and then we find a man with a limp coming to his mistress's rescue.'

'Do you have any idea of how many men walk with a limp, Nico? Do you know how many polio victims there are? How many with a clubfoot? How many cripples? How many war-wounded? Men walking about with a bullet in the calf, or a piece of shrapnel in the thigh?'

'We know that there was a Tareq in the Sharif's entourage,' interjected Boone, 'and all at once we have a Tareq coming to his mistress's rescue. The Sharif gave us the wrong name.'

'Why should he lie to us? Even assuming that it was the same man, what's to stop him using different names? The Sharif does. Perhaps Bizri is his real name and Ghazzawi's his *nom de guerre*. Or perhaps it's the other way around. There's really no need for all this fuss.'

'It's a strange coincidence, all the same.' Mowbray-Smyth smoothed the faded denim of his jeans with his hand. 'It did turn out badly, I'll grant you that, but I think Harry's right. The Sharif, the girl and the man with the limp are more closely linked than we thought. The Sharif definitely told this Randa Bsat that his death was no more than a conjuring trick. He probably used the man with the limp to have his own car blown up, and to eliminate Hammud and Shartuni. I don't see that there's any other explanation.'

'Randa followed the man with the limp of her own free will,' said Boone. 'Those two knew each other.'

'They knew each other!' Fennell turned to Devereux. 'And even assuming that we are talking about the same Tareq and the same man with a limp. What does that prove? The Sharif's old friends thought he was dead. The Apparatus had forgotten he ever existed. Another martyr! And then Boone reminds them of him by kidnapping his mistress? How do you expect them to react? Boone aroused their suspicions. They'll certainly suspect something now.'

Boone had stopped listening. He was thinking of the shout that had rung out when Grégoire had levelled his gun at him. Why did the man with the limp shout? Why did he stop Grégoire from pulling the trigger? For fear that someone might hear the shot? Obviously not. There'd already been a hell of a racket.

'There's been a major cock-up,' Fennell was saying. 'None of this would have happened if we'd adopted the reorganisation plan I drew up.'

218

Brilliant, thought Boone. Guy never lost sight of his goals.

'I don't see the point of preening ourselves in the heat of action.' Briggs had realised that he was under attack now. 'The best thing to do is to try to get to the bottom of all this. We'll have to interrogate the Sharif.'

'Out of the question,' Fennell objected. 'I categorically refuse to subject him to a hostile interrogation.'

The interrogation! That's why the man with the limp spared me, Boone said to himself. My death would have created too many waves in London. Archie would have insisted on interrogating the Sharif. Letting me live and leaving me to carry the can was his way of stopping us from getting too close to the Sharif.

'I think I understand what happened,' he said.

'What did happen, then?' Fennell sounded as though he was pointing out that everyone, including Boone, enjoys a right to self-defence in a democracy.

'The Sharif asked the man with the limp to keep an eye on Randa, and to help her get out of Beirut when the time came. When Randa went to Cyprus, he – or one of his men – followed her closely, like a sort of baby-sitter or guardian angel. When he got to Larnaka, he probably saw and recognised one of Theo Damiano's men, and that worried him. When he saw that Randa was being driven to an isolated villa and not to the monastery, he realised that she'd been kidnapped. He knows that it's Damiano's men who have her. Then he remembers that he has a man in Damiano's entourage, a sort of mole: Grégoire. He contacts him, and Grégoire hurries to Cyprus. The man with the limp now has someone on the inside. The next day, Good Friday, Grégoire reports to Damiano and uses that for going to see the man with the limp. He gives him all the information he has been able to glean: the layout, Randa's room on the first floor, the landing stage, the weaponry, and perhaps a detailed description of me. The man with the limp now knows who he is dealing with. He gives Grégoire his instructions. That night, Grégoire makes sure the guard – Carlos – has been taken out, while the man with the limp and an accomplice head for the villa by boat, so as to avoid the checkpoint in Dekhelia. They reach Randa's room, but the plan goes pear-shaped when I wake up ...'

'Why didn't they kill you?' It sounded as though Fennell wished they had.

'I've been thinking about that. I think the man with the limp knew who I was. He must have known that Damiano was working for me, and he must also have known that the Sharif is with us. That's why he did everything he could to get Randa out without any fuss. He wasn't behaving as though we were his enemies. All he was interested in was getting Randa away from us as quickly and as quietly as possible. Even when it all degenerated into a massacre, he still spared me. He's the one who stopped Grégoire.'

'Why didn't they tie you up when you were asleep in bed?'

'So that I could untie the others when I woke up. If everything had gone as planned, I'd have woken up in the morning to find Joseph, Carlos and Grégoire bound and gagged, and Randa gone. I'd have untied the three Lebanese as fast as I could, and we'd have run away with our tails between our legs.'

'Unfortunately for the girl,' said Mowbray-Smyth, 'and for us too, Joseph must have a hard head, and Harry must be a light sleeper. Harry woke up, Joseph managed to untie himself, and it all turned into a bloodbath.'

'A hard head! A light sleeper!' Fennell guffawed. 'One hard head and one light sleeper, and the outcome is three dead, including the Sharif's mistress. Not to mention the Bunkers, who are simply laughing at us. And why did it all happen? It was all because Mr Boone here decided that it was vitally important that he should "talk", as he puts it, to the girl. I wonder why.' He looked daggers at Briggs.

'The fact remains,' said Briggs, 'that the Sharif did lie to us. We'll have to ask him to explain himself. Harry has to see him to –'

'That is out of the question!' Fennell interrupted him.

'We still have to know. The Sharif swore to us that he didn't know if the man with the limp died along with Hammud and Shartuni. He seemed quite unconcerned about him. Yet here he is, leading an Apparatus commando that kidnaps his mistress. Or frees her, if you want to put it that way, Guy. None of it is clear. We can't go on distributing this product as though all was right with the world, when we know that the Sharif might be lying to us.'

'There's no question of Boone seeing him.'

'In my view,' said Boone, there's a reason why the man with a limp did me no harm. He knew his boss with us, and he wanted to spare him a hostile interrogation.'

'Rubbish,' said Fennell.

'He wanted to spare him a hostile interrogation, same as you, Guy,' Boone couldn't resist adding.

'What are you insinuating?' barked Fennell.

'I think it's time to bring Harry and the Sharif face to face,' said Mowbray-Smyth.'

'Out of the question!' objected Fennell. 'Do you know what the Sharif gave us while Boone was busy getting his mistress killed? A network that is planning something that will make Noah's Flood look like a minor accident! He just gave us a name, of course, just one name, the way he always does. The name of an offshore company based in the Cayman Islands: International Services. It's run by an

221

Egyptian businessman. And a year ago, his company acquired – quite legally – an Italian firm, Segura. And what does Segura do, gentlemen? Go on, I'll give you a guess. Segura is in charge of security at the Santa Giustina dam. Santa Giustina is in the Trentino, isn't it, Alec? Over towards Austria?'

The Caddy Master's father had anglicised his name from Rosetti to Rose, getting rid of the telltale Latin syllable in the process, but he pretended not to catch the allusion. He just pulled a dubious face, as though he really couldn't see why Fennell should ask him such a question. After all, he was Caddy Master, not some tour guide.

'Just imagine,' continued Fennell, not at all put out by his ally's embarrassment. 'The dam holds no less than one hundred and eighty-two million cubic metres of water. One hundred and eighty-two million, gentlemen, that's one sixth of the surface area of the province of Trentino. And Segura has recruited a lot of people since it was taken over by International Services. Can you begin to imagine what the release of this water would do to the happy valleys of northern Italy?' He paused again. 'That's what the Sharif has just given us. And this is the man you want to subject to a hostile interrogation, Nico.'

Nico! Boone remarked to himself that you had to have the pedigree of a John Nicholas Jocelyn Mowbray-Smyth to turn up at a meeting of the Royal & Ancient dressed like a hippie, and to get everyone to call you Nico, even old Syd. Alessandro Rosetti, on the other hand, had become Alec Rose and wore the same grey suits day in, day out. He so wanted his dark – almost black – suits to look English, but they only succeeded in bringing out his Neapolitan origins. Funny place, England. The immigrants wanted into the system, and the toffs wanted out.

'Guy's right,' agreed Devereux. 'An interrogation might put his back up and make him dry out. That can wait. Yes, it can wait. The Prime Minister is extremely pleased with this operation. It really isn't worth sabotaging it.'

'Boone's already tried,' retorted Fennell. The director's words had acted like a stimulant on him. 'Boone and his famous local operators. Personally, I've never liked these Pros, mercenaries who fear neither man nor God. If it were up to me –'

'Theo Damiano has always been straight with us,' Boone interrupted him.

'Straight! Straight, my foot. And now we discover that one of his men – this Grégoire – was in the pay of the Apparatus. This Damiano's a double-crosser, a traitor, that's what he is!'

'Anyone can make a mistake, and we are not in a particularly good position to preach. When it comes to traitors and double agents, England takes the biscuit.'

'Don't be so insolent, Boone!' Rose was outraged. He was patriotic to the point that he used to send the late Queen Mother a birthday card every year.

'I think you need a bit of a rest, Boone,' said Devereux. 'Take a holiday.'

'You hear, Boone?' This was Fennell's moment of triumph. 'Take a holiday. A *long* holiday. Here at home in London. South of the river. In Wandsworth. You aren't even going back to Beirut to pack your bags. We'll do that for you. You are absolutely forbidden to cross the Thames to come to the Clubhouse. You are absolutely forbidden to take an interest – close or otherwise – in the Clubhouse, to use the Service's facilities, and to solicit your personal networks, Levantine, European, religious or secular, black or white. You drop everything, Boone! Do you understand?'

Boone turned to look at Briggs. But Briggs was looking at Fennell and saying nothing. Boone concluded that his boss had got what he wanted. Without saying a word, he and Guy had struck a bargain. All it took was an exchange of glances. They had made a deal: I'll ditch Boone, the deal said, and in exchange you put off your plan to reorganise the Service until the cows come home. But be careful, Archie also seemed to be saying, one step out of line and I'll let Boone loose on you.

So that was that. Boone wouldn't be seeing either Lebanon or Maria for a long time. It was Practice for him now. Or pen-pushing in Russell Square. A complete failure. The Boone system was taking in water from all sides, and Harry simply couldn't bail fast enough.

33

'Once Khorasan had fallen into the hands of Genghis Khan's men, the Khwarezmians retreated north to the safety of the desert. But the great Persian desert was as powerless against the Mongols as the walls of Samarkand and Bokhara had been. Swelled by the desertion of the Turkish contingents, Genghis Khan's armies marched resolutely on Khwarezm, driving tens of thousands of prisoners before them at lance-point to act as a human shield. As the great empty spaces had not succeeded in slowing down the advancing invaders, Jalaleddin Mangoberti, commander of the armies and the son of the last Khwarezmian Shah, opted for the high ground and narrow spaces. With his few remaining faithful warriors, he slipped into the passes of the north, where animals sank up to their bellies in the snow, where men's beards froze when they got out of the bath and where the cold made the water tanks burst even though they were covered with sheepskins. He hoped that the frozen peaks and steep-sided valleys, burning cold and thin air would eventually calm the murderous ardour of the Mongols, who were howling at his heels like some devastating wind. The prince did not know it, but he had started a new life as an adventurer. His nomadic existence, which was to be a life of perpetual flight and hit-and-runs, would take him from the Caucasus to India, back to Georgia and finally to Iraq, where he would meet his death. The man who had spent fourteen years of his life fighting the most formidable army in the world finally succumbed to the knife of a worthless little Kurdish brigand.'

Boone had promised Maria that he would put his enforced stay in London to good use by helping with her research on the last of the Khwarezmians, and by correcting the thesis she was writing in English. For the last two weeks he had been immersed in the life of Mangoberti. Like him, Mangoberti was a loser. Working on Mangoberti helped him to forget his anger and resist the temptation to ring Archie or Nico in the hope of picking up some scraps of information about an operation of which he was no longer part.

He was busy correcting Maria's grammar when the doorbell rang. He pretended not to hear, but the intruder was persistent, ringing for a third time. Finally giving in, he got up to answer the door. He had no intention of buying anything from anyone. Opening the door, he found himself face-to-face with Theo Damiano, wearing his little silver cross in his buttonhole and carrying a well-worn Gladstone bag. It was the sort of bag that inspired trust, the sort that any con man can buy for a couple of pounds at a flea market.

'Good morning, sir,' said Damiano, politely raising his moorland. 'Perhaps you remember me.' He'd apparently rehearsed his cover story. 'I was in the neighbourhood, and I recalled the very stimulating conversation we once had about St Augustine. I just thought you might be able to spare me a few minutes of your time.' The street was empty, but the Padre seemed to want to go on with his act, audience or no audience.

'Well?' said Boone once they were behind closed doors.

'Well,' sighed Damiano, sinking into the first chair he could find.

He looked tired. Boone noticed that he had dug out some flannels and swapped his Italian moccasins for English-looking Oxfords. Going to the window, Boone looked up and down Benderley Road again.

'I haven't been followed, Harry. Her Majesty's *mukhabarat* are not on my tail, and I tried fifteen different houses before I came knocking on your door. No luck, I'm afraid. There are two churches and a cemetery in the area, but people around here don't seem to be very keen on religion. And these bibles ... They weigh a ton. When I think of the astronomical quantity of gospels, missals and catechisms your great-uncle carried all the way across Egypt and the Sudan! The man was indefatigable. Another Gordon. An ecumenical Gordon. That's faith for you, Harry! I can still see him in his big black Humber. A pre-war model. Nothing could stop your great uncle, not hostility, not irony and not incomprehension ...' He fell silent and looked around the room in search of some relic, but nothing caught his eye. 'It's funny that he never wanted to go back to Ireland. When I think that he's now at rest in an Egyptian cemetery in Asyut ... You really are a strange lot ... Everyone else wants to go home. The Jews waited two thousand years to go home; "return" is all the Palestinians talk about. But you lot! You don't just become expatriates. You even have yourselves buried in foreign lands.'

'How did you find me?' asked Boone, taking out a bottle of whisky.

227

'Maria –'

'Maria ... And how is Maria?'

'Maria is well. Maria is bored. Maria wants you not to stay away too long.'

'If only it were up to me ... When did you get here?'

'A few days ago.'

Boone didn't ask how he had got to England. He guessed the old man had flown to Dublin and taken the ferry from there, probably travelling on a Maltese passport.

'Staying in London?'

'Oxford, Harry, Oxford. I've found a room near St Antony's.'

St Antony's? Why St Antony's, wondered Boone. Why not Campion Hall? It would have been more appropriate after the Oriental Library in Beirut – the same Jesuit atmosphere.

'What's the damage on your side?'

'Oh, not too bad. You see, I was right to use two different teams. While the police were looking for whoever it was who had rented the villa and the cars, we were able to get off the island without any trouble.'

'I wish I could say the same.'

'You're lucky that Joseph managed to free himself and give you a hand.'

'I don't know about that, Theo. Perhaps it would have been better if he'd stayed safely tied up in bed. That way, we'd have avoided all the killing.'

'Harry, Harry...' Damiano had put on his 'contrite' expression. 'Joseph is really sorry he left you in the lurch. But you were unconscious and, after all the shooting was over, he didn't have much time to untie Carlos and escape with him. They had to leave on foot, you know. Taking the car was out of the question. Joseph

228

couldn't hang about. Not with three corpses on his hands. You can understand that, can't you?'

'What I do understand is that your Joseph saw fit to leave behind a live body alongside a few dead ones, so as to slow down the police. Very clever, Theo.'

Damiano tried to protest.

'No, I mean it. Very clever. If the police had turned up to find three bodies and no one they could question ... But with a witness on the spot – me, as it happens – there was no reason for them to rush off on a wild manhunt. Bravo! He's a real professional, your Joseph.'

'What do you expect? Joseph thought that, with your passport, you'd be all right. Or at least in a better position than him or Carlos, with their highly suspect Lebanese passports. Whereas you, with your British passport ... The Republic of Cyprus, come on ...'

'And leaving me behind was your way of getting the Clubhouse involved, wasn't it? You cover yourself for this mess, and for the car-bomb at the Cité Sportive, in case someone has the bright idea of making the connection ... Well done, Theo!'

'Harry...'

'Drop it. I suppose you're here to talk about Grégoire.'

'Yes, Grégoire.' Damiano took the whisky Boone offered him. 'You know, when he unexpectedly turned up in Cyprus, he came from Athens. I'd sent him there to meet a source we'd been handling for years. A source Grégoire had been handling for years, I should say. A Syrian communist living in exile in Sofia. Someone must have contacted Grégoire and told him to get to Cyprus as fast as he could, someone who must have known where he could contact him.'

'So your Grégoire was a double agent.'

'Grégoire and the Apparatus? Doesn't make sense, Harry. No sense at all.'

'So he didn't handle Islamist sources?'

'Just Palestinians. Palestinians, and former communists.'

'Was he in the know about the car-bomb?'

'Of course not.'

'He didn't know anything?'

'He's never had anything to do with the Apparatus, or with Islamists in general. Neither directly nor indirectly. Strange, isn't it?'

'You say he didn't know about the car-bomb?'

'You're not listening to me, Harry! If Grégoire had been working for the Apparatus, the Islamists would have flooded me with false information. They've never done that, which leads me to conclude that Grégoire wasn't working for them. Perhaps we should be looking at Syrian communists. Perhaps that's the answer.'

'What's a Syrian communist got to with all this? And one living in Bulgaria at that.'

'There's something else ...' Damiano got to his feet. The other body at the villa ... Joseph identified it. Someone he knew. He wasn't a Muslim, Harry, still less an Islamist. He was a Lebanese Christian. His name was Nidal Tabet, and he worked as a driver for a dentist in Beirut, Dr Simon Zehil. And, wait for it, this Simon Zehil is none other than the chairman of the Lebanon-USSR Friendship Association. Now known as the Lebanon-Russia Friendship Association, of course. What do you think of all that?'

'You're sure of your facts? You're sure the other body in the villa was the same Nidal Tabet?'

'Of course I am. Nidal Tabet vanished from Beirut on Good Friday and no one has heard from him since. After all, not everyone gets to disappear on a Good Friday and then reappear three days later ...' Damiano suddenly went quiet and sat down again. 'Lord forgive me for my blasphemy,' he said, sinking into in his chair as though he wanted to make himself small in the face of the wrath of God. But as it seemed to be taking its time coming, he assumed that he had been forgiven and recovered his power of speech. 'There's something funny about this business. We start dealing with the Apparatus and the Islamists and end up dealing with Christians and a pack of communists. So what's going on?'

'I don't know.'

'A French officer who'd been posted to Lebanon once said to me: "Whenever I think I understand everything about this place, I say to myself someone hasn't explained things properly." So, what haven't you explained properly, Harry?'

'Nothing at all! I admit that it's a bit strange to find Christians working for the Apparatus, but why shouldn't they? You have enough Muslim sources, don't you?'

'Sources, yes. Field operators, no. I'm quite prepared to believe that the Apparatus might use Christians, but not communists.'

'What does it mean to be a communist these days? There aren't any communists any more. The Soviet Union is dead and buried. People do the best they can, and get money from wherever they can. And if it's the Apparatus that has the money, why not the Apparatus?'

'You're such a cynic, Harry!'

'Coming from you ...'

'Where does this leave the woman, then?'

'What woman?'

'Randa! Randa Bsat!'

'What about her?'

'Nothing. It's her father, rather ... Her father was in the party. The Communist Party.'

'Randa's father was a communist?' Boone swallowed his whisky in one gulp.

'Randa Bsat. Father: primary schoolteacher. Party member in Sidon. European-style nuclear family: father, mother and three children. Two boys and a girl ...' Theo Damiano was rattling off information as though he were reading from a police file. 'Fifteen years ago, the Ministry for Education transferred Mr Bsat to a new post. And where does he find himself?' He looked at Boone in the way of a schoolmaster encouraging a diligent yet shy pupil. 'In a village in the western Bekaa. And precisely which village? Mastaba, Harry! The Sharif's village!'

'They knew each other for fifteen years? They knew each other from the village?'

'It's a very touching story, Harry. Randa is ten and young Ali – our Sharif – is twelve. They meet, get to know and like each other, and they eventually fall in love. But their families don't approve. It's not a good match. His father is a direct descendant of the Prophet, and he's the village imam. He and all his household are symbols of religion and tradition. Whereas her father is a communist schoolteacher who represents secularism and modernity. A bit like Don Camillo and Mayor Peppone ... You know, Harry ... Guareschi? Right, so you don't know. Let's just say it's a bit like the Montagus and the Capulets. Our turtledoves are torn between their love and their families. Five years later, their lives are turned upside down. The car-bomb in Mastaba solved their dilemma for them. The rival families were decimated. Both of them, finally united in death. Young Randa came out of it without a scratch on her. A real miracle. Ali Al-Husayni – our Sharif, Harry – was seriously wounded and taken to the hospital in Nabatiyeh. When he came out of hospital, he joined the ranks of the Islamists and began to make a career for himself in the Apparatus. Young Randa was taken in by some nuns – Canadian missionaries – who eventually paid for her to go to university. You can imagine the rest. Years later, our two friends meet again, perhaps by chance. He is in the Apparatus, and she is a student. Why doesn't he marry her? Perhaps he thought she would damage his career, or perhaps she didn't see him as husband material. But still he sets her up in a ritzy apartment, protects her and pays for her upkeep. A sort of secret garden.'

Boone said nothing.

'The story couldn't be stranger, Harry. It doesn't match the usual profile of an Islamist militant. Too many unexplained mysteries, too many grey areas. And when we do finally find someone who can tell us a bit about the Sharif, they come down on us like a ton of bricks, and at considerable risk to themselves.'

'You mean someone panicked?'

'Someone who apparently didn't want us stirring up the past. Someone who didn't want us to grill this Randa. But who? And why was it so important to stop Randa talking about a dead man?'

'No idea.'

'And what's the connection with Grégoire, with Nidal Tabet and with Randa's communist father?'

'I don't know, Theo.'

'Very odd, don't you think? So strange that I thought it would be a good idea to take a close look at our friend the Sharif. It's a strange tale, Harry. It begins ten years ago. One day, the entire village of Mastaba gathered together in memory of one of its sons, who had had the unfortunate idea of visiting Galilee as a tourist in arms. So that day all the people in the village, believers and non-believers, gathered to honour their martyr and the leaders of the Islamic Resistance who, by sending him off to get himself killed in the Holy

Land, had opened up the gates of Paradise for him a bit prematurely. Yet someone else, who apparently had an axe to grind with the Islamists, seized on this opportunity and blew up a truck packed with six hundred kilos of explosives, that had been parked in the village square. The explosion blew the Islamists to pieces – and, unfortunately, almost the entire population of Mastaba along with them. A real hecatomb, Harry. Mastaba has been deserted ever since.'

'We already know all this.'

'But we don't know anything more about him. That's what's so surprising. The day after the bomb, the dead and wounded were taken to the hospital in Nabatiyeh. That's where the Sharif was treated. Given that Mastaba is deserted and that the survivors have scattered, I said to myself that the hospital would be a good place to start looking. But I was wrong. Just imagine. A year later, the records were destroyed in a fire. It's impossible to get hold of the Sharif's medical record. Gone up in smoke. Just like his village. Just like his car. The Sharif we assassinated was a ghost, Harry!'

'All this is just speculation, Theo!'

'But you have to admit that there's a strange symmetry between his entry into public life and his tragic end. It all begins and ends with a car-bomb. One explodes and he appears, and then another one explodes and he disappears!'

'There's no need for symbolism, Theo. Soon, you'll be making numerical analyses based on dates of birth and what have you.'

'Our late friend the Sharif wasn't exactly what we thought he was. I smell a rat.'

'We've got no proof. And if I don't have proof, I'll never manage to sell your story. I need proof.'

'You'll get it. You'll get your proof if I have to spend everything I have getting it. I want to know who I'm dealing with, Harry! I'm not going to spend the rest of my days looking over my shoulder. And I imagine you'd like to get back to Beirut and my niece. Maria won't wait for you indefinitely, you know.'

'Don't stir up trouble, Theo.' Boone now feared for the Sharif's safety.

'I didn't come to ask for your permission, Harry. A few years ago, you dropped me unceremoniously. I owe you nothing. I want this business cleared up. My security is at stake.'

'I'll talk to them about it, Theo.'

'Do. Do talk about it, Harry. Here ...' As he stood up, he gave Boone a scrap of paper. 'You can reach me at this number between six and eight any evening.'

'Is that where you're staying?'

'It's the number of a pub. The only thing that worries me is that Mrs Rees – she's my landlady – might find out that I go there on a pilgrimage every day. She thinks I go to a prayer meeting. If you can't get hold of me, leave a message...' He glanced at the biography of Mangoberti that Boone was correcting. 'Say it's from Bertie,' he added. 'I'll understand, and I'll meet you at three the next afternoon, in the Renaissance room in the Ashmolean.'

At the door, he wedged his hat on his head and smiled broadly and asked: 'Are you sure you won't take one of my bibles?' Then he was on his way.

34

'I thought you were on holiday, Harry.'

'I am, Archie. I am on holiday.'

'I thought we'd asked you to keep out of this business.'

'Damiano came to see me. I couldn't very well shut the door in his face.'

'So the Padre is lying low in England, is he? Until things calm down, I suppose. Where is he now?'

'I don't know,' Boone lied. 'He wouldn't tell me.'

'No prearranged meeting?' Briggs waved his hand to get rid of the smoke from Boone's foul-smelling cigar. 'No fallback rendezvous? I'm surprised.'

'He said he'd be in touch.' Another lie.

'And you've dragged me all the way to Windsor to tell me this nonsense. Is that why I'm getting my shoes and trouser bottoms dirtied? Is that why I'm walking along the muddy banks of a river in spate?'

'I suppose you think it isn't important enough?'

'Important? One thing matters to me, and only one thing. Does Damiano know that the Sharif isn't dead?'

'No.'

'You've not been letting him into our secrets, have you?'

'I haven't said a word.'

'Good, good ... I know how upset you must be feeling. And I know that frustration can lead to indiscretion. So be careful. No slip-ups, if you please.'

'What do you think?'

'Impressive.' Briggs was admiring a squadron of ducks that had just made a perfect landing on the water. 'Very impressive.'

'I'm talking about Theo's story. About Grégoire, Nidal Tabet, Randa's father and the village where Randa and the Sharif grew up.'

'To tell you the truth, I don't think anything about it. I'm not paid to think. I'm paid to provide solid evidence. And I don't see anything solid in what you've just told me.'

'The Sharif lied to us.'

Briggs didn't answer. His eye had caught an apple tree. He had a weakness for apple trees at this time of year, when the buds, still closed but full of youthful promise, gave the old trees a rosy halo that transfigured their grey bark. They reminded him of the Italian girl he had seen in Piccadilly a few weeks earlier.

'He lied to us,' Boone said once more.

237

'Have you ever known a source that didn't lie, Harry? Do you know of a single source that doesn't have a little something tucked away as an insurance policy?'

'Then there's Randa. She was our only link with his past, and as soon as we get our hands on her, someone panics.'

'Yes, *we* panicked. There was a wave of panic in Russell Square that day.'

'Then there's his defection. You and I thought that people like him don't defect. He surprised us. Atypical behaviour.'

'Atypical? It's a good word, "atypical". But the suggestion that he should defect didn't come from him, did it. That was our idea. Guy's idea, to be more specific. All this is very weak. It doesn't stand up.'

'And what about Tabet, Archie? And Grégoire? And Randa? They're all atypical.'

'Listen to me –'

'Atypical,' muttered Boone, sounding like a runner out of breath.

'Listen, Harry. You're obsessed with this business. I asked you to rock the boat a bit to destabilise Guy. But you rocked it so much that I fell out, and Guy found himself in complete control. In control, and ready to send me to the bottom.'

'I did everything you asked.'

'All I wanted was for you to help me get a foot inside the door.'

'I did get your foot inside the door. I stuck my neck out for you. You came to me, and I didn't let you down. Return the favour. I need to go back to Beirut.'

'You didn't help me get my foot inside the door. You kicked the bloody door down. You were like a bull in a china shop. You see plots everywhere. Shall I tell you what I think? I think you've stopped seeing things for what they are.'

'It's *you* that can't see things for what they are! All of you! You're so bloody obsessed with the dividends you're getting from this operation that you can't even envisage the possibility that there might be something behind all this.'

'Something behind all this? What do you think that something might be? So the Sharif's a double agent, is he? He's been telling us nonsense, has he? I suppose the networks he's helping us roll up are packs of boy scouts. And the signed confessions are film scripts. I suppose the explosives we are digging up are marzipan. Do you know who he's seeing today? Do you know who's coming to visit the descendant of the Prophet in his Cornish retreat? An Italian admiral, no less. And next week it's the Israelis' turn, though they'll of course pretend to be Dutch, so as not to offend his sensibilities too much. The whole world wants in on this, Harry. The whole world wants to see this rare pearl. Everyone agrees that the Sharif's intelligence is exceptional. Careers are being built on it. The holy man is bringing home the bacon for a whole swath of the intelligence community, which didn't know where to turn after the end of the Cold War.'

'You owe me –'

'You've gone too far. If you want to go under, you do so by yourself.'

Leaving him standing there, Briggs did an about turn and set off for the station, skipping between the puddles as he went.

Boone was beside himself with rage. Bureaucratic logic had taken over from field logic. Right from the beginning, they'd been less interested in the Sharif than in the intelligence he could supply. *How many reports today? How shall we issue them? And to whom? What do our friends think? What can we ask them for in exchange?* The source had eventually become immaterial, vanishing into the flow of intelligence it was coughing up. The source could just have easily been the man with the limp, Sheikh Hammud, Dr Shartuni, or even Colonel Kamel. What did it matter? Espiocrats aren't sophists. They're less interested in sources than in products. They had decided that this particular product was very high quality. Very good for promotion. They didn't give a damn about the Sharif's underlying motives, his personality, his past, his friends or his love affairs. They were interested in all that only to the extent that it might affect his product. So long as he went on producing, everything was fine.

A ball rolled up to his feet, followed by a breathless little boy who came to a halt a few yards away from him. An Arab kid, he thought to himself. He seemed to be weighed down by the pair of enormous Nikes he was wearing. The child gave him a big smile. Someone had no doubt told him Western adults are nice to children. Boone quickly disillusioned him by kicking the ball in anger. It landed fifty yards away in the bushes. The little boy looked at him in horror. His world had collapsed around him. Arms swinging, head down, off he went in search of his ball, dragging his hurt and his oversized Nikes with him.

Boone walked on until he reached the bridge that divides Windsor from Eton and lit a cigar as he went over to the other side. He was now north of the Thames. Without realising it, he had just crossed the Rubicon that the Royal & Ancient had warned him not to cross.

In the main street, a poster in the window of an antiques shop announced that an amateur theatre company sponsored by the venerable school would be performing Heinrich von Kleist's *Penthelisea* in the town hall that Saturday. Boone remembered having seen the play at university. He could remember the Greeks and the Trojans locked together in a struggle in which neither side showed any pity. Then, on a battlefield already red with blood, they suddenly saw the fearsome Penthelisea at the head of her Amazons.

As the horsewomen rode at full charge towards them, the clash of arms ceased. Neither the Greeks nor the Trojans were sure what to do. 'Join us, Penthelisea!' shouted the Greeks. 'Penthelisea, join us!' screamed the Trojans. But, deaf to all these expressions of hope, Penthelisea hurled her Amazons to attack both the Greeks and the Trojans, cutting them all down with no discrimination and sweeping away their Manichaeanism with one strike.

Looking at the poster, he suddenly realised that he was no different to the Greeks and the Trojans. He too had become caught in a Manichaean prism, and he had gone on seeing and perceiving the whole business and everything relating to it through that prism. What if I forget about the Greeks and the Trojans for a while, he wondered. What if I introduced a Penthelisea into this twosome game? Thought of as a game for two players, Theo Damiano's story didn't hold up. But what if the game for two players was a smokescreen? What if there was a third party involved, a Penthelisea playing them off against each other?

Grégoire. If this was a game for two players, Grégoire must have been recruited by the Apparatus. But if it was a different kind of game, it was conceivable that some third party had been manipulating him. What about Nidal Tabet? If he wasn't just a mercenary who sold himself to the highest bidder, it was conceivable that he had remained true to his old loyalties. The man with the limp? He didn't figure in the Apparatus's organisational chart, yet he was very close to the Sharif. And Randa. The liberated Americanised woman stood out like a sore thumb. Boone was quite prepared to believe that an Islamist who was the son of an imam and a descendant of the Prophet might just have room in his life for a bit of love on the side, but now that he knew that Randa and the Sharif had been friends since adolescence, he felt less inclined to accept that

241

libidinal explanation. It just didn't make sense. And what about the Sharif? Boone had been surprised when he decided to defect. Yet he did. Contrary to all expectations, he had agreed to come to England. Then there were the Americans. Why had the Americans shown no interest in the Sharif? Could he have been an American asset?

Boone felt that this business extended far beyond the framework of relations between the Clubhouse and the Apparatus. Someone else was involved. The Sharif and the man with the limp knew whom. Perhaps Randa had had her suspicions too. But who was it? Who was playing Penthelisea in this game between the European Greeks and the Asiatic Trojans?

Crushing his cigar stub underfoot, he concluded that he had no idea. If he wanted to get back to Beirut and to Maria, if he wanted to get his system up and running once more, he would have to find answers to all these questions. He was glad he had lied to Briggs, glad that he hadn't given him Theo's address. That kept him one step ahead. One little step ahead, before Alec Rose's people turned up in North Oxford and intruded upon the privacy of Mrs Rees and her lodger. Boone had made up his mind. Briggs had thrown him away like an old sock; so he would betray him in turn.

35

The eleven-eighteen from Paddington drew into the station just before twelve thirty, only ten minutes behind schedule. Boone was greeted by a typically damp Oxford, with its mixture of spring rain and swampy emanations from the sodden clay-like ground.

He should have taken the bus, if only because it would have made it easier to check if anyone was on his tail. But as he came out of the station, he ignored the old red double-decker that was coughing itself to death at the bus stop and set off on foot. He'd been away for a long time and felt the need to immerse himself in the city at ground level, without the distance and height a bus ticket would have bought him.

Crossing Hythe Bridge, he ignored the new business school ziggurat and walked up George Street as far as Magdalen, turning left into St Giles. His original plan had been to go for a walk in the park, but he changed his mind when he reached the corner of Woodstock and Barnbury. The drizzle that had been falling since he left the station had turned into heavy rain, and in the unlikely event that someone was following him, that someone would find it difficult to understand why he was prepared to get soaked to the skin just for the sake of a nostalgic walk in the park. It would have been out of character. He wisely decided to put off his little excursion for another day, and to throw his hypothetical tail off the scent, he went to Brown's.

Oxford's trendy café-restaurant was packed. It had been a success for more than twenty-five years, and Boone couldn't really explain why. Perhaps it was the happy mixture of American food, English music and Viennese atmosphere. Or perhaps it was the fact that its customers were always moving on. With a life expectancy of nine terms, they didn't really have time to get tired of it. Whatever the explanation might be, the fact was that Brown's was bursting at the seams. A docile Boone took his place in the youthful queue blocking the entrance, but not for long. An enterprising young meeter and greeter soon noticed him, smelled money (all things being relative) and suggested Boone might like to take an *apéritif* while he was waiting. Boone ordered a double whisky; the young man seemed impressed. Five minutes later, a beautiful young black girl rewarded him for his prodigality by taking him straight to a little corner table at the back of the room. It was a good place to watch the timeless dance of his successors as he sipped his whisky and chewed a pastrami on rye. The town's present masters looked exactly like the old ones. He sat and watched the incessant ballet of waiters and waitresses, punctuated by the sound of the swinging doors leading to the kitchens as they came and went. They walked through the doors with a ghost-like grace. He then settled his bill, left the expected tip,

244

and made way for three students who couldn't believe their luck: no one had ever been seen to have a meal and run away so quickly.

Outside, it was still raining. If the rain is cold, it's winter; if it's warm, it's summer. That's the way it is in the British Isles, Boone thought to himself, dreaming of the Mediterranean he couldn't go back to. He recalled how, in classical times, the influence of the climate had been invoked to explain the melancholy of the English: all those little drops of rain found their way through the skull and the soft tissues, penetrated the veins and eventually affected both the brain and humours. Erasmus spent time in Oxford before he wrote *In Praise of Folly*, and Robert Burton wrote his *Anatomy of Melancholy* in the city.

When he reached the Oriental Institute, he noticed that people still came and went as they pleased. Readers took out the books they needed and then filled in the borrowers' slips. Having obeyed the polite notice that asked them to put the slips in a box, they then left the premises without any further checks. The whole system was based on trust, and it seemed to work. It was said that the Oriental Institute lost fewer books than the most secure and computerised libraries in the land.

Once inside, Boone consulted the catalogue at B for Barthold, V. V., *Turkestan Down to the Mongol Invasion*, London 1928, reprinted in 1958. He reckoned he might as well make sure his cover was perfect. Armed with its call mark, he looked for the book on the shelves and then found a quiet seat at the back of the reading room.

He spent an hour with Barthold, conscientiously taking notes on behalf of Maria. Shortly before three he treated himself to a small yawn, stretched and stood up. He left the room, leaving his book and notes in full view on the desk: a tired reader was taking a break.

In the hall, he took the stairs to the first floor and set off briskly down a corridor lined with half-open doors. At the end of the corridor, a closed door barred his way. That did not stop him from taking a firm grip on the handle and pulling it hard. The door opened, and he gave a sigh of relief. He was now on 'the bridge', a narrow passageway linking the Oriental to the neighbouring Ashmolean. Having crossed over, he pushed another door, which opened as easily as the first. Some things really never change in this university, he remarked to himself. When Boone was a student, the story was that the doors were left open to allow an adulterous curator at the Ashmolean to have secret rendezvous with his lady-love, a librarian at the Oriental. Twenty years later, for reasons that were totally different but just as covert, Boone could still use the lovers' bridge as a shortcut. He wondered if they were still having their affair, if the doors were left open in their memory or whether common law had finally prevailed. Whatever the truth of the matter, the doors were still open, and that suited his purpose.

He entered the archaeology section of the Ashmolean Library. Taking the Griffin Staircase, he went down a corridor and through the main reading room into the Byzantine Hall. Then he went up the Evans Stairway, cut through the Flemish Room and reached the Mallett Gallery where he found the Padre, absorbed in a Raphael study of St Jerome.

'Well then, Harry?' Damiano asked, without taking his eyes off St Jerome. 'Did you talk to them?'

'I did.'

'And?'

'Nothing doing.'

'What do you mean, "nothing doing"?'

'I mean they're not interested.'

'Not interested?' Damiano stopped looking at St Jerome. 'Are you telling me that they don't think there's something fishy about this business?'

'They're not interested, that's all.'

'But you told them? About Nidal Tabet? About the dentist, Dr Zehil?'

'I told them.'

'Did you tell them about Grégoire? Are you sure you told them that it was impossible for him to have been recruited by the Apparatus?'

'I told them, I told them ...'

'And still the penny didn't drop?'

'They don't want to know.'

'Perhaps they don't, but I need to. I'm not spending the rest of my life over here! I have to find out who I'm dealing with.'

'As far as they're concerned, we're dealing with the Apparatus.'

'And what do you think?'

Boone took his time before replying. He knew that once he had committed himself, there would be no turning back.

'Perhaps you're right, Theo. Perhaps we are dealing with something other than the Apparatus.'

'That's more like it.' Damiano went off to admire one of Rapahel's studies for *The Presentation in the Temple*. 'But the question is who. If it isn't the Apparatus, then perhaps it is the Centre. Perhaps it is Moscow.'

'The idea that the Russians might be involved in this business is frankly absurd.'

'It's the *why* that escapes me, Harry. Why should anyone go to so much trouble to stop us digging up the past of a dead man? Why?'

Boone said nothing. He knew that he needed Damiano. He knew that he had already decided to tell him everything, come what may. But he was putting off the final decision, like someone choosing the right moment to commit suicide.

'Listen.' Damiano had come to a sudden halt in front of a Michelangelo drawing of a battle. 'I think I've got it, Harry. It's to do with the explosion.'

'Which explosion? There have been so many, Theo.' Boone assumed that the scene of carnage had been the source of Damiano's sudden insight.

'You remember the operation against the Sharif? All those unexplained deaths? At the time, you accused me of being heavy-handed, and I accused you of having put another bomb in the Sharif's car.'

'I remember.'

'You still think I overdid it with the explosion?'

...

'Do you still think it was me?'

'No. I don't.' said Boone at last.

'Was it you?'

'No, it wasn't us.'

'It wasn't you? It wasn't to protect the mole you have inside the Apparatus? So who was it? The Apparatus? Why should the Apparatus want to get rid of its favourite son? If it wasn't the Apparatus, was it the Centre? If it was the Centre, why should the Russians hide behind you and me in order to assassinate the Sharif? I don't understand!'

Boone desperately wanted a smoke. He knew that the time had come for him to go over to the other side.

'I know who planted the second bomb,' he said.

'You know? Who was it? The Centre?'

'No, it wasn't the Centre, Theo.'

'So it was the Apparatus.'

'No, not the Apparatus.'

'Then who was it?'

'The Sharif had his own car bombed.'

'The Sharif? What are you trying to tell me? Why should the Sharif –'

'He's not dead. That's why.'

'He's not dead? What do you mean, he's not dead?'

'I mean he's not dead. He's over here, in England. I got him out of Beirut just after the car-bomb.'

'You mean ...' Damiano grabbed a button on Boone's jacket and twisted it. 'You mean that all this business ...'

'... was a smokescreen. A fake assassination to cover our tracks. The second explosion was his insurance policy. But he wasn't insured with us. It was his way of making sure there would be no evidence left behind. No *corpus delicti*. Just after the explosion, he quietly met me at the Passage du Musée.'

'Bloody hell! You're saying it was a setup? And I fell for it? Me, the Padre? I fell for it like some amateur?!'

'He offered us his services.'

'He offered *you* his services! Why you? After all, England doesn't count for much these days. Why not the Americans? Why make a deal with the monkey when you could make one with the organ grinder?'

'Apparently he had nothing to give to the Americans. And a lot to give us.'

'That's strange. That's very strange. Unless those old Anglo-Arab ties have something to do with it – the Arab Revolt and what have you. Come to think of it, Lawrence was Irish. Same as you.'

'Stop talking nonsense, Theo, and make your mind up. Either he's a Russian agent, or he's an American agent. He can't be both at the same time.'

'And just like Lawrence, you thought you were pulling the strings when somebody else was.'

'I did what I was told to do throughout. He planned the entire operation: where, when and how.'

'God in heaven, Harry!'

'You and I were just pawns. He chose me, and I chose you. And to make it perfectly clear that he didn't exactly trust us, he blew up his own car.'

'Now you tell me? A walk-in who organises his own defection? But this has the Centre written all over it, Harry. It reeks of the Soviets. It's classic stuff. Nidal Tabet, Dr Zehil, Grégoire and the Lebanese-Russian Friendship Association. I understand it all now.'

'Don't get carried away. Your story still doesn't stand up. You see, he's been giving us high-grade intelligence. Nothing that we haven't been able to verify, check and exploit. Whole networks, arms dumps, safe houses, cut-outs, bank accounts, the lot ... He's given us operations too. He's the best Islamist source we've ever had, and I don't believe for one moment that he's a Centre agent.'

'Who's to say all these operations weren't Russian-inspired?'

'Come off it, Theo! And even if they were, why should the Centre give them to us on a plate?'

'You're being blind, Harry. You still think in terms of the Cold War and a binary world. You think that ideology explains everything, and you're forgetting about geopolitics. I suppose you think that the new ideological affinities between Russia and the West have done away with age-old geopolitical realities?'

'That's possible,' Boone admitted, thinking of Penthelisea. 'It's quite possible that I'm being blind, as you put it. But how can we be certain? We've got no proof. Just hypotheses.'

'Then we'll have to go and find some proof.' Damiano had already embarked on his new campaign. 'We'll have to go digging into the Sharif's past until we find out where and when he might have been recruited by the Centre.'

'Can you check a name for me, Theo? Tareq Ghazzawi, also known as Tareq Bizri.'

'Is he involved in this?'

'I think he is.'

'I'll check. But this is going to cost ...'

'I don't have a budget. I've been sidelined.'

'You must have a bit of money put aside, Harry. For the house in Dlebta, maybe.'

'Maria would kill me if I spent that.'

'If you don't, you are not likely to see your Maria again. Or Dlebta, for that matter.'

Boone said goodbye to the house in Dlebta. 'I'll try and scrape together fifteen or twenty thousand dollars for you.' After all, he thought to himself, the Boone system is well worth the sacrifice.

'I'll get to work right away.' Damiano had suddenly perked up.

'Here.' Boone gave him a scrap of paper. 'Don't lose it. These are the numbers of four telephone boxes in London. Call me as soon as you have anything. I'll be at the first number at thirteen-hundred hours next Tuesday, at the second number at fourteen-hundred on the following Tuesday, at the third at fifteen-hundred the Tuesday after, and at the fourth at sixteen-hundred on the fourth Tuesday.

251

Then we go back to the first number at thirteen-hundred on the Tuesday–'

'Not Tuesday, Monday.'

'Agreed.' Boone didn't understand why Damiano preferred Mondays to Tuesdays, but he wasn't in the mood to argue. 'If I need to contact you, I'll phone the same pub at eighteen-hundred hours on Thursday. I'll use the name "Bertie".'

'Not Thursday, Friday.'

'Fine.' Boone was beginning to understand why the Padre was changing the arrangements. He wanted his signature on this. Deciding the operational details in person was his way of letting Boone know that he was in charge now.

Back at the Oriental Institute, Boone plunged again into V. V. Barthold, but he couldn't keep his mind on Central Asia. He was more interested in his own insane quest, a bloody quest that had left behind a trail of bodies: Randa, Shartuni, Hammud, Grégoire, Nidal Tabet and all the other victims, innocent and otherwise. Still the Sharif eluded him. How many more deaths would it take to satisfy his tantalising desire for the Sharif, he wondered. How many more betrayals to save his system?

36

The weeks following the betrayal in the Ashmolean passed very slowly, in time with Boone's intermittent research on Mangoberti and the deposed prince's arduous journeys through the mountain passes of Transoxiana. The Khwarezmian's headlong flight helped the Irishman forget about his Lebanese quarry – assuming he really was Lebanese – and there were days when he almost convinced himself that Mangoberti would defeat the Sharif, if not the Mongols.

Soon, however, the media came to the Sharif's rescue and made a point of reminding Boone of him. The police forces of Europe appeared to be having a good season, and the papers were having a field day. In London, the police announced the arrest of a man who was apparently planning an Islamist remake of the original Guy Fawkes Night. It was rumoured that the secretary of an MP representing a Midlands constituency was involved in this gunpowder plot. In Rome, the Prime Minister, who had come under fire for making disparaging remarks about Islam, proudly proclaimed in vengeful tones that 'his' secret services had foiled a plot to sabotage the Santa Giustina dam. In Barcelona, customs officers stated that they had found twenty kilos of C4 in a shipment of *halva* addressed to an Oriental delicatessen. Police at Roissy airport let it be known that they had arrested a ground service worker who, while vacuuming the cabin of an airliner, had tried to conceal a knife in the toilets for the benefit of someone who apparently knew just where to find it. At the Calais terminal, a group of Kosovar refugees had been arrested in possession of a home-made bomb that they had apparently intended to detonate in the Channel tunnel. In Moscow, the President himself announced that co-operation between the Russian and Western secret services had made it possible to foil a bomb attack on the Metropole hotel. London, Paris, Rome and Madrid were pressing for military action against Islamist targets everywhere, while Berlin and Brussels were still preaching caution. Europe was divided.

The Clubhouse would be joyously celebrating its fifth birthday this year, and some would no doubt be dreaming of knighthoods and rehearsing for the mirror and the admiring gaze of their wives the bow they would be making to the Queen. And they owed it all to the Sharif, to his source. *His* source, which the Royal & Ancient had stolen from him and used as a stepping stone.

Week after week, he waited for Theo's phone call on the appointed day and at the appointed time. But Theo never rang. Perhaps Theo was no longer in England, he told himself. Perhaps Theo had been caught. Perhaps Theo had nothing to say to him. Perhaps Theo had found nothing that could console him for the loss of his deposit on the house. Perhaps there was nothing for Theo to find.

Shortly before four on the second Monday in June, Boone made his way on foot to Clapham to wait for Theo's call at box number four, on the west side of the Common. He wasn't very hopeful. He was just finishing his second round of the allocated phone booths, and seemed resigned to starting the third. As he approached the phone box, he wondered if he was late, because he thought he could hear the phone ringing. He wasn't the only person to have heard it, either: a woman with lifeless hair who was walking her dachshund had heard it too. She stopped and stared at the phone box, unable to decide what to do. Boone solved her dilemma by rushing to the phone, giving her a big embarrassed smile. His look seemed to say: It's for me. It's my wife, my girlfriend, my mother; my phone card has run out.

Yes, Theo, yes, it's me, he said once the dachshund had dragged its owner away. You were just about to hang up? Really? I'm late? Not really. Barely twenty seconds. What about you, Theo? How many weeks late are you? How many interminable weeks, days, hours, minutes and seconds? Do you have some good news for me? So you do have good news. I can tell from your voice. You sound like the Padre again. This is the voice you use on special occasions. You want us to meet? Let's meet right away, then. No? Why not? Are you expecting someone? Someone who's bringing you something? What about tomorrow? No? Next Monday? Why wait so long? Well, it's your decision, Theo. Next Monday is fine. Observatory Street? You mean in Oxford? Yes, I know it. Number 59? OK, Theo, Number 59. The door will be open and I can walk straight in? OK. Just after one, did you say? Why just after one? Why not one on the dot? Oh, all right, why not? You're the boss. Ever since the Ashmolean, it's you who's been in charge. So, as you wish. Next Monday, just after one, 59 Observatory Street. And I'll come in without knocking.

37

The following Monday, Boone dutifully caught the eleven-eighteen from Paddington again. Coming out of the station, he turned left and then left again into Worcester Street. He had decided to approach Observatory Street from the residential west rather than from the academic east. More discreet, it seemed to him.

The most sordid section of Walton Street had yet to come under serious attack from the property developers, and the rows of decrepit little Victorian houses looked like something out of Dickens. Boone was suddenly stopped by an old woman, who must have been the same age as her house: the years had treated both of them harshly. She stood on the doorstep, wrapped in a shawl that had seen better days and waved to him as though she were flagging down a bus.

'Do you have a match, please?' she asked in a broken voice.

'I don't have a match, but I do have a lighter.'

'My gas fire has gone out.'

The temperature was approaching twenty degrees Celsius. But maybe not for old bones, thought Boone.

'I'm all alone,' said Old Bones.

Boone wasn't sure what to do, but decided he couldn't just ignore her. Besides, he was a bit early for his 'just after one' appointment, and he would have given a lot to know what anyone who might be following him would make of this impromptu halt.

'It really is very kind of you.' She had come back to life all at once. 'Come in, I'll show you.'

She led him into a narrow hallway. The staircase was cluttered with all kinds of boxes and carry bags. Boone assumed she had arthritis, and had abandoned the upstairs room to sleep downstairs.

'There.' She pointed in the general direction of something.

'There' was a tiny dark room. The only furniture in it was a battered armchair and a low table. Pride of place was taken by a dried-up banana skin and a chipped and stained mug. The heater stood where Boone might have expected to find a television, against the back wall facing the armchair.

'Can you see it?' The old lady sounded worried.

Boone realised that she must be practically blind, using sound to find her way around: the sound of his footsteps on the pavement, the sound of his voice when he answered her, and the sound of the rusty hinges when he opened the gate.

'I can see it.' He bent down to examine the heater.

'I've lived all alone ever since my husband died. He was a packer at the University Press. Mr Hopgood.'

When Boone found the right switch he turned it on full, waited for a moment and then applied the flame from his disposable lighter to

257

the central panel. Nothing happened. He tried again, listening closely for the hiss of gas. Still nothing. He sniffed discreetly. Nothing. Perhaps the gas company had cut off the service. Perhaps she hadn't paid the bill. He was wondering what attitude to adopt when he caught sight of an electric lead connecting the heater to a wall socket. He couldn't believe it. The old lady had wanted him to light an electric heater with a match.

'I'm sorry,' he mumbled as he stood up, 'but I can't light it with this. I think you must need matches for this kind of heater. My lighter won't do the trick.'

'I think so too,' she agreed, not at all put out. 'But thanks all the same.'

'You're welcome. Do you want me to shut the door on my way out?'

'No, no. Leave it open. I'll wait for another gentleman to come by.'

Boone didn't like to think how many years she'd been using the same pitiful strategy for company. Ever since Mr Hopgood died, presumably.

As he went on his way, he smiled at the idea that, if someone had indeed been following him, his tail would be pretty puzzled by now: What on earth had Boone been doing in that dump? A safe house? A secret meeting? And if it was a meeting, why had it been so short? A letter drop, perhaps. Should he go on following him? Or should he wait for the mystery person he'd met inside to came out? And who was this old woman? What if she came out? Should he follow her? Accidentally knock her basket over so he could search it? Boone imagined his tail writing down Mrs Hopgood's address. He imagined his colleagues discreetly asking her neighbours questions: It's for an opinion poll, about the telephone, about the gas, about senior citizens, about pensions.

Further to the north, Walton Street began to look very different. In Jericho the house fronts were brightly painted and the roofs well-maintained. Once, penniless old age pensioners used to rent out rooms to students who found it hard to make ends meet. Not any more. The middle classes had invaded the place. Well-off students no longer spent their money on rents: they bought, and then played at being landladies for the benefit of their less well-endowed colleagues. Having been driven out of the university by the government, the class system was happily rebuilding itself *extra muros*. And what better place than Jericho?

In Observatory Street, the houses remained true to the old British tradition of town planning. They all looked the same and weren't numbered in sequence. It took Boone a good ten minutes to find what he was looking for, a little house that resembled hundreds of others, though the gaudily painted doors gave some of them a certain individuality. The door to Number 59 was painted yellow. Boone did as he had been told, and entered without knocking.

In the hallway, a dusty hatrack was adorned with a colourful woollen scarf and an acrylic hat – forgotten relics of a winter that no one missed. Further down the hall, a cork notice-board invited the visitor to buy a bicycle, sample the Lebanese cuisine of a Syrian restaurant, find a lost cat and wash the cups after using them.

'Harry? This way, Harry!' Theo's proprietorial voice was coming from a half-open door opposite the notice-board.

'Come in, come in!'

Boone found him sitting behind a huge table that doubled as a desk.

'Welcome to the Centre for Lebanese Studies, Harry.'

An armchair; a sofa; a *kilim*; a fireplace; part of the wall taken up with bookshelves and the rest of it with prints of Orientalist

259

paintings: it all looked more like some mad professor's den than a research centre.

'Have a seat Harry. We won't be disturbed.'

'There's no one in the ... in this Centre?'

'Well, there's usually a director, but he's away. He's gone to London to try and persuade some very wealthy Lebanese expats that charity is its own reward. I wish him luck.'

'You took your time, Theo.'

'Were you getting impatient? It's not been a piece of cake, you know. The sod covered his tracks very well.'

'Did you find anything?'

'I found your Tareq. Tareq Ghazzawi, alias Tareq Bizri.'

'And?'

'He's one of your Sharif's flunkeys. A sort of odd-job man. The interesting thing is that, in his teens and when he was still just Tareq Ghazzawi, he used to flirt with the Lebanese left.'

'Another communist?'

'I don't know about the communist bit. He was never a Party member. A fellow-traveller, more like it.'

'But that's not so surprising, is it? A lot of disenchanted lefties joined the ranks of the new Islamist movement. I even know of Christians who've converted to Islam.'

'True enough. But the deeper we dig, the more communists and fellow-travellers we find.'

'Apart from Ghazzawi, what else did you find?'

'Do you know this?' Damiano waved a large green book at him. 'This is Volume Four of a five-volume encyclopedia of Lebanese villages. Just for fun, I looked up "Mastaba". You know, this book lists every family by village and by hamlet. Which is how I learned that the sons of Mastaba had a long-standing tradition of emigrating to West Africa. Now, who is the great specialist on Lebanese emigrants to Africa?'

'I give up,' said Boone, when he realised Damiano really was waiting for an answer.

'My good friend Professor Beasley.' Anyone he had talked to for more than ten minutes was one of Damiano's good friends. 'Remarkable woman. She teaches at the University of Oklahoma, and I had the pleasure of meeting her here in Oxford just last month. I was getting interested in Mastaba's families and Phyllis – I mean Professor Beasley – knows all about them. So, obviously I couldn't resist. "Where did they go?" I asked her. "They're in the Ivory Coast," she told me, "and their patriarch down there is a certain Khaled Kotob." Then she told me his story. Our friend Khaled Kotob went to Abidjan in the sixties, and for a long time he worked as a peddler. Used to go off into the bush with a pack on his back. He gradually became the inescapable middleman between the towns and the countryside. He made a lot – and I mean a lot – of money. He cosied up to the whites, then to the blacks, and now he's a pillar of the local economy. So I said to myself that it might be worth my while talking to him, before car-bombs begin to go off in Abidjan.'

'Good thinking.'

'I remembered,' Damiano continued, as ever enjoying the sound of his own voice, 'that at the time when everyone was up in arms about the late president of the Ivory Coast because he had built a basilica, the ERA – represented by your humble servant – sent him a message of congratulations and support. Always a good policy, Harry. These people remember things like that, and they are not ungrateful. Not like some ... So I called in a few favours my old Ivorian friends owed me, and made contact with Khaled Kotob. I sent Joseph to see him. Believe it or not, Joseph has discovered a new passion. He's writing a book about Lebanese emigrants to the Ivory Coast. Joseph had all the recommendations he needed. He mentioned Professor Beasley here, and Oxford there, and Mr Kotob proved to be perfectly charming. Charming and talkative. So Joseph learned that, fourteen years ago, Mr Kotob made a triumphant return to his home village. He had a road built at his own expense to improve Mastaba's links with the outside world; he also financed the construction of a new mosque and a new school. Mr Kotob remembers the teacher very well – especially the teacher's wife. He remembers the imam and the Al-Husaynis, too. The Kotob family worked the Al-Husaynis' land for centuries, and Mr Kotob was obviously delighted to show his old lords and masters how wealthy he'd become and how generous he could be.'

'You got all this in writing?'

'Better than that.' The Padre waved a large brown envelope at him. 'I have a tape of the interview Mr Kotob gave to Joseph. And that's not all.' Opening the envelope, he took out a set of photos and slid them across the table to Boone. 'I have photos! No triumphal journeys without photographs. Take a look, Harry. Mr Kotob testing the tarmac on "his" road ... Mr Kotob being welcomed by the notables of "his" village ... Mr Kotob posing in front of "his" mosque ... Mr Kotob with "his" schoolteacher and the latter's family ... Mr Kotob with "his" imam and his sons ... The imam's wife and daughters aren't in the photo, of course. Khaled Kotob gave Joseph all the negatives for his book ... For posterity!'

As he glanced through the photos, one in particular caught Boone's eye. Two adults, one clean-shaven and looking very smart in his city suit, the other wearing a short beard and the white turban of a descendant of the Prophet, were surrounded by five boys who looked to be between the ages of eight and sixteen. The Sharif must have been thirteen when it was taken. Boone immediately ruled out the eldest and youngest of the five boys and concentrated on the other three. One of them must be the Sharif, he said to himself as he tried to recognise the man he knew in one or the other of these shy teenagers who were smiling for the camera. That's him, he decided at last: the one at the far right. That's the Sharif. Perhaps it was the faraway stare. Or perhaps it was because he was standing slightly apart from the others. Aloof. Atypical.

'Look at this, Harry.' Damiano had stood up and was pointing at another photo. 'Juliette ... Randa ... Randa with her father, her mother, her two brothers and Khaled Kotob. Look at Kotob, Harry! Posing beside Mrs Bsat, proud as a peacock. Good-looking woman, isn't she?'

The teacher's wife was indeed beautiful. She bore a strange resemblance to her daughter. It was as though Randa had died twice, and twice a violent death.

'Your Joseph's done a good job.' Boone put the pictures back on the table. 'Researching Lebanese immigrants in Africa was a brilliant idea.'

'It's not over yet.' Damiano sat down. 'In fact, this is just the beginning. Now we're in a position to pursue our quest in Lebanon. Joseph has a letter of introduction from Khaled Kotob, and Kotob has given him the names of people from Mastaba who still enjoy the benefits of his largesse. He's a very generous man, this Khaled Kotob.'

'So you can ask more questions.'

'All with Khaled Kotob's blessing. The name alone should open doors and loosen tongues.' He replaced the book on its shelf. 'We'll find out who's behind all this Harry, and then we can go back to

Lebanon without any fear of being shot ... But I'll need money. You've no idea how much this business has cost me already.'

'Oh yes I do.' Boone tried his best to look sympathetic.

'Believe me, Joseph's plane ticket alone –'

'I know,' Boone interrupted him. He suspected that Joseph's ticket had been a present from some sympathetic thug in the Ivory Coast.

'A small fortune, Harry.'

'May I have the negatives?'

'Take them, take them. But don't forget the money.'

Boone didn't even try to hide his annoyance. 'I'll see what I can do.'

'And take care of the negatives,' said Damiano as he showed him to the door. 'Take good care of them, please. After all, if we do draw a blank, I can always cut my losses by writing a book in honour of Mr Kotob, can't I.'

Boone didn't react immediately, but walking down Woodstock Road towards the Bodleian, to get on with the research he was doing for Maria, it did cross his mind that the Padre might already have pocketed a small advance from Mr Kotob.

Oxford got older during the vacations. Whenever the university town swapped its term-time residents for seasonal visitors, the average age of its inhabitants shot up. Bikes then gave way to multi-wheeled containers that disgorged their hordes of tourists into the streets. The tourists then spread through the venerable city in typically national configurations: American tides, British queues, German detachments, Italian processions, French medleys and Asian clusters.

When he reached Broad Street, the sight of all the visitors making for the Bodleian made Boone change his mind, and he decided to go straight to the station. But as he turned into the Turl he bumped into

264

a Teutonic battalion that was heading slowly but steadily in the direction of Exeter. Despite his efforts, he found himself bringing up the rear. As it drew level with the college, the military unit began to redeploy for an assault on the gate, and the Irishman took advantage of a gap in the German lines and a very un-Teutonic moment of hesitation to take French leave.

At Carfax, a transatlantic wave stared at the medieval tower, waiting for the Jack o' the clock and the carillon before ebbing away.

'*Fortis est veritas,*' someone said, pointing to the city's motto.

'Are we far from the hotel?' asked someone else.

The man spoke with a drawl. Putting his hand to his pocket, Boone felt Theo's envelope. The American's Southern accent had just given him an idea. He walked over to the nearest pay phone and dialled a number.

'Hello?' The woman at the other end of the line sounded harassed.

'Sarah? It's Harry.'

'Harry! No, not now, Pam, not now. Stop it, will you! Sorry, Harry ... Where are you calling from?'

'London,' lied Boone, praying that the chimes of Oxford weren't about to start ringing.

'You're in England? Just a moment, Harry ... Pamela! I said not now. Take your brother out into the garden! Harry ... Why do you never ring, you naughty boy?'

Naughty boy! She hadn't changed. The same old tendency to treat him like a child. The same maternal tone. Twice a mother, and still she wasn't satisfied.

'Children all right?' he asked. 'Pam and ...'

'Jack, Harry, Jack. Pamela and Jack are fine, as you can hear. It's me that's not fine. They wear me out.'

'How's Lew?'

265

'Lew's fine too.'

'Could you give me his work number? I need to talk to him.'

'So *sir* isn't calling to ask after me. *Sir* merely wants to talk to my husband.'

'Sarah ...'

'Well, Lew isn't in the office today. He's here. You've caught him between two planes. I'll put him on.'

'Thanks, Sarah.'

'You will call again, won't you? You will call to ask after me?'

'I promise,' Boone lied. He had never understood why she insisted on treating him as though he were a childhood friend.

'Pamela!' The former Mrs Boone was shouting now. 'Stop teasing your little brother. Out into the garden with you! Sorry, Harry, I'll put Lew on.'

Boone sighed. Thanks to Pamela and her long-suffering little brother, the conversation had been shorter and less painful than he'd expected.

'Harry?'

'Lew ...'

'How are you, Harry? What can I do for you?'

'I think I need to pick your brains about software.'

'Sure. What's it about?'

'Missing children, Lew.'

38

'How's the rhubarb pudding?'

'Delicious, Lew. Just like the roast pork. How the hell do you find these places?'

'It's an American knack. When it comes to good traditional food, you can always rely on an American.'

Ten years of living in London had had no effect on Lew Gates's accent. Boone suspected that he worked on it for the sole purpose of reassuring his multinational yet hardly cosmopolitan employers.

'When the bigshots from headquarters do us the honour of a visit, this is the sort of place they like to eat in – quiet atmosphere, flowery curtains, oak furniture and obsequious staff.'

He signalled to a waiter. Boone noted that he wore the same crested signet ring, and the same cufflinks. Only the Rolex changed. It got steadily thicker as the years went by.

'Let's have coffee in the bar,' said Gates, as he watched his guest take out a crumpled little cigar.

At the table they had done no more than exchange polite remarks, as suits two well-brought-up men who had shared the same woman for a while. As usual, Gates had been especially friendly towards Boone because, deep down, he felt a bit guilty for stealing Sarah from him. And as usual, Boone had been extremely polite to Gates because, deep down, he was grateful to the American for having taken her away.

As they left the dining room, Gates went to the cloakroom to collect a battered satchel that reminded Boone of the one poor Shartuni used to proudly carry around.

Once they had been served coffee, Gates settled into his armchair and crossed his legs. Boone caught a fleeting glimpse of his hand-sewn Ivy League loafers.

'I've been working on your photos, Harry.'

'It's really very kind of you. I do appreciate it.'

'No need to thank me. It was fun. You know about the system, don't you?'

'Vaguely. I read about it in the paper. Something about trying to find some children ten or twenty years after they went missing. They aged their photos, or something of the sort. The article mentioned your company.'

'Yes, well, we developed the software. Not that there's anything new about the idea of aging portraits. Composite photography has been around since the end of the nineteenth century. One of Darwin's cousins, the eugenicist Francis Galton, was experimenting with it as early as 1877. But he was just physically manipulating the features by matching up or superimposing different pictures. What we can do now is quite different. You interested in how it's done?'

'Very,' lied Boone.

'Well, the human face is made up of a structure and a canvas. The structure consists of bone and cartilage, and doesn't change much after the first fifteen or twenty years of your life. The canvas consists of muscles, organic tissue and skin, and shifts and changes over time. All you need to age a portrait is a camera, a computer and the right software. The camera converts the image into digital data, the computer stores and rewrites the data and then the software manipulates the whole lot. You include basic parameters, like the bone structure, the canvas, the environment, diet … Stop me if I'm boring you.'

'Not at all,' Boone lied.

'Then you feed the parameters into the computer, which permutates every possible combination and gives a final result. Obviously, it's a lot easier when you have a photo of an adult whose bone structure is similar to that of the child, because then you have a point of reference. That applies to your two group photos. In one, we have the little girl's father and mother and in the other we have the father of the five boys. The system obviously has its limitations. Imponderables and extrinsic factors we know nothing about may have modified the child's physiognomy: serious illnesses, fractures, scars, loss of teeth, malnutrition, and so on.'

'And has your Michelangelo software been a success? Is it selling well?'

'The *Leonardo* software … To answer your question, yes, Leonardo is selling very well. The police, the UN, NGOs … What about you? Still living in the shadows?'

269

So much for discretion, thought Boone. Sarah would tell anyone who was ready to listen that her ex-husband was a spy. She was as open about it as though he worked for the Foreign Office or the BBC.

'These photos ... I suppose they're for work, Harry. I say that because I have to admit that the cherubs you gave me don't look like choirboys any more. They're so sweet when they're little, but ...' He leaned towards Boone. 'Where the hell did you find this lot? And who the hell wants to find these children?'

'Can I see the photos?'

'Of course.' Gates took them out of his satchel. 'Ah, the girl. Now I would like to find her. She's a real beauty. She must be about twelve in the photo you gave me, don't you think? Well, this is what she looks like after fifteen years.'

Boone feverishly grabbed the portrait from Gates. The texture was a bit strange and the grain too even, but it was definitely a portrait of Randa, Randa with long hair. A little fat in the face, perhaps – what could one expect from a well-fed American computer programmer? – but it was she.

'Congratulations, Lew. Your Leonardo works miracles. I saw this woman not so long ago, and I can assure you that this is a very good likeness.'

'You saw her? You know her? Lucky devil! Tell me, is she really –'

'Can I see the rest?' Boone was annoyed. So Lew Gates thought he could share Randa with him the same way they had shared Sarah.

'Here ... these are the two group photos you gave me, and this is what I've turned them into ... there are eight portraits in all.'

'Why so many?'

'You asked me to do six: the five boys in the first photo, and the girl in the second. But as there were two other boys in the photo of

270

the girl, I thought I'd do the lot. All the children, I mean. Perhaps I shouldn't have.'

Boone wasn't listening. He'd found a portrait of the Sharif. Clean-shaven, and without the scars on the right side of his face – Leonardo couldn't have known.

'Tell me ... I made a bet with myself that this man was the little boy of twelve or thirteen you can see on the far right. Has Leonardo proved me right?'

'Let me see,' said Gates, taking the photo from him. 'What reference number have we given this one? G? Let's have a look ... G, G ... No, you're mistaken, Harry.'

Boone was disappointed, but pointed to another of the children in the photo.

'Hmm ... No, it's not that kid either. You have one answer left.' Gates was beginning to sound like a game-show host.

'This one, then? But to be honest, that surprises me.'

'You're right. To be surprised, I mean. You're not even getting warm, Harry. You're cold.'

'But the eldest is too old, and the youngest is too young!'

'True. In fact, your friend – let's call him Mr G – isn't in the photo.'

Shit!

'He isn't there,' repeated Gates.

Of course he isn't! Randa wasn't his mistress! And she wasn't his first love either!

'Your Mr G is in the other group photograph.'

They were brother and sister! Randa was his sister! That's why he'd been protecting her. That's why he'd set her up in the flat in the Rue d'Australie.

'Here ... look ...'

271

That's why the man with the limp was keeping an eye on her. That's why he went to Cyprus. To stop me finding out. *I am not a kept woman.* That's what she was trying to tell me. But I thought it was a misplaced sense of modesty.

'You got it wrong, Harry.'

Of course I got it wrong. And I'm not the only one. The Apparatus got it wrong too.

'Subjects A, B, C, D and E are the five boys in the first photo ...'

The Apparatus knew about Randa's existence. The Apparatus thought it was doing the right thing by turning a blind eye and tolerating the escapades and libidinal excesses of its darling Sharif.

'As for subjects F, G and H, they are the girl and the two boys in the other picture.'

That's why he used bombs to cover his tracks. But he'd forgotten about the African connection. He hadn't taken into account Khaled Kotob, the Padre, or the basilica that had enabled the Padre to make friends in high places in the Ivory Coast.

'You didn't ask me to do subjects G and H, but I did them anyway. In case they came in useful.'

He hadn't taken the random element into account either. There was no way he could have known that Lew Gates would be so zealous.

'A little present, so to speak. With Leonardo's compliments.'

Thanks for the present, Lew, Boone said to himself. And a big thank you to Leonardo, too. The Leonardo system had bailed out the Boone system. Harry Boone could almost feel the damp Mediterranean air on his skin, and Maria's spicy taste on his lips.

39

'So our Sharif isn't a noble Al-Husayni after all. Just a common, garden-variety Bsat!'

'A communist, Archie. A young communist activist. Son of a communist cadre. Infiltrated by Moscow into the Apparatus.'

'And he is no more descended from the Prophet than Alec Rose is descended from Queen Boadicea!'

Thanks to Leonardo, Harry Boone's exile in Wandsworth was over, and Briggs was officially welcoming him back to Russell Square. Indeed, he was proudly celebrating his return by offering him a drink. He was doing more than welcoming him back – he was adopting him.

'But why, Archie? That's what I don't understand. Why should Moscow mount an operation like this? Why use one of its agents to pass on information about Islamist terrorists and their financial backers in the Gulf?'

'Why?' Briggs poured whisky from a carafe into two tulip glasses. 'I'll tell you why. Moscow would like to crush its southern Muslim neighbours once and for all, that's why: Chechens, Ossetians, Tatars, Bashkirs, Dagestanians and what have you.' He added a drop of water to the whisky. 'Moscow would like a free hand. Moscow wants complete freedom to napalm and cluster-bomb all these rebellious populations to its heart's content. The only thing is that Europe didn't quite see it that way. Human rights and the right to self-determination: that was the philosophy of the day, wasn't it? Hence Slovenia, of course, followed by Croatia, Bosnia, Kosovo and Macedonia. Moscow has learned a lesson from the Balkans. Moscow isn't Belgrade, and Moscow is pining for the Caucasus and Central Asia, from whence it was driven out when the Soviet Union imploded.'

'So the Centre lets the Sharif loose on us. To poison our minds.' Boone sniffed at the whisky. The water had brought out the iodine in it. He swallowed half his drink at one gulp. The smoky, peaty taste caught in his throat. Islay, he reckoned. Probably Lagavulin.

'Poison our minds?' said Briggs, taking note of the almost poisonous amount of alcohol Boone had just swallowed. 'Not really. No, I don't think so. Moscow didn't do it just to poison our minds, as you put it. It was to enlighten us. Yes, to enlighten us.'

'Enlighten us?'

'After all the publicity we've given to our recent successes against the Islamists, you won't find many Europeans protesting when Russia goes on an indiscriminate Muslim-bashing expedition in its "near-abroad". Nor will Europe have much to say when Moscow finally extends its influence to most of Muslim Central Asia.'

'Moscow's raising its threshold of impunity.'

'Human rights, the right to self-determination, the right to be different ... all that's history now. As you can well imagine, after the arrests in Europe, the trials, the frozen bank accounts, the checks on companies run by Arab princes and Muslim businessmen and the blacklisting of charitable associations financed by Gulf sheikhs, Europe's relations with its Arab neighbours will never be the same again. Not for a long time, anyway.'

'To say nothing of our own Muslims: London, Bradford, Marseilles, Frankfurt, Berlin ...'

'A real headache ... Do you know how many Muslims there are in Europe already? I mean, how many European Muslims? I'm not talking about the Bosnians and the Albanians, Harry. I'm talking about Brits of Asiatic stock, Frenchmen of North African stock, Germans of Turkish or Kurdish stock ... The Americans don't have this problem. Unlike Europe, they can get by without the Muslims.'

'Whereas Europe, with its aging population, depends upon Muslim labour, just as it depends upon Muslim oil and gas.'

'Not to mention our defence industries, which rely on the Gulf markets, and our banking system, which lives off the money deposited by Arabs.'

'It really is a poisoned chalice.'

'You'll have noticed that Lukin didn't just send us a job lot of intelligence. Not at all. It was all carefully planned well in advance. Every piece of information we got from the Sharif followed on from the last, and led to the next. Lukin handed us the information about the Palais de Justice operation to give us an appetite. Then he cut off the supply. He let us get so hungry that we literally threw ourselves at his Sharif. Then, once the Sharif was in England, he steered us away from the Americans and gave us Europe in exchange. He allowed us to hook the French, and once the Entente Cordiale was re-established, he made us distrust the Germans and the Belgians.'

'His masterstroke was to get us believe that we were giving him intelligence, when in fact it all came from him.'

'As you say, a real masterstroke. Because when someone gives and someone receives, it's the giver who becomes attached to the receiver. Giving always makes you feel good, and giving intelligence to the Russians made us feel good. We became fond of them because, by accepting our gifts, they confirmed our self-image.'

'When I think that Lukin had the nerve to invite Guy to Moscow to thank him in person for the intelligence he was supplying. Intelligence that came from one of his own agents!'

'Classic stuff.' Trying hard not to smile at the trick Lukin had played on Fennell, Briggs looked around the room and its furniture with the critical eye of a man who knew he would soon be moving into something more spacious and impressive. One man's sorrow is another man's joy. 'Classic stuff Practice should be teaching,' he continued, having finished his survey. 'Lukin completely fooled Guy with that one. Frustrated by Van Dusen, Guy flung himself into Lukin's arms and Lukin led him by the nose.'

'And let him take all the credit.'

'It reminds me of what a Secretary of State once said about Washington: "You can get a lot done in this town, provided you let someone else take all the credit." That's precisely what our friend Lukin did with Guy. A real spymaster. Guy didn't stand a chance.'

'What about the Americans?' asked Boone. 'Do you think they were in on it? Do you think they knew that the Sharif was being run by Moscow?'

'That would at least explain why Van Dusen was so lukewarm,' Briggs said cautiously. 'I don't know what he heard from Langley, but it seems to have been enough to put him off.'

'And the Sharif never gave us anything of real interest to the Americans.'

'Of course he didn't,' whispered Briggs, as though not even his office was safe from Washington's ears. 'Can you imagine what would have happened if he'd spilled everything he knew about the Islamists' American targets? We would have lost him, Harry. He would have been too much for us to handle. Too much even for Van Dusen and his pals. One of those innumerable committees Washington is so good at would have got its hooks into him. Can you imagine Langley lying to Congress? Or telling the gentlemen on the Hill that the Sharif is a Russian asset? That Moscow has staged a beauty of an operation to cause chaos in Europe and poison our relationship with Islam?'

'Or, worse still, that Moscow had kept quiet all those years and left the terrorists free to target the West, including America. That the Russians might have known all along.'

'That they said nothing, and let the terrorists get on with their business,' Briggs added.

Boone recalled how shocked Julian Le Pelley had been by the Sharif's comment: 'In our line of work, curing is always better than preventing.'

'Moscow had to avoid that at all costs, Harry. And the best way was to make sure that the Sharif gave us nothing – absolutely nothing – that might bring him to the attention of Congress.'

'But if the Americans did have their doubts and did suspect that the Sharif was a Russian agent, why didn't they say anything to us?

They could have had a word in Guy's ear. They could have warned him. We are allies, aren't we?'

'Allies?' sneered Briggs, looking around him furtively. 'Who needs allies when there's no worthy enemy? The Soviet Union is dead and buried, and so is the special relationship so dear to our masters. Nowadays, the Americans merely use us as we once used the Aussies and the Kiwis.'

Boone noted that Briggs had delicately refrained from adding the Paddies and the Jocks to the cannon-fodder list.

'You mean the Americans knew? They were colluding with the Russians?'

'The bipolar world has had its day, and the circular world is taking over from it. The centre of the planet is being displaced to the periphery, towards Washington, Moscow, and possibly Peking. We are the old centre, Harry, we and our Muslim neighbours. Neighbours, and enemies.'

'So the Russians and the Americans agreed to lobotomise Islam by raising the spectre of terrorism.'

'The same way they once lobotomised Europe by raising the spectre of the atom bomb,' Briggs said.

'Then Europe is no more than a side issue?'

'Nothing happens over here anymore, barring chaotic demographic movements. The main flows of energy have been bypassing us for a long time now. They're beyond our control. They've moved north towards Russia, east towards China, south towards the Indian Ocean and west towards the Atlantic.'

'The Old World is no more than a playground,' Boone mused.

'But not just for any old game,' Briggs consoled him. 'For the *Great Game*, Harry. The Great Game we once played with the Russians. In

Persia, remember. In Afghanistan, too. Now the Americans are playing it, and the next Kipling will be an American.'

'And when Islam has finally been brought to heel, they'll turn on each other again.'

'We're not there yet. For the moment, they're on the same side.'

'We've stumbled into a family quarrel,' Boone said.

'As you say, a family quarrel. After all, half the terrorists we are fighting these days were trained and armed by the Americans to fight the other half, who were trained and armed by the Russians ... Just a family argument, as you put it so nicely. Or, to be more precise, an argument over an inheritance. It's all about controlling the flow and the price of oil. It's all about pipelines and outlets from the Caspian and the Gulf.'

'"Who shut up the sea gates?"'

'Who did what?'

'Nothing ... I was citing the Book of Job,' Boone said.

'I'd forgotten you went to a church school. But yes, you're right ...'

'The meek might well inherit the earth,' Boone quoted the Bible again. 'But of course, the mighty are keeping the mineral rights for themselves!'

'History repeats itself. And as the Sharif's mentor, Karl Marx, so nicely put it, it's tragedy the first time round, and farce the second.'

Well, the joke is on us, thought Boone as he drained his glass.

40

Boone drove fast, too fast for the liking of Briggs, who was sitting beside him in what the French call 'the dead man's seat'. But Briggs raised no objections, just as he had raised no objections when Boone lit one of his disgusting little cigars. The latest meeting of the Royal & Ancient had granted Harry Boone a certain level of immunity, and Archie Briggs was not the man to spoil his subordinates' triumphs. Not too quickly, anyway. When they reached Exeter the road narrowed and, to Briggs's great relief, Boone took his foot off the accelerator and quietly joined the queue of vacationers heading for the sea. Crossing Dartmoor, they were seriously slowed down by a convoy of Dutch holidaymakers feeling quite at home in the flat landscape. After Truro, the traffic became even heavier. It was as though all the motorists on the peninsula had agreed to escort them that day. Boone was now crawling along, and Briggs wasn't complaining. But this period of respite did not last long; as their escort bid them farewell just before Helston, Boone reclaimed the empty road. He drove at top speed along the increasingly narrow lanes, which grew darker and darker as the overhanging trees closed down on them. The road led to the house Fennell had requisitioned for his darling Sharif. Boone followed it without ever hesitating or slowing down to look at a signpost, as if he knew the way by heart. He felt like a wandering hangman who could unhesitatingly find death row in a prison he had never set foot in. Have-rope-will-travel. An execution, he thought. That was it, he was going to an execution. No, it was a vivisection, more like. He'd have preferred to be going alone. He could have done without Briggs, the forensic pathologist. But he couldn't get rid of Briggs, who had rushed to his aid in his moment of victory and jumped on the bandwagon. Briggs was determined that Boone's triumph would be his own.

As they approached the house, everything indicated that a change of regime was taking place. Harmless-looking vans and unmarked cars, which were so anonymous as to look suspicious, were taking away the technicians and the sophisticated equipment. Fennell was pulling the plug, pulling out his troops. Catlow and Le Pelley – two of the troops Fennell had forgotten to pull out – came to meet them, and Catlow was obsequious enough to open Briggs's door for him. Briggs silently acknowledged the tribute and got out of the car with the dignity of a prince-regent. The transfer of power was well in progress. As they reached the door, he could not help himself from stopping to admire the fine plant with trumpet-shaped flowers that was happily climbing the front of the house: *bigonia grandiflora*. He was particularly struck by the contrast between the orangey flowers and the grey stone. He'd so often seen these splendid flowers being totally overwhelmed by the red brick walls along which they were made to climb. Once he'd finished admiring the *bigonia,* he finally deigned to follow the potbellied man and his pipe-smoking acolyte inside, where Simon Blaker was waiting for them. The Rookie looked grumpy. He greeted them in an almost inaudible voice and remained standing by the empty fireplace, looking as superfluous as it did on such a fine day. At a signal from Briggs, he left them and returned a few moments later with the Sharif.

The man who had been the Clubhouse's star had let his beard grow. Presumably to lend a very Islamic air of authority to his teachings, thought Boone. He looked around the room at the serious faces, ignored Briggs who was sitting in Fennell's chair, and turned straight to Boone.

'Harry, my friend! What a nice surprise!'

Whatever he was saying, he wasn't really surprised to see him there. He knew that something was amiss: all that gear being packed up; Guy, who had vanished; Simon, who was avoiding him; and his guardian angels, sticking closer to him than ever. The long leash he had been on for the last few months had been made tight. Then there were the silences, too. The silences of men who have suddenly lost the power to make decisions. He hadn't been taken in. He had known that all this meant newcomers, and a new authority. The new authority was apparently vested in his old friend Harry, and this dumpy little man with not even a name to himself, whom he'd already seen in Cyprus and who had unceremoniously taken over Guy's favourite chair. Still ignoring Briggs, he strode across the room towards Boone, hand outstretched. Boone had only a few seconds to make up his mind. Should he keep his distance and give him time to prepare his defence and his lies? Or should he pretend, smile at him, hug him and give him affectionate slaps on the back? He told himself that he had enough aces up his sleeve not to be forced to play that game. So he held out a limp hand that expressed rather more than the well known British dislike of all physical contact.

'I thought I'd never see you again ...' the Sharif shook his hand vigorously. 'I've been constantly asking my friend Simon about you. Haven't I, Simon?'

My friend Simon, indeed! So the Sharif hadn't been slow in finding the chink in Fennell's armour – Simon Blaker, the Arabic-speaking Rookie. He had turned him into an ally. *You and I are alike, Simon. You and I have read the Qur'an. We're not like them, Simon.*

'Haven't I, Simon?' repeated the Sharif, without letting go of Boone's hand. 'Haven't I been asking after Harry?'

The Rookie didn't answer. Boone assumed he was missing his books and regretting his disastrous foray into the land of the living.

The Sharif was still staring at Boone. *And where the hell did you get to?* His eyes looked both smiling and inquisitorial. *Did you go back to your mistress's bed and your* dolce far niente *as I hoped you would, or have you been busy digging up dirt all this time?*

'Are we moving house?' he finally asked, having despaired of bringing Boone's hand back to life.

'Yes, we are,' replied Boone, retrieving his hand. 'But first, I need to talk to you.'

'Right!' ordered Briggs as he got to his feet. 'Everybody out!'

He left the room, pushing the others ahead of him like a shepherd driving his flock.

'I have something for you.' Sitting down on the couch – their couch – Boone ostentatiously produced an envelope. The Sharif sat down beside him. Boone realised that he always sat beside and never opposite him. Never facing him.

The Sharif leaned slightly towards him with the attentive look of a source about to be asked a question. Taking a photo Boone was handing him, he looked at it, frowned, looked at it again, raised his eyebrows and finally tried to smile. *So you weren't on holiday, after all,* he seemed to be saying.

'That's a photo of my village that you've got there!'

'Recognise anyone?'

'Of course.' He lit a cigarette. 'That's my father, God rest his soul, and standing next to him is, if I'm not mistaken, a millionaire from Africa who was paying a nostalgic visit to his birthplace ... This must have been taken some fifteen years ago. Where did you find it?'

'What about this one?' Boone handed him another photo. 'I'm willing to bet that's you, there on the far right.'

'Just a moment ...' The Sharif frowned again. He had moved much closer to Boone, and their shoulders were touching. 'On the right, did you say? No, that's not me. That's my brother Ahmad.'

'Are you in this photo?'

'Of course I am,' he replied without the slightest hesitation. 'That's me, beside my father.'

So you're still lying, said Boone to himself. Perhaps you don't know that I know.

Putting the photo on his knee, the Sharif puffed on his cigarette and then noisily exhaled. He was looking through the French window.

'They're all dead ... The car-bomb attack.'

'I know.'

'Do you have any more photos?'

Wouldn't you just like to know what other photos I've found? You'd love to know what clues I've dug up.

'Look ... Do you recognise anyone here?'

The Sharif's hand didn't shake when he grabbed the photo. He was wearing his candid look again. *Curious? You think I'm being curious? You bet I'm curious. Who wouldn't be?*

'Of course I do,' he said cheerfully. 'That's our teacher! The teacher, his family, and that emigrant from Africa again ... His name escapes me ... He gave the money to build a new school and a mosque.'

'What about the kids? Recognise them?'

'That's the eldest, Rafiq,' he said without batting an eyelid. 'That's the girl – Randa, I think her name was. And that's the youngest. Can't remember his name. I remember Rafiq very well. We were in the same class.'

'Are they dead too?'

'Yes, the same day as my family ... The same car-bomb ... All of them except the girl.'

'Look at this.'

Boone produced a black and white photo.

'It looks like me. But it's a recent photo. It's been retouched. That's what I would look like if I'd never been wounded.'

'It is a photo of you. To be more specific, it's a computer projection using a photo of you as a teenager.'

'Is it? A computer?'

'New software. It's used to find children who went missing when they were very young, years after they went missing.'

'Does it, now?'

'You want to see what your brother Ahmad would have looked like today, had he survived?' Boone handed him more black and white prints. 'And your brother Muhammad? And your brother Abdullah? And your brother Abdulmajid. You don't look much like your brothers, do you? Your father doesn't look much like you either, come to think of it. Perhaps you take after your mother.'

'Perhaps,' lied the Sharif. He'd never heard of this software before. Boone's bluffing, he was thinking. Boone may suspect something, but he had no proof. Perhaps these were just photofit pictures, he was thinking.

'And there's Randa ... Randa Bsat, as seen by a computer that has looked at a photo of her when she was ten.'

Taking the photo, the Sharif stared at it without any emotion, as though it was a photo of a perfect stranger. He wouldn't give anything away. He was willing to fight to the death. But Boone was tired of playing this game. He decided to put all his cards on the table and administer the *coup de grâce*.

'She was beautiful,' he remarked.

'Yes, that's true. She is very beautiful.'

'*Was.*'

'What do you mean, *was*? She's not dead, not to the best of my knowledge. She survived the car-bomb in Mastaba.'

'She may have survived the Mastaba explosion, but unfortunately she didn't survive what happened next.'

'What do you mean by that?'

'I mean she's dead.' Boone looked him straight in the eye. 'It's over ... It's all over ... Randa is dead ...'

The Sharif held his gaze. He knew – intuitively knew – that Boone wasn't lying. He methodically sorted out the photos and gave them back to their owner. He seemed to have lost all interest in them. In fact, he seemed to have lost interest in everything. Stubbing out his cigarette, he immediately took out another. Boone imitated him and lit another of his little Dutch cigars. For a long time they both smoked in silence. Boone watched the Sharif, and the Sharif watched his cigarette burn away as though it were an hourglass. He was smoking with a generous intensity, as though it was his first cigarette of the day, or perhaps his last. Driven by the binding agents, the cigarette was burning fast, and when the smoke began to dance around his fingers, he delicately stubbed it out in the silver-plated ashtray Simon Blaker had given him. He then looked straight at Boone and smiled sadly. He seemed to have come to a decision.

'When? When did she die?'

'Almost four months ago.'

'How did she die?'

'A shootout. She was caught in the crossfire.'

'In Beirut?'

'Cyprus.'

'Were you there?'

'I was.'

'Who else? Anyone I know?'

'Tareq Ghazzawi. The one you call Tareq Bizri.'

The Sharif said nothing. He didn't even want to know who had been firing at who that day. He was miles away.

'It was an accident,' said Boone.

'Why keep it from me?'

'They were afraid of losing their source. They believed in you.'

'They believed in me! What about you? Did you believe in me?'

'For a while.'

'For a while ... When did you begin to have doubts?'

'When I realised that you'd lied to us about the explosion that destroyed your car. I could understand why you took your own precautions and booby-trapped your own car in case we skimped on the explosives. I could understand that. But I couldn't understand why you didn't tell us about the accomplice you hired to help you with the operation – especially when you had no qualms about telling us that you'd booby-trapped the briefcase to keep Hammud and Shartuni quiet ... Then I realised. You could booby-trap the briefcase yourself. But when it came to the car, you needed help. Planting three or four hundred kilos of explosives in the car of a "personality" like you, isn't something that can be done just like that, and it can't be done discreetly ... To do that, you needed an accomplice: Tareq ...'

'His name is Tareq, but you're right, his surname isn't Bizri. It's Ghazzawi.'

'So you lied to the polygraph about his surname, but you did give us his real forename. That way, you managed to hide the fact that you were lying.'

'That's right.'

'If you'd told us he was called Ghazzawi we could have done some digging. We'd have found out that not so long ago, he was still close to the Communist Party.'

'True.'

'You said nothing about the wicked things you did at the Cité Sportive so as to keep Tareq from us. When there's an accomplice, the secret is out. An accomplice means there's a conspiracy. And you had to avoid that at all cost.'

'You're right ...' The Sharif seemed to be regretting his decision. 'But I had no choice. I was concerned lest your Western and pseudo-democratic scruples make you skimp on the explosives. So I used Tareq to help me booby-trap my car.'

'Because a failed attack on your car would have upset your plans.'

'A failed attack – one that didn't pulverise my car – would indeed have drawn undue attention to me, and I'd have had less room for manoeuvre. It would have made it difficult for me to disappear.'

'On the other hand, you couldn't admit to us that you had an accomplice, and you couldn't tell us who he was.'

'It was a risk we had to take.'

'Tough luck.'

'And now you know. How did you find out?'

'I found a photograph of you and Randa. The software did the rest.'

'And where did you find this photograph?'

'In Africa.'

'Africa? So England is still a colonial power!'

More of an ecumenical power, Boone said to himself, thinking of the Padre.

'Where in Africa?'

'At the home of that millionaire emigrant.'

'At the home of a millionaire! How ironic! You see, the class struggle isn't over! What was his name again?'

'Kotob.'

'Yes, that's it, Kotob ... Khaled Kotob. It all comes back to me now. What exactly do you know?'

'I know that you're not Ali Al-Husayni. I know that you're Randa's brother. Her elder brother.'

He stood up, took a few steps in the direction of the French window and then moved away from it, as though he was afraid that Boone might misinterpret his sudden interest in the exit. 'My name is Rafiq,' he eventually said, staring through the window. 'It's funny ... It's the first time in ten years that I've dared to say my own name. Even Randa didn't call me that. My younger brother was called Raja. Rafiq, Randa and Raja. My father was called Rabih. He was a rational man, was my father. He left nothing to chance.' He sat down beside Boone again. 'It all started on that day in June, ten years ago. It all started with the bomb in Mastaba. It was Tareq who thought of the switch. He was working as a nurse in the hospital in Nabatiyeh at the time.'

Hence the fire that destroyed the hospital records, thought Boone.

'I didn't know it at the time, but Tareq was already my controller. Still is, come to that.'

'So Tareq was your Centre controller!'

'Tareq came to see me the day I was taken to the hospital,' he said, lighting another cigarette. 'I was in terrible pain. I was very frightened. I thought I was going to die. Tareq told me that my sister Randa was safe and sound, but that my father, mother and brother had been killed. And then he told me that Sharif Hasan Al-Husayni had died too, along with his entire family. I didn't understand why he was telling me about the Sharif and his family. He told me that the bodies were unrecognisable. That they'd been taken to the hospital only for statistical purposes. That they had to be buried before nightfall, as tradition demands. It was a golden opportunity for Tareq. All those charred corpses torn to bits and being buried in a hurry. All those disembodied identities that just needed new bodies, new faces ... And then I realised why he was telling me about the Sharif and his son. He wanted me to take Ali Al-Husayni's place. Ali was the same age as me. We were about the same build, and his body had been pulverised in the explosion.' He put his hand to his face. 'I had been disfigured. I was almost unrecognisable. The opportunity was too good to be missed. So when one of the doctors finally got around to taking a look at me and asked me my name, Tareq immediately told him that it was Ali Al-Husayni, that I was Sharif Hasan's son. The doctor wrote all this down, and Ali Al-Husayni's body took on my name in the mortuary. We'd pulled it off. I was Sharif Ali Al-Husayni, the son of an imam and a descendant of the

Prophet. No more flirtations with the Party, no more communist father. I had acquired an ancestry and pedigree, and Tareq had his source inside the Islamists. The legend was perfect: same age, same build, same life. Made to measure.'

'But why send you here? After they'd taken so much trouble to give you a legend, to protect you, to infiltrate you into the Islamists, to help you rise through the ranks of the Apparatus ... Why?'

'The Apparatus is finished!' He stubbed out his cigarette. 'The Apparatus has been abandoned by the Arab princes who used to finance it. The Apparatus is on the point of being betrayed by the various secret services that have been protecting it and using it. They're all too happy to clear their names with the Americans by giving up their co-religionists. So the Centre decided to sell its shares in the Apparatus – before they fell in value – and to invest elsewhere. Or, if you'd rather put it that way, Moscow is selling its dinars and riyals in order to buy euros.'

'But why us? Why not the French?'

'Because the Centre needed a credible channel, that's why. And who could be more credible than the British? After all, it's a well-known fact that Britain is lukewarm about the European Union. So when London begins to distill intelligence that is of particular relevance to Islamist terrorism in France, Spain and Italy, no one suspects a thing. On the contrary, it's seen as an encouraging sign that Britain is abandoning its Atlanticism and turning to Europe. And when, shortly afterwards, Britain describes the Germans and the Belgians as bad Europeans and accuses them of having reached secret agreements with the Islamists, it already has its Continental allies in Paris, Madrid and Rome.'

He was getting carried away now. He seemed determined to prove to Boone how superior he was. And he was succeeding. *You*

291

may have sophisticated software that can age photographs of children, he seemed to be saying, *but when it comes to intricate setups, we're still streets ahead of you. Your economic system may have prevailed,* he seemed to be implying, *but when it comes to intelligence, you've still got a lot to learn.*

'The British were so excited about the intelligence the Centre was supplying that they couldn't contain themselves, and suddenly discovered that they were Europeans after all. They were so thrilled with the credit that same intelligence bought them in Russia that they actually began to dream of being the godfathers who would sponsor Russia's membership of the European Union. Without realising it, they were playing into the hands of the Centre by dividing Europe, integrating Russia into Europe's security system and raising the tension between Europe and its Muslim neighbours.'

'And Europe isn't Islam's only neighbour.'

'Exactly.' He was taking an obvious delight in unravelling the operation to the man who had unmasked him. 'Europe isn't Islam's only neighbour. There's also Russia. And Russia needs to buy time. It needs time to recover. Russia is perfectly willing to let Europe flirt with its former European colonies, because they're unmanageable at the moment. But then there's the East. Russia wants to rebuild its forces in the East, in the Caucasus and Central Asia.'

Enter Lukin, Boone said to himself.

'Russia needs Europe to give it a free hand to crush the centres of Islamic revolt in Greater Russia and to bring the old Muslim republics back into the fold.'

'But why did you agree? After all, communism is finished now! Everything's changed!'

'That's true. Communism fell when the Wall came down. Yes, everything's changed. But only for you. For us, it's worse than it's ever been. Look at what religion has done to Lebanon. Eighteen religious communities at each other's throats for eighteen years. Look at what religion is doing to Israel. Jewish fanatics born in New York are stirring up Muslim fanatics born in refugee camps. And what about Afghanistan? Look at what the nice romantic Mujahiddin did with the arms you gave them to fight the communists.'

'The Russians are no better. They use religion the same way everyone else does. Their priests consecrate their bombs and give the mafia their blessing. Why did you do it?'

'We make our choices and stick to them.'

'But things have changed, damn it!'

'Think so? Only names have changed. Soviet Union, Russia, what's the difference? Geography hasn't changed. Nor has human nature. I'm still the same, I haven't changed. Nor had Randa. She was still the same. Don't let them fool you. Nothing has really changed. Nothing has changed, and before long you'll be rebuilding the Wall you were so happy to knock down. To keep the Fourth World off your patch. To protect your pathetic way of life. To preserve your petty-bourgeois comforts.'

Boone was used to dealing with monosyllabic sources and to having to shake the tree in the hope of some meagre fruit. He found all this prodigality overwhelming. Did all spies long for just such a moment, he wondered. Is this what they really want? To confess, to be absolved? Something he had heard when he first joined the secret service came back to him: 'A source is like a bottle of ketchup. You shake it and bang it and nothing comes out. Then, all of a sudden, it all comes out at once.'

'You've done a good job.' The Sharif said it in such a humble tone that he sounded almost arrogant. 'I take my hat off to you. But tell me something. What good does it do you to know that the Centre's conned you?'

None at all, Boone said to himself. He's right. It doesn't do us any good. We're like Wellington. Wellington may well have beaten Napoleon, but he couldn't undo what Napoleon had done. A cop, that's what Wellington was. A good cop maybe, but still a cop. What about us? We're cops too. Not intelligence officers. Clever cops, maybe, but always one step behind. Cops with no visibility. Blind cops, working the bloody field in bloody Braille. Myopic moles. And who are we dealing with? A spy? No, not just a spy. The Sharif was much more than a spy. He was a strange mixture of old Bolshevik systemization and youthful Islamist fervour; a cross between Soviet subversion and Oriental thirst for martyrdom; the worthy child of a sanctified scientific materialism. Was that where the future of the world lay? The very idea chilled Boone to the core.

'I'm your prisoner all right, Harry Boone. But I'm not the loser. You are.'

Boone was only too aware of it. He'd unmasked the Sharif, but Moscow's operation would go on without him. Its victims would make sure it reached a successful conclusion. Fennell, Devereux and Walker would take over now, with one eye on their reputations, the other on their pensions.

41

Boone and Briggs were following the setting sun down the grey-green cliff. It was like following a hearse, thought Boone. The pace was being set by Briggs, who looked both solemn and jubilant in his lounge suit. He looked about as sincere as an undertaker at a luxury funeral.

'What I don't understand,' Boone was saying, 'is why they didn't foresee the African connection.'

'You forget that we're not dealing with an Illegal. At least not in the strict sense of the term. This operation wasn't planned by the Russians. It was an impromptu response to the car-bomb in Mastaba. Pure opportunism, with all the virtues – and vices – of spontaneity. The initiative came from Tareq Ghazzawi, not Moscow. Lukin merely inherited the operation, and just ran it. Impeccably, I must say.'

'Impeccably. But before long, I'll know all the ins and outs of this business, and I'll also know about the Americans.'

'Oh no, you won't!' Briggs warned.

'What?'

'You won't know anything. You won't know anything, because we don't want to know anything. After such a fiasco, can you imagine the Royal & Ancient running the risk of endangering the few special ties we still have with Washington? Walker and Devereux would like to forget about this whole business. The Sharif – we'll go on calling him that, if only for the sake of appearances – will give us nothing about the attacks on the Americans. He won't give us anything because you won't ask him for anything. Understood?'

Harry Boone understood. So Briggs had got his promotion by agreeing to act as a liquidator. Boone made a mental addition to the list of the links that would ensure that Moscow's operation was a success: Walker, Devereux, Fennell, and now Briggs.

'After all,' Briggs was saying, 'we've had a major success, haven't we? All those Islamist networks, arms caches and explosives, all the plots we've foiled, all the financiers we've fingered. All that's real, concrete and solid, isn't it? The fact that he was acting on Moscow's orders when he gave us all that doesn't make much difference. Whatever anyone says, the operation was a success in intelligence terms. A real Birdie. Better than that – an Eagle.'

'An Eagle? Why not an Albatross while you're at it?'

'In political terms, I grant you that it's been a real disaster. An air shot. But politics isn't our business, is it? We're in the intelligence business.'

'So nothing will change?'

'Guy's come off rather badly ...'

Poldhu Point had just come into view. It was the site of the Marconi monument, commemorating the first transatlantic telegraph. The monument symbolised the very special relationship between two countries divided by a common language. Hands reaching out across the ocean as a young Rome takes over from a valiant Greece that had run out of breath. What better place to admit that the Cousins had once again conned their English relatives, thought Boone.

'All in all, Guy miscalculated badly,' Briggs continued, relieved to have reached the sandy beach with no mishaps. 'He's no longer in our masters' good books. Oh, nothing tangible for the moment, but there are some unmistakable signs. You know Walker called him "Fennel" the other day? "Fennel", not "Fennell". "Fennel" as in the plant ... Different musical sound, isn't it? Wrong emphasis on the wrong syllable.'

They were indeed playing a different tune, said a pensive Boone to himself. He silently recalled Plato: 'When the music changes, the walls of the city shake.' The music had indeed changed, but Fennell's American friends hadn't bothered to tell him. So the walls of the city had shaken, and Fennell had fallen. Humpty Dumpty ...

'What about the Sharif?' Boone asked.

'The Sharif? Well, he's not much use to us now, is he? After everything that's happened, we can hardly send him to do the rounds of the friendly services. We obviously can't send him back to Beirut or anywhere else in the Middle East with our apologies to the Arabs: "Let's forget about all that and turn over a new leaf." And we can't keep him here indefinitely, can we? Sooner or later, he'll want to start singing. To the press, for instance. That would get us into a fine mess.'

'So?'

297

'Well, officially, he's already dead, isn't he? Officially, he's been dead for six months. Some at the Clubhouse would very much like to see his physical state match his official state. Do you follow? They're tempted to do what doctors often do: bury their blunders by six feet under.'

'You want to kill him?'

'That's entirely up to you, Harry.'

'Me?'

'You set up a nice little debriefing for me, the sooner the better. Make sure you leave out anything to do with the Americans. And once you've finished with him, we'll put him in cold storage.'

'In prison, you mean?'

'We can scarcely turn him loose. So we'll put him in cold storage until his audience forgets about him, and then we'll discreetly ship him back to his friends in Moscow. We'll send him back to Lukin.'

'Who will of course keep quiet.'

'As I was saying, Harry, all that's up to you. You make no waves, and I'll try to curb the bloodthirsty instincts of Walker and Devereux. Then you can go back to Beirut. Agreed?'

What the heck, Boone said to himself as he kicked at the sand. Why shouldn't I agree? Why jump over the fence when I can happily sit on it? And he added another name to the mental list he'd made: Walker, Devereux, Fennell, Briggs, and now him. The Boone system had just claimed another victim: Harry himself.

With Thanks to

Vassili Barthold; François Bourgeon; Rupert Brooke; Catherine Casley; David Cornwell; Winston Churchill; Peter Cross; Bruno D.; Gilles Deleuze; John G.; Giovanni Guareschi; Félix Guattari; Alfred Hitchcock; the Houzel brothers; Marc I.; Veronica Kemp; Rudyard Kipling; Heinrich von Kleist; André-Jean Lafaurie; Chibli Mallat; Karl Marx; André Miquel; Dominique Mongin; Georges N.; Yasin Omari; Vincent Pelletier; Plato; Lolita Romanov; Vita Sackville-West; Vladimir Serioguin; William Shakespeare; Georges Simenon; Margaret Sironval; Perla Srour.